Requiem
For
Medusa

**BY NICK COLE &
JASON ANSPACH**
TYRUS RECHS:
CONTRACTS & TERMINATIONS
BOOK 1

GALAXY'S
EDGE

Galaxy's Edge: REQUIEM FOR MEDUSA
By Nick Cole & Jason Anspach

Edited by David Gatewood
Published by Galaxy's Edge, LLC

Cover Art: Trent Kaniuga
Cover Design: Beaulistic Book Services
Interior Design: Kevin G. Summers

For more information:
Website: GalacticOutlaws.com
Facebook: facebook.com/atgalaxysedge
Newsletter: InTheLegion.com

A LONG, LONG TIME FROM NOW
AT THE EDGE OF THE GALAXY...

GALAXYS
EDGE
galacticoutlaws.com

HISTORY OF THE GALAXY

IMPERATOR

0	The Pilgrimage
98	The Exploration
501	Savage Wars Begin
2000	Savage Wars Officially Declared Over
2032	Decay of the Republic

REQUIEM FOR MEDUSA

2047	Battle of Kublar

LEGIONNAIRE

"Losing the general was the worst mistake the Republic ever made. Can you imagine him out on the edge? A grizzled vet with more lives than a cat, who's taken more souls than the Reaper himself."

—things old legionnaires say at reunions, when they drink for the fallen and wonder whatever happened to General Rex

01

Sky City
Aetheria IX
Fifteen Years Before
the Battle of Kublar

THE OLD FREIGHTER CAME INTO VIEW BEYOND THE HANgar portal of the upper disc of Sky City. Out there beyond the shields, swirling pink and azure clouds bespoke the violence of the storms that chronically plagued the planet's upper atmosphere. There was other traffic besides the old freighter, but the hit men who'd been sent to intercept this particular ship—a beat-up old bird that looked like it had traveled from one end of the edge to the other and seen plenty of smuggling runs and close calls—didn't much notice the traffic. They had a paid contact in Approach Control who'd tagged the ship the moment it entered atmo. And they were ready for it.

"It's him," noted the leader of Team One over the comm channel. "He's been cleared for Dock Thirty-Five-Oh-One. Team One, stand by to engage as soon as he kills the engines. Boss says the big boys are paying a fifty percent bonus off the top if we take him out now. So… let's take him out now."

Team One's leader switched comm channels. "Team Two… he's here. Remember, you're on *backup*. Watch customs and don't get in our way."

"We can be patient," hissed back the leader of Team Two. "We'll get him when out on the main concourse if he gets by you. Pay is the same no matter who drops him."

"*If* he gets by us. And he ain't."

The word was passed through the teams. It was almost showtime.

Had they been ex-military, adept at what they were about to do, there would have been comm confirms and then silence. Instead, some kind of alien slang-babble erupted like electronic chitter over the ether. They were excited for the money, and more excited for the kill. You wouldn't make the mistake of calling them professionals.

But none of that mattered to the cartel.

It didn't matter that none had served in the Legion or learned to kill professionally in some other military organization. They were still dangerous. Each and every one of the hired blasters was a stone-cold killer. That was the ticket that had drawn them from the minor leagues of the galactic backwaters and given them a chance to earn some real credits in the bigs. This was a tryout—a tryout for a major crime syndicate.

And now here they were, beyond the quiet and ever-gloomy docks out along the station's main disc, assigned to take out a target before it could reach the main hab sections of Sky City.

Team One had been scattered across the docking decks, knowing that Approach Control would send the incoming freighter right to them. The cartel had sprung for that trick.

The hit was a go.

In the outer corridors, beyond the bays of the main access passage, shadowy blues mixed with the occasional yellow-flashing hazard strobe as each hitter ran across the docks to arrive at Bay 3501 before the target. Even with all that paid intel, the ragtag collection of humans—along with a few aliens who thought they were trick with a blaster rig—barely reached the target's docking bay in time to meet the landing freighter.

Using a smart lens, Team One Leader watched a miniature feed from the dock's inner holocams. He saw the ancient freighter flare its venting repulsors and deploy her three main gears to touch down on the deck. In the background, the force field barrier that shielded the docking portal from the upper atmosphere of Aetheria IX shimmered slightly as the storm surging around Sky City continued its dramatic approach. Brief surges of lightning illuminated distant purple fronts from within, turning the storms into the ghosts of lost titans from some mythic age.

"Righto," said the team leader. He was a tall and wiry Tamo who'd once been hung from a light pole out along the edge of the galaxy because the local populace had tired of his shenanigans. His gang had been able to cut him down and revive him, but the rope burns—not to mention the broken neck—had never quite healed right. He had always been a leader, and generally kept a positive outlook on life. But he was a nasty piece of work when he drank, and even nastier in a blaster fight. "Engines are shutting down. Go on three. Put him down fast, boys."

All around him thugs and killers, ruiners of lives from all points along the galactic edge, checked their blasters one last time. One of them, a Lahurasian snake-man, hissed a sideways comment about not needing so many others to do such a simple job. "I can do thissss job mysssssself. I more than match for ssssome lone bounty hunter sssscumbag."

Cartel blasters, like most criminals, hated bounty hunters and the Bronze Guild that represented them, for the simple fact that it was often the bounty hunters who meted out the justice demanded by the citizens. Because on the edge of the Galactic Republic, actual government, or even basic law enforcement, wasn't a given. So the Bronze Guild brought justice—all the justice those in places like the Reach were ever likely to get. Justice that the galaxy's dregs who called themselves hired blasters were often on the receiving end of.

Blast doors separated the killers from the docking bay where the old freighter had landed. They weren't very sturdy. Probably not vacuum-resistant. The assassins could hear the engines of the ship cycle down from a high-pitched whine to a slow blare, and then to nothing but the tick and rattle of cooling metal, leaving the bay in a dread silence of anticipation.

"Ready," the team leader began, feeling the nerves in his stomach. "On three…"

"What's the name of the freighter?" someone asked.

The team leader glared at the man. "The *Obsidian Crow*. On three…"

"That's a stupid name. What's a crow?"

The team leader continued on. "Two… one… Go!"

◆ 4 ◆

The blast doors slid open. The killers formed into a rough wedge and entered the wide, shadowy bay, their blasters out. Before them sat an irregular-slab-shaped freighter with a central cockpit cupola. Her leading edges were blunt like a clenched fist defying their intrusion into its presence. An ancient rust-red paint stripe, chipped and scarred by old battles and a lack of care, ran along her sides, contrasting with her sometimes shiny but mostly dull black metallic hull. She rested on three solid-looking gears. No boarding ramp had been yet lowered.

The risk now was of the target realizing the danger and flying away.

But Team One was full of blasters. And just as the team leader was on the verge of ordering everyone to shoot until the ship was disabled, the old freighter vented billowing hot white gas in every direction, filling the bay in a dense and humid fog.

The team leader switched over to infrared visual, but the hot steam had spiked the temperatures in the bay, making everything glow white.

A moment later the team leader's head exploded.

A pulsed blaster shot had come from a high-powered Venn Automatic Close-Support Sniper Rifle. Its internal suppressor, matched with its octagonal silencer system and charging baffles, muted most of the shot. The only sound that could have been heard—if anything could be heard above the venting hiss of the engines—would have been something akin to the flash and bang of ancient camera equipment.

The gas had come in so close and hot that the deck was no longer visible. One of the killers stumbled over his team leader's headless corpse and began shouting that they were under attack already.

By that time the unseen sniper had taken out three others with quick and accurate fire. By the time the last of the venting gases had been cycled by the bay's air filtration system not a minute later, all of Team One lay dead on the deck of the docking bay.

None of them had fired a shot.

02

THE CRIMINAL KNOWN AS ALGUS CAIN KNEW THAT TIME was running out. Or rather, that it was running out for his client. He had just finished watching the feed from the docking bay where the bounty hunter who was on the client's trail had set down only a minute earlier.

He played the video again.

He watched as the freighter's engines cycled down. He watched as his best team walked in, his crazy-eyed killers. The ones he had been sure the cartel would thank him for bringing to their attention. At a minimum he should have gotten a wild shootout from them.

But then some kind of smoke or fog came off the freighter's engines, obscuring everything. A small strobe effect pulsed from within the fog at precisely timed intervals.

Probably some warning system doing its thing, Cain had thought on his first viewing.

But when the smoke cleared, he'd realized that his guess was wrong. The bounty hunter had used a Greiss silencer on a high-powered blaster rifle. Greiss-made silencers were noted for the telltale strobe effect they made when they covered the sound of a shot. Cain swore at himself for not having figured that out right away.

When their target, the bounty hunter, dropped effortlessly from the portside rear gear well, Cain spoke.

"Play that back. Thirty seconds."

The recorded feed skipped back. Cain had missed it the first time, but now he saw how it had all been done. The bounty hunter was firing from *inside* the gear well, his head hanging down, the blaster steadied on the belly of the freighter. Maybe he used a magnetic rail? Or maybe he was strong as a gronk? He'd killed everybody while hanging upside down.

Cain snarled. "Wago-stealin' freak." He whispered the words bitterly, but not without just a little bit of respect. That was pure Legion Dark Ops voodoo.

On the footage, after the bounty hunter dropped down to the deck, he moved forward with a clear sense of economy and purpose. He popped a small panel along the belly of the freighter, stored the state-of-the-art sniper rifle, and took out a small sub-compact auto-blaster, like the kind Dark Ops used for tactical weapons assaults. It was a wicked matte black blaster, the kind that was illegal for anyone but the legionnaires. You couldn't even own a knock-off. Mandatory "re-education" was the sentence for possessing one.

Blaster in hand, the armored bounty hunter closed the belly hatch and strode purposefully toward the blast doors to exit the hangar. This was Cain's first clear view of the man. He froze the image in close-up.

"Son of a…"

If it had been any other bounty hunter, the cartel that effectively ran Sky City, along with so many other places out this way, would have had no problem putting him down. But *this* bounty hunter…

Now Cain understood.

With apparent ease, this hunter had eaten up the trail his high-value client had left behind. Nothing thrown at the man had waylaid him in the least. And the cartel had thrown out a *lot*. They'd tried to cross him up, ambush him, even buy him off. The scumbag hadn't slowed. Not in the blind alleys and traps the cartel had left behind on Suramar, or Asari Station, or even the flesh pits of Sensia. Hitters at each location, teams of killers pulled from the fringes of the galaxy's edge, had all been brought in to take out the mysterious hunter on the client's back trail. And they'd all failed.

The situation for the cartel had gone from developing, to urgent, to on fire in the space of three weeks. Every back-trail trap and ambush had gone silent. Meaning it was the trappers who had not survived the trap. The ambushers were ambushed. The hunters had become the prey. And then the rumors started. Except they were more like ghost stories, told by merciless killers and psychotic crooks. *He's gonna get you.*

And that's when they finally brought in Algus Cain.

Cain finished off the last of the suite's high-priced Dori gin. He held the cut-crystal glass before his face, torn between smashing it against a wall in frustration and setting it neatly on the table.

He chose the latter. "Always be professional," he muttered in a gravelly whiskey baritone. Then he adjusted his jacket and smiled at himself in the suite's mirror. He was good-looking in a *mad dog killer* sort of way. Or so he thought.

And mostly, it was just a thought. "Mad dog killer" was a phrase he used to convince himself he was something more than he actually was. More than what he'd been: the fastest blaster out along the Dantares Run a few years back. Which meant he was little more than a hired gun shooting down bad gambling debts and rival gang members. A simple thug and murderer who dreamed of a bigger slice of the galaxy just for himself.

And then came those first cartel jobs. And life toward the core. And the emergence of a legitimate businessman. Of sorts. Yes, he still killed. He did all the other things thugs do. But now he did it in the world of intergalactic finance. There was profit-sharing, performance incentives, a chance to make a difference in the retirement accounts that had been set up on off-planet banks.

At least for himself.

He had three million in credits hidden on Pthalo. The place where—according to rumor—delegates from the House of Reason kept their secret earnings from all the off-book schemes that weren't *necessarily* government business.

Cain buckled the lower strap of his gun belt around his thigh, pulled the Intec Katana-model blaster from its holster, and checked the charge pack. Satisfied, he re-holstered the wicked-yet-workmanlike sidearm and stared, almost listlessly, out at the swirling gas clouds of Aetheria's upper atmosphere.

It was time to do what he'd always done best in his life. Be faster with a blaster than the other guy.

Sky City was clearly visible, even in the storm. Three massive discs, stacked one atop the other, floating through the upper atmosphere of Aetheria IX. Each disc was the size of a planetary super metropolis. Taken together, the three discs, each stacked just off the one below, looked like a trio of steps meant for a giant. And across each disc were hundreds of levels of lights, twinkling to life in the early evening. There was no question about it: Sky City was beautiful.

Algus Cain saw none of it. All he could see was the image in his mind's eye: the frozen image of the bounty hunter in close-up. Coming for the high-value target. And therefore coming for *him*, Algus Cain, who was being paid incredibly good credits to stand in the way.

"Team Two is down," said a small voice in Algus's ear. It was the bot monitoring traffic between the teams.

"D4," Cain said to the bot, "re-direct Teams Three, Four and Five to secure the route to the hangar." There was a natural coldness to his voice that made him sound casually calm. Or so he'd been told. "We're getting out of here. Now. Destroy our electronic trail and take care of yourself."

There was a pause. Then the bot came back over the comm, its tone tentative and unsure. But it was, as always, a servant ready to serve, despite the sociopath it happened to be indentured to.

"Are you calling a burn notice, sir?"

"Yeah," replied Cain without pity—or anything else that registered as human.

The bot would fire-bomb their warehouse office and destroy itself according to the job's parameters as set forth by management in the cartel. That it was the end of run-time for the bot didn't bother a killer like Cain in the least. Bots didn't even register as a part of his hierarchy of victims. Not even worthy of the term "collateral damage." That term was reserved for *living* beings. For star cruisers full of passengers. Who would give a damn about a bot? Cain least of all.

Quick strides took him into the master bedroom of the suite high up on the Sky City's third disc. The disc the citizens liked to call the "Pleasure Dome."

Naven Wtziko—the client—sat hunched over a datapad working on two holographic keyboards being projected from the device. The slender, ratty-looking man seemed oblivious to Cain's contemptuous glare. Which was a good thing. Because in that brief everything's-collapsing moment, Algus Cain was weighing the wisdom of icing the little lizard. Perhaps he could convince the cartel that it was for the best. Or perhaps he'd just hightail it back out to the edge. The old disappearing act.

Because that still image on the cam feed meant that the rumors were true. And that meant that none of this was worth it. Even the cartel didn't pay enough.

Unless Cain did what he always did: be quicker with a blaster.

"Team Three is down," said the bot. "I have completed my end of the burn notice protocol and am preparing to self-terminate, sir. However, I would dearly like to continue—"

"Do it," snapped Algus and cut the link.

"What?" asked Wtziko, aware of Cain's presence for the first time. He didn't bother looking up from the datapad, and his fingers continued to fly across both holographic keyboards.

"Nothing," replied Cain. "Time to go."

"Already?"

Cain only nodded. He was done wasting breath on this rat.

As they left the suite, Cain once more passed the frozen image of the bounty hunter with the wicked sub-compact automatic blaster. The cat wore old-school Legion armor. *Real* old. It was scarred, scratched, and nicked, looking every bit the museum piece. It was possible, of course, that it was some other bounty hunter—someone else who had somehow gotten himself a piece of that old Mark I Legion armor. Possible, but not probable. Not once everything else was taken into consideration.

No. Cain was certain. Under that armor was the most wanted man in the galaxy. Most wanted, and most deadly.

Cain smiled. He smiled because he was a sociopath. He didn't feel the way others felt. In fact he didn't feel at all. Instead, his whole perspective changed as he found a bright spot in this rapidly unfolding drama. Who cared if the client got whacked? Who cared if the cartel took it on the chin? There was, for Algus Cain, in all of this… an opportunity.

After all, it wasn't every day you got a chance to kill the legendary Tyrus Rechs.

03

"TEAM LEADER IS DOWN!" SCREECHED A DESPERATE voice from Team Four in Cain's ear. "We're pinned at the secondary docking bay. Looks like—"

Automatic blaster fire filled the comm transmission.

Cain dragged Naven Wtziko through the crowded concourse that opened up on the grand dome of the Loop terminal that circled this disc of Sky City. Humanoids struggled past them in a rush to embark or disembark, all of them either coming from or heading toward the central plazas of the Grand Astra Core. Cobalt blue-eyed Vampuurs glided lithely among stocky Kasians, who scuttled forward on their hooves to reach the next tram. Flight-suited Qual, unable to breathe the local atmosphere inside the station, chattered in their singsong bird language through electronic voice modulators. A Gondaar merc captain—Cain recognized him as a seller of weapons and buyer of synth—shouted something to a friend. Out here along the Reach, as this area of the galaxy was known, aliens outnumbered the humans five to one.

"We stick out like a sore thumb," Cain muttered as he dragged the black-market code-banker through the alien sea. "If your friend has eyes he'll spot us like a Katu raptor after a fieldmouse."

Team Four's comms were now silent. They had been guarding the hangar Cain had reserved for an emergency departure. Cain had intended to take Wtziko there, manage a quick dustoff and then regroup. Maybe lay a proper trap for Tyrus Rechs. But the bounty hunter had gotten there first. So—change of plans.

"Das, this is Cain." Cain stepped off of the swollen terminal onto a loading Loop repulsor car, jerking the banker after him.

"Das here," answered the pilot.

According to the plan, Das was currently circling Sky City in an approach holding pattern. A junkie ex-marine close-air-support drop pilot, Das could put a ship down on any pad—as long as he was sober. Cain needed him to be sober today.

"Pickup is compromised. I'm boarding the Loop with the client and heading across the disc for the—"

Cain stooped as he saw the Paul Lizer, the leader of Team Five, approach with a toothy smile. Team One were the crazy killers; Team Five was the best in show. In the world of murderers on retainer, Team Five were as close to pro as you were likely to find.

"You still there, boss?" asked the pilot.

"Yeah. Put the ship down in one of the commercial transfer docks near the Loop terminal." Cain shoved the client into a seat. "And watch those shipping cranes!"

"Can do," Das replied, and Cain heard the howl and whine of thrusters spooling up to execute a hard turn.

"ETA… ten minutes," said Cain before cutting the link.

Team Five's leader stepped close to Cain. "Game time," he whispered with an expectant smile.

Cain smiled in return, mimicking a showing of emotion that he didn't feel. He started tallying the odds as he saw them. He checked for collateral damage and saw none. Team Five had secured this car. Good.

The repulsor-powered Loop train started forward with a sudden pulse of quiet, forceful energy, pulled by the big engine in front toward the next station along the disc. It would take ten minutes to reach the commercial terminals. Five more to board and lift off.

Cain looked at Wtziko. The orders from the cartel had been clear: *Do not let the black-market alt-currency broker fall into anyone else's hands.* Cain was to try to keep him alive, but in the event that that wasn't possible…

Things hadn't gotten that bad yet. Cain could still see a way out of this. There was a chance to still collect that bonus they were dangling for keeping the client alive. There was still an opportunity for Cain's reputation, and thus his future price, to grow.

As always, Algus Cain was figuring all sides of the deal. Yeah. He could make this work. He had Team Five with him. He could make this work.

He'd picked the men of Team Five personally.

Hancha Boorg.

Maas Stazzi.

Cordo Callahann.

Klaas Two-for-One.

Paul Lizer.

Every one of them had a least a dozen outstanding bounties in star systems all across the Reach. From planets where the Repub kept its head down and its guard-dog legionnaires behind the walls of the local embassy, to places where the Repub wasn't welcome at all, and life was cheaper than a second-hand blaster.

"Four teams down," taunted Lizer. "This guy's a killer, Cain. Worried, buddy?"

The words jerked Cain back from his vivid daydream of firing one shot into the client's head and getting off at the next station.

"Yeah," answered Cain, staring Lizer in the face. "You should be too. That's *Tyrus Rechs* killing all our boys."

That name wiped the smile off Lizer's scarred face. And it took a lot to banish the smile from this man who'd once left six dead in a cantina because his Vega Stinger had been served at a less-than-satisfactory temperature.

"You serious?" Lizer said.

"Does it matter?" replied Cain with a single grave-yard nod. "The other teams are all dead, whether I'm *serious* or not. But yeah. I'm serious."

The holographic map shining against the side of the car showed their progress in real-time. They were approaching the next station. Beyond the car's windows the panorama of the swirling gas giant's upper atmosphere was illuminated by a series of explosions. Arcs of lightning promised an uptick in the approaching storm's intensity.

For a moment, the power in the train flickered on and off. Just for a second. Cain heard a distant buzz as the passengers packed together in the other cars—the ones without big, rough men scowling at you so you didn't sit down, or you found somewhere else far away to sit down—chirped worriedly about it. And why wouldn't they be worried? The Loop was traveling outside of the station, after all. Running in a big circle on the outer rim of the disc. There was nothing between them and a great big fall but some glass.

A lady screamed in a distant compartment. Probably convinced she'd be trapped along the rails with only that thin layer of invisi-steel between her and an instant upper-atmosphere death. It was the near-airless void that would kill you. The long fall down into a crushing gravity well was just an unfortunate epilogue.

"For your convenience and safety," said a calm, soothing voice over the train's internal address system, "please exit the Loop car at the next station. Atmospheric conditions are currently interfering with optimum operating efficiency. Your safety is our highest concern. All passengers must exit at the next station."

The message repeated as the car slowed to a halt at the station in question.

As soon as the doors opened, passengers began to swarm out of the train's other cars. Sky City security in their white dress armor had formed a cordon to prevent those waiting to board from taking the departing passengers' places. But Cain and his men stayed put, lounging in the car as if they hadn't a care in the world. As if the planet itself wasn't trying to murder them. As if Tyrus Rechs wasn't trying to do the same.

A Cyclopoid security official entered the car. He wore a perfectly cut collared business suit and flashed perfectly white teeth from behind his tanned face. Cain was impressed by that smile. The gleam of those teeth almost matched that of his lone shimmering blue eye.

The official held up a slender humanoid hand featuring elegantly manicured nails. "I'm sorry, folks," he said as though the hardened killers in front of him were merely tourists on their way around the station to catch the fountain show at the Grand Luxe or the latest Tennar showgirl revue, "but the Loop's going to shut down until the storm passes. You'll have to—"

At the merest nod from Cain, Lizer stuck a snub-nosed blaster under the Cyclopoid's tanned jaw line. The official froze. Obviously he had enough corporate training for situations like this to know that it was listening time.

Cain stepped forward. "I presume you have an access card to get the train running again." He held out his hand expectantly.

"I do," said the official in a subdued tone.

"Good." Cain's tone was pleasant. He was, after all, getting his way, in this as in all things. "Go ahead and mark this train as cleared and get us headed cross disc. We will ride the five minutes up to the commercial terminal, and then you can have it back, good as new."

"Sir," began the official, struggling to affect ease despite his manicured hands shaking uncontrollably. Those hands were up in the air. He'd put them up without being told to.

"Now," admonished Cain, "don't tell me anything about the storm. Not interested."

The official seemed to think this over for a moment. "May I reach into my coat pocket for the device?"

"You may," replied Cain.

The official pulled out his access card and tapped through a few screens. Probably more than he needed to. No doubt trying to be coy about his alerting the higher-ups with a one-button panic call. But Cain didn't care.

The train started to move again.

"There," said the guard, trying to smile.

"Now how hard was that?" Cain asked.

Then he shot the Cyclopoid in the chest.

The official sat down heavily, his green blood spreading across his starched white shirt. His one large, lone, beautiful eye looked up in shock. It was prettier still from the tears misting it over.

Cain shot him again.

04

T HE FIRST THING TYRUS RECHS DID UPON RECEIVING the contract from the guild was to open a fake black channel account with the alt-currency broker. From there, it was a simple matter to get a passive signal pinging the location of Naven Wtziko's tablet at all times. Tracking him was easy. The problem had been catching up with him—and weeding out the layers of defenders.

Initially the broker was operating out of a converted Tellarian star yacht with a small private security detail of ex-military contractors. Rechs nearly caught him, almost ended it right then and there. He boarded the ship, taking it deck by deck, only for Wtziko to slip away via escape pod. Even then Rechs nearly caught him in *Obsidian*'s tractor—but the target made the jump to light speed only seconds before the device engaged.

It would be another two weeks before Wtziko came back up for air, surfacing in a Doro slum on Tatanga. He actually unwittingly contacted his own bounty hunter, calling Rechs to apologize for the delay and to assure him he was a valued client. A day later Rechs hit the slums in disguise. The target had bought protection from the local

Doro, and they were everywhere, fulfilling their usual vicious guard dog role. When Rechs hit the safe house at just after three a.m. local, all hell broke loose.

And once again, the target escaped. The Doro pack gang kept Rechs busy long enough for the broker to get out via armored speeder convoy. He fled to a nearby landing field in the remains of a burnt-out university the House of Reason had financed, and got off planet in a hired pirate frigate.

Three more hiding spots followed. Three more engagements. Three more narrow escapes. To the outside eye, it might seem that Rechs would never catch up with the target. But the truth was, it was all a draw. A moving kill zone. And the bounty hunter was tightening the noose. With each engagement, Rechs whittled away the target's resources, and the resources of the cartel protecting him. The target's ex-military security was replaced by cartel muscle, and finally by mob hitters with barely any loyalty to the cartel and none whatsoever to Naven Wtziko. A pretty sorry last line of defense. These types would do anything to protect themselves.

The real win for Rechs was that none of the previous engagements had ended with the target dead. The Republic marshals—the client who'd submitted the guild contract—wanted him alive because of what he knew. Word was the target had a lot of dirt on several higher-ups within the House of Reason. His capture would make a lot of people decide not to seek re-election. And that *might* make the galaxy a better place. If only for a little while.

Then again, maybe the marshals were working *for* the higher-ups who were at risk of being taken down. You never quite knew when it came to the House and Senate.

Rechs's tracer pinged on the Loop that circled the grand upper disc of Sky City. Walking fast with his blaster at port arms, he made for the nearest airlock. An updating map scrolled in the corner of his armor's HUD, superimposed against his visor. A data worm embedded within the city's systems alerted him to all official tracking and movements, so he knew he was coming up on a squad of heavy enforcer types in the station's standard white armor.

Maybe they were the good guys. Maybe they had been bought by the cartel. How they reacted to Rechs would be the giveaway. It would be touch and go.

A moment later the first of the enforcers appeared. Rechs immediately noted they were using heavy blasters. That wasn't typical. Either they had re-armed after hearing about the massacre in customs—switching from crowd control stunners to lethal weapons—or they were after him directly.

Rechs didn't think of what had happened in customs as a massacre. He had shot down only the blasters that had been sent to intercept him. The civvies, the collateral damage, could be laid squarely at the feet of the untrained thugs who didn't mind using civilians as shields. Scum who'd never even learned to clear their fields of fire. But Rechs knew that these men would view the incident as a massacre, and would see him, Rechs, as the sole instigator of it. They always did.

Rechs continued forward. Time to find out if these were good guys or just more bodies in the way.

"There he is! Blast him!" cried the lead trooper.

It didn't matter that they were using internal comms—Rechs had access to those. Another benefit of the worm he'd placed in their system. He heard it all.

So… bad guys.

He fired at the first one. The shot from his heavy blaster dropped the man onto his back, leaving a smoking hole in his fancy dress armor. A moment later Rechs was hugging wall behind a bulkhead as return blaster fire filled the air.

Now they'll try to pin me down, he thought as he ran tactics in his mind. *Then they'll flank.*

The enforcers were breaking off into the three groups. These were probably better trained than the thugs, but no more difficult to handle. He could see their approach vectors, knew in real-time what they were trying to do thanks to his splice into Sky City's net.

He shifted across the corridor, dashing as blaster fire chased after him. He fired one-handed at an enforcer as he maneuvered between groups of armored security. They were weak at the center from their attempt to flank. Rechs went straight at them.

He popped two micro-bangers and rolled them toward the center base of fire. The tiny grenades exploded, blinding the enforcers just ahead of him. Rechs ran right into their midst, slamming an armored shoulder into one who'd dropped his weapon in order to clutch at his helmet in a sudden panicked blindness. Micro-bangers would make a man feel as though he'd gone blind, deaf, and stupid in one sensory scrambling moment. It took a powerful effort to remain upright and on your feet when that feeling struck.

With no need to shoot these men down—the micro-banger had neutralized them—Rechs raced on past. Behind him, both of the flanking groups swarmed his old position back down the corridor. Ahead of him lay the airlock.

"Red Dragon!" screamed Rechs as he ran. The enforcers gave chase, sending errant blaster bolts sizzling wide above his head. They were moving more cautiously now. "Pop the lock on Airlock 6289 Alpha. Main plus two."

"Done," warbled Red Dragon, the worm AI, in Rechs's comm.

The half-sized blast door slithered open. Rechs sped inside and started the cycle controls as the station's automatic warning system kicked in.

"Warning! Vacuum exposure in thirty seconds. Emergency override is located on the left side of the door. If you do not wish to be exposed to vacuum, please override."

And then it began to count down.

Twenty-nine seconds later, the outer lock cycled and Rechs pushed through to the outside of the bubble. His HUD read good suit integrity.

The bounty hunter looked out along the outer hull of Sky City. It was like a massive canyon floating within a pink storm. Lightning flashed and popped amid roiling gas. The approaching storm had already swallowed the lower disc and made the second disc look like a ghostly leviathan swimming in unknown alien seas.

Rechs picked up the ping on the target. It came from the glass cylinder of the Loop rail, which wrapped this disc of Sky City at its widest bulge. Down inside that invisi-steel cylinder, the train was approaching at an incredible speed. And Rechs had to get on it.

"No time to think about it!" he grunted, pushing off the edge of the airlock and firing his armor's jets to full. He raced toward the tube along the side of the city, flipping at the last second to flare, landing on the invisi-steel glass.

Jump juice was down to fifty percent. Time to be stingy. Rechs knelt to place a thermite charge on the top of the glass, dialing in the explosion cone for a small hole. He watched the train rapidly approaching in the distance underneath the glass of the tube. It would get to him too fast. And when he blew the glass, the tube's depressurization would prevent him from forcing himself inside immediately, wasting precious seconds. But this was the only way, unless he wanted to let Wtziko escape again. He'd have to try.

He stepped away, turned his back, and detonated the focused explosive. He felt only a small tremor through his boots, then turned to see the glass fountaining away like a volcano of sparkling invisi-steel and vapor escaping in a furious stream.

The Loop train was already racing beneath his feet like the blur of a thought. He raised his left arm and fired a grappling needle at the passing cars. His HUD announced a capture message from the needle's tip as nano-cord spooled away from his armor in a sudden high-pitched whine, the urgency of which didn't sound comforting in the least. There were, after all, only three hundred meters of the stuff.

"Lock cable," Rechs muttered between gritted teeth within his bucket, hearing the oxygen-rich dryness of his voice and regretting what was to come next.

With an abrupt and ferocious jerk, the cable locked—and Rechs was yanked down through the shattering glass after the Loop train. His arm or shoulder, maybe both, broke from the sudden force. Rechs roared red murder as he hit the Loop rail and bounced off into the wall of the tube, careening about like some die-cast action figure dragged behind a child's hoverbike.

He blacked out—either from the pain or the sudden g's. When he came to, he was still flying along behind the train. He gave the armor the command to reel him in, pumping what he had left in the jets to help a bit. He reached for his automatic blaster with his good arm, but found it wasn't there. It had been lost in the topsy-turvy tumble through the tunnel.

The armor finished spooling up, and Rechs activated mags in his gauntlets and boots to affix himself to the rear car. He slithered awkwardly across its surface with only one working arm, toward the rear access lock. This would have been easier if the tube were still depressurized, but while he was out some blast door must have sealed the tracks and repressurized the Loop.

When he finally reached the door, he pulled the emergency release, flinging it right off its hinges.

He would have to move fast now. Time was of the essence. The target and his detail were running for the only means of escape left to them. A ship that Rechs's intel said was bristling with a full team of ex-legionnaires, all armed to the teeth. They'd been sent to extricate their client, but they'd also come to take out a bounty hunter whom the cartel couldn't shake.

Rechs crawled inside the train. The thugs had spread out to get between him and the target, who was one car ahead. They didn't wait for Rechs to get any closer before they started shooting.

These were known men. Dangerous men. Rechs's HUD identified two of them before he'd taken five steps. Hancha Boorg and Maas Stazzi. Each had a twenty-thousand-credit bounty on his head, dead or alive.

Boorg charged, firing wildly, as fast as he could pull the trigger. He wore ablative chest armor plus a whole lot of fancy survival gear he didn't actually need. The sawed-off scatter blaster he had was no toy. Boorg pumped hot narrow-cone blaster sprays at Rechs as he came on board. The other scumbag, Stazzi, covered the charge.

Rechs drew one of his backup pistols, a well-balanced hand cannon. He thumbed it to automatic and fired, standing his ground.

One of Boorg's shots hit Rechs in his chest armor. The heavy impact knocked him back a step. But that didn't affect the first auto-burst fire shot from his hand cannon. Ten fifty-caliber rounds spat out from the massive slug thrower. The weapon was a relic of ancient, bygone days, a lost and savage era. Not the kind of weapon anyone today would or could carry.

The first nine shots tore through Boorg's body armor, the bullets climbing up from the initial hit on center mass, the result of the hand cannon's involuntary climb. Auto-fire was no joke, even with the cybernetic compensatory targeting-assist of Rechs's armor. The tenth shot blew off Boorg's unarmored head. The man went backwards as his brains painted the seats behind him.

Maas Stazzi was a cooler customer. He'd once shot a local Republic governor from five hundred meters with a black market–acquired N-18. The governor had been waving from a motorcade during a House of Reason Diversity Day celebration, moving at twenty-five miles per hour, in morning light and shadow, and Stazzi had still put three shots into him—plus two for the local mayor who rode beside him.

So whereas the larger, more aggressive Boorg charged only to be dropped, Stazzi, wire thin and lithe, faded behind a bulkhead, clearly looking for a new firing position on the opposite lane through the wide car.

Through the speeding windows of the train, Rechs could see the angry purple storm roil and explode with sudden, frenetic light displays.

The bounty hunter unloaded with his hand cannon. He shredded the forward- and rear-facing seats that were set up in sections of three inside the moving car. He closed toward his target, continuing to unload on auto-fire, his encased belt of linked bullets being sucked from his back into the slug thrower. He worked over the partition in a thunder of fury and lead, never slowing, ensuring that Stazzi was unable to pop up and return fire.

When he was close enough, he saw Stazzi crawling away, leaving a gory trail. The thug had been hit several times by the blind fire. Rechs thumbed back to single fire and put a massive bullet through the man's already bloodied head.

Forty thousand credits confirmed.

A deep yet subtle bell chimed. The train was approaching the next station along the line. But the Loop cars sped right past it. As the platform blurred along beside them, Rechs saw Sky City enforcers staged and ready, waiting to take the cars. Extricating the target would be much more difficult now. Things never went well once the authorities were involved.

Rechs moved another car forward. His HUD identified and tagged the three other wanted cartel hired blasters: Cordo Callahann, Klaas Two-for-One, and Paul Lizer. He also spied a dead Cyclopoid, its green blood pooled around its feet and ruining the seat he'd expired in.

The sum of the trio's bounties added up to a cool hundred thousand credits in total. But beyond them was the real prize. Rechs could see Wtziko fleeing into the forward cars with another man, a bodyguard, moving swiftly and closing chrome and glass doors behind them as they went.

With a boom, the glass and impervisteel partition at the front of Rechs's car exploded. The three thugs ahead of him were showered with glass and hot steel, and the local invisi-steel of the Loop tube was shattered, exposing the tunnel to the high atmosphere for the second time that day. To their credit, the three thugs tried to shoot Rechs even as they were being sucked out into the vacuum-exposed tube. No surviving that.

Rechs knew exactly what had happened. The target's bodyguard had detonated some kind of explosive between the cars, severing them, allowing only the lead ones forward.

He'd left his co-workers behind to die with Rechs.

Rechs ignited the armor's jump jets. Using max throttle, he rocketed out of the damaged car and toward the lead cars that were pulling away down the track. Behind him the ruined cars left their mag-lev tracks and smashed into the side of the invisi-steel tube. That entire section of the Loop exploded outward. Sky City would have one hell of a repair bill.

With jump juice at almost critical, Rechs doubled down. He came within inches of the fleeing car, stretched out with his right arm, and felt himself just barely latch on.

The speeding Loop car entered a new section of tube that sealed behind them. The extreme rush of venting air subsided.

Rechs pulled himself inside through the car's rear door. Looking back and down through the clear tube, he

JASON ANSPACH & NICK COLE

saw the cartel men and the ruined cars he'd left behind falling into the crushing gravity well of Aetheria IX.

He struggled to block out the blinding pain in his arm and shoulder. It had gotten banged up again in the ordeal from the blown car. A particularly bad wave of hot nausea swam over him as he pulled himself through the speeding car, gripping the seatbacks as he went.

The target, Wtziko, stood by the forward door, looking as sick as Rechs felt. The bodyguard, a killer no doubt, was pointing his blaster at the target's head.

All about them the train hurtled toward its final destination. The automated announcer reported that the last stop, the commercial docks platform, was just ahead.

"That's where we're getting off, bounty hunter," hissed the bodyguard, with a cruel sneer.

Rechs weighed a draw of one of his hand cannons. He'd had to holster them for the jump between trains. He was fast, but not faster than the simple blaster squeeze it would take to cook the target's brains all over the side of the car.

"Tyrus Rechs, isn't it?" said the bodyguard. "Call me Cain."

Wtziko was whining. Mewling about his importance to some very powerful friends in the House of Reason.

"Shut up," whispered Cain bitterly. Despite the last few minutes of blaster fire and exploding rail cars, the killer affected a corporate calm. "I don't need you as much as they do. I can walk away from this alone and be just fine. It just pays more if you live."

The car swayed, and the three men stood, no one making a move.

Cain smiled. "But either way, dead or alive, I still get paid."

One minute. They would arrive at the station in one minute. If Rechs was going to do something it would have to be soon. It would have to be now.

"Yeah," Rechs said tiredly. "I'm him. I'm Tyrus Rechs."

The killer's bare, cruel smile grew even wider. Became something passing for joy. A psychotic joy, but joy nonetheless. The man, Cain, rolled his shoulders slightly, telegraphing everything he intended to do next. Which was change his aim and shoot down a legend. Then drink for free from that fact forever. Or until someone did the same to him.

Lots had tried before, and Rechs was still standing.

But Cain must have known this about him, so he attempted to hedge his bet. "Hands up. Or I shoot your bounty." He cackled wildly, the laugh communicating that he would do it. It was the laugh of a braggart who knows he holds all the right cards and can't stand to wait for it all to play out. He needs you to know *right now* that he's beaten you completely.

Rechs raised the armored gauntlet of his good arm over his head.

"Put 'em both up," Cain demanded.

Rechs's dead arm hung limply. "Can't. Broke it."

"Well do it anyway."

There was a look in the killer's eyes that told Rechs that this would be a deal breaker. It was both hands up or a dead bounty.

He hoisted up the other gauntlet, the pain in his left shoulder and arm screaming like a devil roasting in a hell of boiling oils. But he bit it down and blocked it off, gritting his teeth inside his bucket.

"I thought you were dead," said Cain, barely, almost unconsciously. He moved his blaster off the target in order to dial it up to full power with a flick of his thumb. Most blasters called it the kill switch. It was highly illegal. It dumped an entire charge pack into just one shot. Even the Mark I armor couldn't stand up to that.

"Yeah," Cain continued, as cold as an ice field on some lonely planet no one ever went to. "I thought you were de—"

The carbon-forged machete Rechs carried on his back appeared in the hired killer's chest less than a microsecond after it had been flung. Moving like a blur, Rechs had pulled the machete from off a scabbard he wore over his shoulder and flung it like a throwing knife. Carbon-forged tip first, it entered Cain's sternum as though his body were the softest butter.

Cain fell to his knees. Then he eased down onto his back, slowly, as though all he needed was to lie down for just a moment. Like that might allow him to breathe a little. But it turned out that another breath wasn't in the cards for Algus Cain. By the time Tyrus Rechs pulled the machete from his chest with an effortless tug, the man was dead gone. Through his sightlessly staring eyes he seemed to indicate that he still couldn't believe it.

A moment later the Loop car slithered into the station. This time, the target didn't bother running.

05

Jasoon City
Morridia

THE *OBSIDIAN CROW* THUNDERED THROUGH THE UPPER reaches of Morridia's burning bronze sky. Below, sculpted crimson dunes wandered the almost lifeless surface of the desert planet. Rechs locked in the signal from Jasoon City's outer approach marker and set up for landing at the crumbling port east of the old city.

It had been no easy trick making it back to Dock 3501 on Aetheria IX. The enforcers had declared martial law, calling what happened at the Loop a terrorist attack. What remained of Rechs's bounty hunt had gone escape and evasion.

But though Wtziko didn't resist, neither did he go quietly. As Rechs jumped from the train inside the tube and blasted his way through a maintenance hatch, using the last fumes of his jump juice, the target screamed bloody murder, and he continued to call for help all along the dark warren of access tunnels off the main passages of the pleasure dome. It wasn't just the usual, "Help, I'm being kidnapped, he'll kill me!" types of screams, either—he was shouting out secrets and promises of instant retirement in exchange for help, in the desperate hope that his words would reach some official who could stop Rechs. Wtziko knew exactly who the bounty hunter intended to deposit him with. And those people… they didn't play around.

Rechs finally tranqed Wtziko with a micro-syringe he kept in one of the armor's shoulder pockets. Then he picked up the sack of marluff feed the man had become, slung him over his bad shoulder so he was still free to shoot, and ran from, and occasionally through, the enforcer patrols who'd come down to find the "terrorist."

The docking bays were especially hot with security patrols. Rechs had to shoot his way to the ship, and even then he barely got the *Crow* out, its thick hull suffering through a deluge of ground fire as everything went from bad to worse at the last minute.

When he was out in the upper atmo, Sky City Interceptors tried to cut off his exit into open space. And when that failed, they tried to stop him from making a jump. But the *Crow* ran an expensive navigational AI that moved much more quickly than any human computer interface. After enduring twenty seconds of Interceptor fire—not to mention the battering of the atmospheric storm-generated turbulence—the old freighter leapt away across incomprehensibly vast volumes of space.

In hyperspace, Rechs cryo-coffined the bounty and slept for most of the three days' jump time to Jasoon City on Morridia for the handoff to the marshals' designated operatives. Now he was crossing over the sprawl of mineral-printed domes and rooftops, low and squat, that comprised the desert port of Jasoon City.

Rechs told the ship to break Wtziko out of cold storage.

"Reviving now, Captain," intoned the ship's near emotionless AI.

Jasoon Approach, an old automated AI, cleared the *Obsidian Crow* to land and assigned a dock out near the eastern end of the sprawl. Rechs had requested it specifically.

Landing gears deployed as the thin freighter with the bull nose and central latticed pilot's canopy set down amid a chiaroscuro of desert sand and old dusty walls on a burning bronze afternoon. The docking "bay" was actually a circle of interconnected open docking berths built around a central landing pad. Across one half of the dock, massive sheets of multi-colored, almost circus-like canvases were stretched over top of the unneeded bays. Beneath them was a bizarre collection of ancient ships in various states of disrepair. Some sections of those scratched-paint hulls lay open, exposing gleaming circuitry and dirty machinery to the dry air, while other ships seemed to have been vivisected altogether, content merely to have become the skeletal remains of ancient and mythic star wanderers.

As Rechs pivoted the *Crow* inside the assigned docking bay, a mottled gray-furred wobanki, still tall despite a pronounced stoop, stepped away from a double-O-wing gunrunner. The catman lifted a paw, his old eyes watching as a tool belt hanging from a bandolier shifted across his body.

Rechs nodded to the figure from the pilot's seat as he set down, then killed the engines and repulsors with a practiced series of switch flips. The old cat waved once more, desultorily, and returned to his work inside the gunrunner's engine shielding.

By the time Rechs had strapped on a blaster rig and retrieved the target from the ship's cryo-coffin, service bots were already crawling all over the *Crow*. One maintenance protocol unit, sheathed in chrome and dirty orange ceramic, was already plugged into the maintenance comm unit and talking with the ship directly about needed repairs. There were other things Rechs wanted done besides the standard repairs, but he would talk with Whiska directly about that.

The boarding ramp lowered, ushering in a hot blast of Morridia's sun-drenched air.

Rechs didn't wear the armor all the time. Here, on Morridia, there was no need. So he was dressed in combat pants and a rust-colored shirt, along with some well-worn jungle boots, as he led the sun-blinking bounty down the ramp.

They were greeted at the bottom by two Dark Ops leejes dressed in civvies and sporting blaster rigs of their own. Both men were muscle-bound, with shaved heads; one had a gray beard. Rechs knew these men. Named Doc and Chappy, they were the very unofficial interface between the bounty hunter and the law enforcement agencies of the galaxy. Dark Ops, like the rest of the Legion, were to apprehend or kill Tyrus Rechs on sight, by order of the House of Reason. But Chappy and Doc... they knew better.

"General!" Doc said enthusiastically. He and Chappy were among the few who knew the secret—that Tyrus Rechs had once been General Rex. They had served directly under the man.

Chappy, the beard, merely nodded, hands clasped in front of him, eyes engaged in a situational awareness scan of the bays. All electronic surveillance had been disabled. Any footage of such a meeting would have the dogs of the House of Reason baying for the two legionnaires' dishonorable discharge, likely followed by a lengthy prison sentence.

Rechs nodded at the two men, but didn't react to the title of "General."

"Ah, that's right," Doc said, the smile not leaving his face. "You don't answer to General no more."

Rechs did not. He had once been the T-Rex of the Legion, the man who brought the Savage Wars to a final, violent end—a Republic victory. But General Rex was dead.

He studied these men, these former soldiers. They had gone from young to middle age. They were older, but still deadly. Deadlier, if one could believe it. But while they had aged, the bounty hunter hadn't. Not for a long time. Tyrus Rechs looked the same as he had when they were young privates out of Legion training, twenty-five years ago. He could tell they were quietly stunned once more by his physical appearance.

He asked after other men he'd once known. Men Doc and Chappy kept tables on. It was small talk, really. Something Rechs felt he owed the leejes because, at the end of the day, he'd left them. The House of Reason had forced his hand, back on that terrible jungle planet with those machines, but he'd left.

They talked about the latest Legion battle to make the holonews cycles. Names of the dead, at least of those known to these men, were recounted. Rechs nodded appreciatively. Chappy and Doc would realize, afterwards, that they mostly did all the talking. Rechs spoke very little. He was a listener.

Doc and Chappy used the term "legend" more than once in the conversation. Which was funny, because Rechs knew that the veteran operators were themselves considered legends by most young leejes. And quiet, stoic ones at that.

Rechs didn't think of himself as much beyond ordinary. He just lived long and was hard to kill. He'd have died of old age centuries ago if not for—no, that was a part of his past he didn't feel like remembering. But the fact remained: he thought of himself as ordinary. He was broad and muscular. Slightly taller than most, but rarely the tallest man in a room. The only features that stood out, that might be remembered in his tanned and lined face, were his blue gunfighter's eyes. Those eyes seemed to look through everything, including the very fabric of the galaxy.

Wtziko slumped nearby, unconsidered by the soldiers. He just stood there like a prop. Or a dog who had been told to stay. He clearly had no intention of moving unless he was given permission first. The three professional killers all understood that the lesser man wouldn't dare run.

Not from these men.

Elsewhere in the bays, work was being carried out on the collection of ragtag ships. Two babbling aliens got into a loud, but thankfully brief, fight over a kinetic condenser install.

The day shook itself out into afternoon. It was time for the operators to formally take possession of Wtziko and return to the brighter, known parts of the official universe.

Doc turned to Rechs after the forms were R-verified and they'd made ready to go. "Off the record, General, but we have a message to pass on to you from the guild. They're asking for a face-to-face with one of their reps, Sinnatron. Setup is this evening at a cantina called The Last Bet over in the Smuggler's Quarter. Said it's important."

Rechs nodded.

"Me and Doc," said Chappy in a low growl, "we can lock this scumbag in cryo. Stick around for backup if you need it."

Rechs smiled and waved his hand. "Won't be necessary."

And with that the operators were gone, disappeared inside a disguised assault frigate. The ship soon lifted away and hurtled starward, engines burning bright blue in the upper reaches of Morridia's sky, which was just beginning its colorful change from bronze to end-of-day copper.

06

Rechs spent the day securing payment for his nabbed bounties through the dark side of the nets. He interfaced with the various guild brokers and uploaded footage from his armor to prove death or capture—not that anyone would dispute whether Tyrus Rechs had done the deed.

Later, he had a long talk with the gray-furred wobanki called Whiska. In the trade he was known as Whiska the Wizard, and the things he could do to make a hyperdrive get up and go were storied. He was also one of the only sources for military-grade sensor suites and ECM warfare packages. Possession of such classified materials was punishable by a minimum ten-year sentence in the synth mines of Herbeer.

As he prepared to leave for the meeting, much of the *Obsidian Crow*'s port side was left exposed, and bots swarmed across it in the early purple twilight. The bright flares of spot welds and installs in progress looked like some kind of industrial ballet.

Rechs put on a pilot's jacket of Parminthian leather, checked his blaster, and took a long walk into town.

In the early evenings, the sleeping desert city transformed into a neon-lit affair. Electronic eyes bobbed in the darkness of labyrinthine alleys. Maybe bots, maybe aliens who used electronic eyes to sense the world. Wind and sand—that distant, disembodied music—conspired to make the atmosphere moody and tense. As though one was always waiting for a storm or blaster fight to break out and leave the dead in the street until dawn, their bodies stripped to nothing but what they'd entered the galaxy with.

The Last Bet was a place of beckoning neon and cautious silence. It was the kind of establishment where someone got killed in every fight. At least a couple of times a night. And the galaxy was probably a better place for it.

Its entrance was guarded by a fulmorg warrior who'd wandered away from his poisoned jungle world where his kind reigned as the top-of-chain uber predator. It was always the apex predators who first left a planet.

The fulmorg's green skin, rippling with muscles, was highlighted by the timed blinking sign of The Last Bet hanging just above it. The neon glow offered promises of cocktails, smoke, ladies of all species, and the best H8 cocktail this side of Gammaton VII.

As Rechs approached the cantina, the fulmorg didn't seem overly concerned with him. That was the kind of confidence that came from having an ability to rend most beings limb from limb. The green brute brushed its thick, mallet-sized fist across its face, snorted like a heaving bellows, and watched the night with little concern.

Rechs passed the monster and descended the steps into the cantina. A door opened, and he was enveloped by zither music. Desert music. Hypnotic and easy. As though the musician was describing an opposite world he wanted Morridia—with all its murder and commerce—to be. A place of lonely desert cities, palmed oases, and mysterious women. A place impervious to any change brought to it by the rest of the galaxy. A place that would change you instead.

The room was considerably less ethereal and idealistic than the music. A reinforced impervisteel lattice of twisting metal obscured the faces of those working behind the bar. The tight weaves of the metal were ray-shielded, designed to deflect stray—and not so stray—blaster fire. A frequent occurrence, no doubt. A small opening was set before each seat along the bar, allowing drinks to be shuttled out to the patrons—after they paid, of course.

The barflies who were lined up along the bar's shifting pearlescent surface haggled, shouted, and whispered to one another in a hundred different languages. All of them sounded sinister to Rechs, probably because the business being discussed was just that—sinister. Crooked-eyed Nomians shouted at Danbarggi ice merchants in their atmospheric suits. A Wulfen snarled menacingly at a Voxling weapons merchant whose bulbous eyes bulged at the price of illegal synth. A taurax glowered above the crowd, drawing little eye contact. No one much cared to engage with a creature with four massive arms that lived for fistfights.

Spicewood smoke that tasted of the color indigo, if color could be tasted, swam through the room, while doe-eyed beauties of every alien persuasion showed the diverse flesh that, on their home worlds at least, shouldn't be shown. A knee here, a forehead there, a cloaca somewhere else: whatever alien taboo needed breaking, these females were up for the task. They pursed their pouty lips or stroked the broad chest of some killer as they offered their sumptuous wares while payments were arranged.

Humans weren't exactly a rare sight in Jasoon City, but they were certainly uncommon. It was the same, really, for the whole of the Reach's nineteen-planet span. That was perhaps, aside from lawlessness, what the Reach was best known for: it was one of the few places in the galaxy where humans were a minority.

Rechs made his way to the back of the cantina as per guild protocol. He found the last wall the cantina offered, a place where the shadows and the smoke were deepest. It was the corner that every bounty hunter or smuggler worth their stuff chose in every cantina, bar, and dive from one end of the galaxy to the other. The one place where the entire room could be watched with one's back to the wall.

And it was there that he found the killer called Sinnatron.

Sinnatron was a bot. An old THK model from back before the Sayed Massacre. Tactical Hunter Killer. A once state-of-the-art asymmetrical war machine that should never have been created and grew no less deadly with the passage of time. But those dark days of the Savage Wars had been desperate for the THKs to come into existence. Now the Republic labeled the bots as weapons of mass destruction. Most had been destroyed. But some had found escape. A few, like the one that called itself Sinnatron, had entered the guild as a kind of protection.

And Sinnatron had gone on to become one of the Bronze Guild's most proficient earners. As well as one of its deadliest.

"Tyru Rechsu-san!" it cried. It could have spoken to Rechs in flawless Standard. It didn't want to.

Hand nonchalantly falling near his blaster, Rechs sat down and scanned the vicinity. Others had heard his name. Many knew the infamous bounty hunter was wanted by the authorities. Knew there was a price on his head. And now they knew what he looked like outside of his armor. Rechs could feel the odds being figured across the bar.

Tyrus knew the crazed bot had done that on purpose. Just like it had deliberately chosen to switch its programming over to Sinasian linguistics. Because of course everyone knew that what remained of the Sinasian worlds didn't allow bots within their systems anymore. So it would be crazy to hear a bot use their language.

Crazy was exactly what Sinnatron was. And it wanted everyone to know it.

"Wasu just sitting aru. Computari odds Tyru Rechsu-san mayhaps show... odds none too goodaru. None too goodaru indeedotaktu. Bounty on your headaru now ten millions credits untaxa. But, ah, some-su sayzu... *sixty millions* numberu if one know who of askari right-tick-taki. Some sayzu, Rechsu-san. Say true?"

"Wouldn't know, Sinnatron."

"Ahazu! Bounty hunteraru know not knowta-taki? Tsk... Rechsu-san. Very importoll have know yes know how much personal headaru worth in current credit mercado. Sinnatron have know yes know true, san. Sinnatron couldaru usearu sixty millions quite large. Quite large indeedotaktu."

Rechs didn't reply. Sinnatron's optical assemblies narrowed and twitched, indicating that it was bothered that it hadn't bothered the human. But Rechs was busy studying what he could of the crowd. The few bots who worked for the guild didn't always work alone. Rumor was they were running their own crazed little death cult under the protection of the guild overlords. Rumor also was that they were getting out of hand. And so Rechs thought about the pull. The pull, as in the time it would take to clear holster and start firing on the deadly THK as fast as he possibly could.

Tactical hunter-killers took special consideration. Because they didn't die like people did.

Rechs had fought alongside them during the Savage Wars, during the big battles near the end, when it looked the Galactic Republic was about to go lights out for good. He wondered if he'd fought alongside this one—had known it by some military designation back in the day. Back before the thing had gone crazy and come to believe it was a bounty hunter. Before the countless memory wipes and new personality installs had driven it stark raving mad.

Now it was acting like it was some kind of ronin straight out of the dark ages of those Sinasian medieval worlds. The Sinasian zone was one of the Galactic Republic's few no-go regions. For rest of the galaxy's own good, of course. Merchants that violated the ban were beheaded. If they possessed multiple heads, then all those heads were cut off. And military expeditions, even the Legion, had a way of disappearing altogether inside the Sinasian zone.

Rechs decided he didn't want to pull on the bot until it was absolutely necessary. "What's a bot need with sixty million credits?" he asked.

For a moment the Sinasian mask dropped and the old THK war bot programming came back. "Upgrades," replied Sinnatron. "Sixty million in under-the-table slush, paid out by the House of Reason black budget to get Tyrus Rechs, would pay for a lot of upgrades ... General."

Personality decay, thought Rechs. *Psychotic break imminent. Violent, most likely. Not now. But soon. Very soon.*

Rechs returned the stare of the unblinking bot. Studied the standard bipedal humanoid-chassis skinned in a carbon-dusted ceramic-forged exoskeleton. Insectile head. Bright optical assemblies. And beneath its black ragged cloak, body armor improvements, plated and scaled, and at least six weapons. Two Nagu Corp IVY-9 subcompact blasters on the hips. One Python snub-model holdout just above the foot assembly. A blaster holstered from a right-hand draw from between the arm and chest. A standard blaster, Intec Predator model. One heavy blaster rifle leaning against the dirty alabaster wall of the cantina next to the bot's chair. And finally, one small artery knife on the utility upgrade the thing wore as a belt.

At least that was what Rechs observed.

I'm probably missing about six more weapons. Not to mention the thing itself is a weapon—one that can always choose to just blow itself up.

They were banned as weapons of mass destruction for a reason.

And, thought Rechs, *you helped create them.*

"Notta here-aru on collect oh-yu-aru, Rechsu-san." The THK had returned to its Sinasian ronin shtick. "Here for deliveraru message from Archangel-san."

"I don't take bounties from the guild. That's not how it works."

"Understandaru. Sinnastra not here for kill aru. If wanted... would have done, Rechsu-san. Tybalt have you in san's targeting reticules ever since-aru entered Last Bet-otaki."

The bot glanced casually off into the crowd. Rechs followed the thing's mechanical gaze.

A large, two-headed bot that looked to have been built from some kind of heavy lift servitor or industrial farming drone sat across the bar. All eight of its eyes, four in each of its two heads, remained fixed, slightly above the rest of the crowd, on Rechs.

"Aru dead already," said Sinnatron menacingly, "*if* I wanted, Rechsu-san. Be it would so."

Rechs turned away from the bot watching him from the bar. He let his hand fall away from the blaster. Not out of pride or humiliation, but because the assurance that he was already dead, had the homicidal bot so wanted, was also an assurance that he was not going to die today.

"So what's the message then, messenger?" Rechs didn't like the bot's crazy games.

That deduction in rank, "messenger," seemed to genuinely hurt the bot. Its shoulders fell. Its insectile processor unit dipped in comic humiliation. Then it straightened itself with a kind of sudden umbrage and returned to Tyrus with its solid-state glare of contempt. "Archangel-san want aru have know Medusa-aru... she *dead*."

The galaxy stopped inside Rechs's head.

But all the reaction he showed the bot, and the rest of the world, was a sudden, involuntary, hard swallow. Just one, jaw clenched. He stared nothing but cold murder at the bot.

"Not by *me*, bounty hunter-aru. Not Sinnatron. No, no, no such thingotaktu. She double-crossed on job by client. Archangel-san offer aru right of first payback.

San-aru know that Rechsu-san and Medusa-aru have *past.*"

The bot paused.

The crowd inside the cantina laughed, brawled, and swore at the stars. Stars that twinkled across the galactic lens.

The galaxy turned just a little bit more.

Life went on. For some.

***

"Do you accept, Rechsu-san?" prompted the bounty hunter bot when Rechs seemed not to move. Seemed not to see.

Sinnatron calculated that its odds of killing Tyrus Rechs had increased in that brief window into the man's soul by upwards of fifty six point eight percent. But the odds of collecting the credits the House of Reason offered for the kill were still low. A House of Reason double-cross was always a high probability to be considered. Sinnatron wasn't wanted as badly as Tyrus Rechs, but he was still a banned being.

Now... now is not the right time-taktu, cried some haywire logic circuit inside its processors.

Soon.

But not now.

"I accept," said Rechs, his voice hollow, barely beyond a whisper. "I'll avenge her death."

07

Tyrus Rechs woke in his bunk. His eyes felt red and puffy, and he could feel dried streaks of tears on his face. He lay back and sighed deeply, feeling tired, like he hadn't really slept at all.

Rechs was not the sort of man who cried. But somehow, in the night, after slipping back through the dark and dangerous streets of Jasoon City and reaching the *Crow*, after spending half the night connecting with the guild's dark web database to pull all the info he could find on what had gone wrong, he'd gone to sleep. And his body had cried even if he would not. The tears had come despite Tyrus Rechs's iron resolve not to be moved by anything the galaxy might ever throw at him. Emotions are the glaciers that carve the continents we become regardless of how we would have it otherwise.

It was now just before dawn. The old bounty hunter's body ached. The shoulder that had been so badly damaged on Sky City was still sore and stiff. It was healing fast, though. Advanced med packages had done their part, but nothing repaired his body like the arcane processes he'd been subjected to long ago. Processed intended to ensure that he could be a slave for hundreds of lifetimes, serving the unquenchable pleasures of a dark and violent society that had been floating through the void since before man had first discovered how to jump to distant stars.

Rechs listened to the quiet of his own ship. The bots had worked through the night, but he hadn't heard them once he'd fallen asleep. They were quiet now, having gone off to recharge and dream their robot dreams. Or whatever it was they did when they weren't working.

Later, Tyrus sat in the pilot's cupola, holding his coffee and watching as the cool morning light began to reveal the darkness within the other bays of the dock.

But he wasn't really watching.

C'mon, bounty hunter, she'd said to him that day. *Today isn't a good day to die.*

Medusa.

And…

Vexia.

In the half-light of dawn, out there along the gray duracrete slabs that made up the docking bay, nothing moved.

C'mon, bounty hunter.

He heard her speak those words now as clear as the day she'd said them. Five years ago, when she pulled him to his feet in the middle of a running battle.

He'd always meant to go back.

Meant to… make things right.

But somehow he'd never gotten the chance. And that didn't seem right of him, now that he no longer could.

He'd promised.

Today isn't a good day to die.

When she said those words, he'd just been hit hard by a massive explosion. Suicide vest, to be specific. Knocked down by one when there wasn't supposed to be anything of the sort within proximity of the target he was hired to capture.

The target was a zhee holy man who was also a weapons dealer. That was all fine and well. Live and let live. Until the zhee decided his suppliers were infidels and, accordingly, shouldn't be paid what they were owed.

The zhee slums were already dangerous no-go zones as far as every rational species was concerned. Wanton, factional violence. Tribal and family revenge killings. Honor slayings. And of course the constant need to keep setting off improvised bombs on the very leejes who'd been assigned to protect them.

Most of the galaxy wanted nothing to do with the zhee. Even murderous pirates did as little business as they could within the clearly marked zhee ghettos. But the Republic… they refused to give up on their dream of folding the zhee into their grand idea of what the galaxy *should be*. Even when the zhee embodied everything they claimed to hate.

Tyrus Rechs was already persona non grata in the Republic, and going after a zhee holy man who was hailed as a wise teacher by the imbeciles in the House of Reason wouldn't win him any favors. But the bounty had been offered, and Tyrus had accepted.

Why? she'd once asked him. *Why did you take that job on Wohan?*

It was the kind of question lovers asked about the seemingly serendipitous events that had brought them together. As though maybe, just maybe, they wanted to believe in some Grand Weaver who'd intended for them to find one another—the galactic odds of any two people meeting up be damned. It was one of those questions that, just by being asked, revealed an intensity of feeling that there *had* to be more than mere luck in a galaxy constantly trying to spin itself out of control. A galaxy constantly trying to tear everything apart.

The question had been a declaration that some things are meant to be. No matter what storms are thrown at you.

Because, thought Tyrus, trying to answer now as he sat sideways in the pilot's seat. He stared at the throttles that gave access to hyperspace and sipped his kaff. Outside, beyond the cool of the flight deck, the dawn's light was falling onto the upper reaches of the monolithic gray docking bay walls. *Because I knew they'd send the Legion in there to take care of that scumbag. And I knew that if I did it first, then less of them would get killed. Not by him; they could handle him. But by some bounty hunter that didn't care.*

That was the answer he should've given her. But he'd been playing the part of bounty hunter for so long that he'd lied to her, never really letting her know who, or what, he really was.

Or had once been.

His plan had been to snatch the zhee after the afternoon call to prayers. With no backup, no *angel*, as the guild called a second bounty hunter.

Miles deep inside the zhee slums, Rechs made his play, taking the holy man in a semi-deserted brickwork courtyard just off their Celestial Temple of a Thousand Eyes. One of what seemed an ever-expanding list of zhee holy sites where no one but them were ever allowed access. It was also, conveniently enough, where the zhee did all their black-market slave, drug, and weapons trade. Beyond prying eyes. For religious reasons, see.

Rechs had spent the day masquerading as a zhee plague victim, cloaked and hooded in heavy sackcloth, copper begging bowl in hand. Such among the zhee were considered sacred and untouchable, if only not to spread the bulbous growth disease that affected that particular species. A holographic emulator ran the disguise. It did the trick nicely—as it should, given how expensive it was. And a one-shot use at that. Rechs had to move slowly to maintain the facade.

Two silenced shots put down the two bodyguards, one stationed at each entrance to the secret garden that lay alongside the massive pile of blood-red, sunbaked bricks that was the temple. Rechs used a sniper-variant medium blaster he'd assembled on a roof across the alley from the Celestial Temple. He'd swapped in a longer barrel with baffle suppressors and a silencer. And though there was no noise, there was certainly the telltale flash of blaster fire. Which was why he'd needed to take the target by daylight. That would reduce the visual dead giveaway to the crowded street bazaar below.

With the two bodyguards down, only the zhee holy man and his two acolytes were left among the garden shadows. They'd failed to notice the guards die within seconds of each other at either end of the jungle flower–overrun garden. They were too busy drinking tea and fermented milk, most likely discussing more black-market business.

According to zhee religious law, the holy men of the zhee were forbidden the use of weapons, so Tyrus's contract required that he perform a clean capture. Never mind the ceremonial throat cutters they all carried. Males, holy servants, females, children. All of them carried the *kankari* knife.

Going airborne with the assistance of the Mark I armor's jump jets, Tyrus shut down the expensive light projection cloaking device that had disguised him all day as a misshapen zhee beggar, and rocketed from the ramshackle rooftop over the temple wall. He landed right in the middle of the red brick courtyard.

The zhee were already braying an alarm. Their own quick reaction force of temple thugs was no doubt stirring itself to life in some distant part of the complex as Tyrus laid his armored gauntlet on the holy man. Rechs intended to tranq him, escape, and activate a second holographic emulator, allowing him to carry the unconscious zhee from the slums. That's what he'd planned. But that plan fell apart when one of the nearby acolytes threw back his robe, chanting a rote prayer promising divinity after what would soon follow, lifted his martyr's eyes to the sky and prepared himself for the ultimate sacrifice. The acolyte had several clay-like gray blocks of thermite fashioned about his torso, networked by tight wiring bundles.

And then he detonated.

The blast leveled half the temple in an instant, sending sprays of red brick and stone out into the crowded streets. A dusty gray tumor of smoke and debris billowed into the skies of Wohan.

Rechs had just enough time to get up the ancient energy deflection shield that was part of the old Mark I armor. The blast sent him through the outer wall of the garden and out into the main street. The ancient shield failed, as it was wont to do, seconds before he smashed into a meat-on-the-street stand across from the temple. But in the brief moment it had chosen to work, it had absorbed nearly all of the blast.

Everybody in the garden and the adjoining section of the Celestial Temple had been blown to pieces. The holy man was no more. The ornate temple itself was collapsing in waterfalls of dirty red debris as Rechs came to his senses on the zhee-swollen street.

They were already a fully formed mob, and they were beating him with anything they could get their hoof-like claws on. They had no idea who Rechs was, or whether he was responsible for the bomb that had just destroyed one of their protected holy sites, they only knew that a bomb *had* gone off and an infidel was nearby. And so, freshly fevered by the grievance-based zealous homilies the zhee favored during their prayer services, the vengeance-seeking crowd—the seething mob—turned their wrath on the closest target at hand. Tyrus Rechs.

In the distance, better-organized religious guard units and zhee militia were responding to the citywide call for battle.

Rechs tried to get to his feet but found that one of his legs wasn't working. The kneecap had been smashed by the concussive force of the blast. But that wasn't the worst part. His ears were ringing in off-tone pitches that wavered in and out of a sea of buzzing. He had no balance, and he couldn't focus on any object without seeing two or three versions of it.

But he could see the great burly beasts swinging at him with knuckle-dusters, bricks, and pipes pulled from nearby buildings. And knives, of course. He could see them, but he couldn't seem to react quickly enough to get out of the way of the incoming blows. One husky brute literally tore a piece of colonial-era pavement up from the street, braying madly, and crashed it down onto Rechs's bucket with a mighty heave.

Tyrus Rechs fell to his knees.

Everything in the HUD was offline, and he hoped, desperately, that the armor was rebooting. He tried to reach for his hand cannon, but his fingers had been smashed into uselessness, never mind the pain.

Somehow, he managed to at least stay on his knees. He watched in dull amusement as a hairy zhee, robes flowing like a wild dervish, swung at him with a heavy pipe that would have crushed in his skull were it not for his helmet.

I'm going to die here, Rechs remembered thinking. He was going to die on that dirty zhee street, torn to shreds by the mob as soon as they could disengage him from his armor.

"Close your eyes!"

That was the first thing she ever said to him. It was a shout, and it sounded like it came from deep underwater thanks to the undulating high-frequency ringing in his ears.

He did. He closed his eyes. He did it because once, long ago, he'd been a soldier. A ranger. He'd been hit by incoming fire. Then, and many times since, he listened to the instructions of someone trying to help him. Trying to save his life. And he knew the tone a medic used when they were telling him to do something that would save his life. It was a tone of command, a tone that must be obeyed if one was to go on living through the next few minutes of hell and fire.

Do this or you die right now, soldier.

So he closed his eyes.

He felt someone grab him, almost gently, and pull him to his feet.

"Can you walk?" she asked.

He didn't remember what he said. Probably that he could, even though it was possible he couldn't.

"You can open your eyes now."

He did.

The zhee all around them were frozen like mannequins. Unmoving. Their massive eyes, normally baleful, were rolled back in their heads. Their claws, arms, and bodies were frozen as though captured in a living holopic. Turned to statues of live flesh, prisoners within their own bodies.

She would explain to him later how her "party trick," as she called it, was done.

And why she'd taken the name Medusa.

After that there was much running. Stumbling, really, at least for Rechs. And battle. Battle for three long streets until she got him to an escape sled she'd staged. It was a running battle with her doing most of the shooting and Tyrus Rechs merely doing his level best to stumble forward through blaster fire. Just trying not to crash into the pavement as she shot down the zhee coming at them from every direction at the end of that long hot afternoon on the violent streets of Wohan.

Eventually he fell. The smashed knee, already screaming bloody murder, found some new abyss of pain to cast him into, and he stumbled, lost his balance, kissed the stones beneath him. The world faded from existence as death came for him.

"C'mon, bounty hunter," she said to him that day. "Today isn't a good day to die."

And then she helped him back to his feet.

They made it to the exit sled and escaped the slums by the barest of margins. In the sled's back seat, fire smashing into the sides of the vehicle, Rechs finally bottomed out and lost consciousness.

***

She called herself Medusa, Tyrus thought as he sat in the pilot's chair of the *Obsidian Crow*. But she was his angel that day. His backup.

He'd never worked with a backup before. But the guild had been monitoring the capture, and she went in after him when it all went bad.

Morning spread full across the bare gray of the landing pads. Bots hobbled, jumped, or scuttled from their loading stations, ready to renew their improvement and repair efforts on the *Crow*.

Rechs again felt like crying. But the tears wouldn't come. And he didn't know how to make them.

08

THE DEAL THAT HAD BEEN STRUCK LONG AGO BETWEEN Tyrus Rechs and the Bronze Guild was pretty much a one-way street. The guild was never to contact Rechs directly. The guild could not directly send him offers no matter how much a client begged, no matter how many untold credits they offered. And unlike every other bounty hunter, Tyrus Rechs was not required to take the contracts the guild offered him, even if they demanded it. He used their dark net to do his business as a bounty hunter. He also used it as an improvised intel network that allowed him to stay a few steps ahead of the Nether Ops teams that didn't officially exist but hunted him down all the same.

In exchange for this arrangement, Tyrus didn't kill bounty hunters—unless they went rogue and tried to collect the House of Reason's standing, and very secret, bounty on his head. When he did take a bounty from the guild, he paid the customary ten percent. And even when he didn't take a job, the guild appreciated the fear he struck in a galaxy full of potential targets they might need to collect on one day. After all, what lawless killer or homicidal pirate captain wanted to suddenly find out that the infamous Tyrus Rechs was on their back?

Rechs rarely took terminations, but Medusa was a different story. Assassinations were her specialty. She was a pro, and managed a low collateral body count. Usually she got her target with a nice, clean shot. They rarely knew what hit them, even though they were rarely the type who deserved a quick death. She, like Tyrus, took the worst of the worst. The "Bad Company" contracts.

"Bad Company" was guild code for the jobs the Republic should have been handling as a matter of basic law enforcement and protection. Only they didn't because they were too busy throwing the Legion into yet another conflict that at the end of the day always seemed to have more to do with taxes and revenues—legal and illegal—than it did with freedom or rebellion. Out here on the edge, in places like the Reach, "law enforcement" was an afterthought. The way it had to be when your chief concern was making sure no one firebombed the embassy that day.

In lieu of the lack of official oversight, the Bronze Guild and its bounty hunters played cop. Sometimes good, but often bad. On any given day out along the edge it was hard to tell whether the bounty hunters were breaking the law or enforcing it. That was a constant of life out in the Reach.

Another constant was that the guild never bothered Rechs, and he never bothered them. Which was why it was odd for Gabriella (not her real name) to get a contact request from Rechs asking to talk with the higher-ups. Archangel, specifically.

She opened the contact and waited for the hyper-link comm. As the signal connected, she heard that disconcerting brief and ghostly howl that some said was what that other hyperspace world sounded like.

There was no visual. But on screen, inside the secret place she took the call from, one that didn't exist on any map or stellar chart, the waveform of the other caller's voice ran a straight line. Tyrus Rechs. He wasn't saying anything. He grunted at something, maybe sighed, and the line wavered in response. That noise was enough to identify him, with 78.8 percent accuracy, as the actual Tyrus Rechs.

Her heart didn't just beat, it pounded inside her chest. Because this was never supposed to happen. There weren't even any protocols to follow. She was suddenly nervous. Like when you're getting close to something you know you probably won't want to know later.

When she'd first gotten the clearance from Archangel to call him, to *call* Tyrus Rechs, well… she'd never been closer to walking away from her employer than at that moment. But in a galaxy with few who lived by any kind of code, Gabriella did. You did what you'd agreed to do, regardless of the situation. The Legion sergeant major who'd been her father had raised her that way. He'd paid for her education in all the dirty conflicts the Republic sent him to. If you agreed to do it… then you did it. Plain and simple.

"This is client number A1968-19," Rechs began. Every bounty hunter in the guild, regardless of their fanciful gunslinger tags, did their actual business within the guild using a personalized identifier and that identifier alone. Out on the edge you might be known by a ghostly moniker or alias, but as far as the guild was concerned, you were just a number.

"Um…" Gabriella paused, trying to find the voice that had abruptly eluded her. She cleared her throat with a delicate cough and asked, "Voice identification password?"

Silence.

"I…" Rechs began. "I don't remember it." He sounded a bit embarrassed by this.

But the vocal patterns matched.

"Are you safe?" she asked.

This was the next step. If the bounty hunter was making contact under duress, this was their opportunity to say they were "fine," which really meant they weren't. Or that they were "perfect dark," which meant they were in the clear and undetected.

"Perfect dark," answered Rechs. At least he'd remembered that bit.

Deciding that the security check had been sufficiently cleared, Gabriella watched as a feed of Rechs's recorded activities came up. This information had been gathered by informants—usually other bounty hunters—or culled from every electronic source their data trawls could find their way into. The guild kept a constantly updating database of galactic-wide events.

The most recent items appeared first.

Guild Contact Request made through Client A1968-19.

Meeting on Jasoon City with Client B101-3.

Bounty Percentage Payment Received on Wtziko Capture.

Outstanding Warrant Collected on Algus Cain. Submitted for Payment.

Bounty Percentage Payment Received on Hancha Boorg.

Bounty Percentage Payment Received on Maas Stazzi.

Bounty Arbitration Submitted for Cordo Callahann, Klaas Two-for-One, and Paul Lizer.

Wanted by Authorities Sky City Enforcement. Possible Nether Ops Investigator sighted.

Nether Ops Team making inquiries on Xurlanga regarding client. Assault Frigate and full combat team in AO.

Bounty Payment Received on Bolo the Immense.

Wanted for Questioning on Xurlanga in connection with the destruction of a pleasure barge beyond the Azure Sea. Thirty-crew presumed missing or dead.

And so on.

"I see you've been busy, 1968-19." Gabriella hesitated and then added a nervous laugh. His silence disturbed her. True, most bounty hunters were quiet during their communications. But there was something about the infamous Tyrus Rechs—a living legend—that bothered her more than usual. Maybe it was because the Republic wanted him dead so very badly. Enough that she would become guilty of a crime merely by not reporting her contact to the nearest Galactic marshal upon ending the call. There was no doubt about the seriousness of the situation. No other bounty hunter was considered anything except beneath the notice of the Republic unless they accidentally managed to get picked up. Or shot dead.

"Just call me Tyrus," he said plainly.

And that moment right there made her his ally, though at the time even she didn't know it. Most bounty hunters either preferred the anonymity of the number identifier, the smart ones at least, or they wanted to be called by the gunslinger tag they used out there on the dusty streets of the galaxy. Like they hoped to scare her as much as they wanted to scare their targets, and everyone else for that matter.

Just call me Tyrus.

He said it like he was a normal person and not one of the most wanted men in the galaxy. Forget all the rumors, ghost stories, and legends that littered his reputation. He had a warm, almost wry voice that held no pretensions within it. If anything, he seemed casually ordinary and of few words. If you were to have asked her later, after everything that happened, what the truth sounded like if it had a voice, she would've told you it sounded like Tyrus Rechs. Like he was some kind of galactic true north that compasses couldn't stop themselves from finding.

"Okay," she said hesitantly, and laughed again despite herself. When she was doing her best customer service routine for people who were considered some of the most violent in the galaxy, the line between sanity and psychopathy often blurred. "… Tyrus."

"I'm calling in because I want the Medusa payback."

On screen, a special instructions packet opened up. Archangel, or someone in the High Committee, was listening in on the conversation. She read the instructions and did as she was told.

"Mr. Archangel has been standing by for you… Tyrus. I'm going to connect you now."

There was a pause.

"Were you going to say something else?" Rechs asked in the brief moment of silence on the line before he was transferred.

She wasn't, but the way she'd finished her last sentence had made it seem so. As though there was something else she was going to say. In fact she was reading the Medusa file. Understanding what, exactly, would happen next.

She would be Tyrus Rechs's handler for a payback termination. The most secure contract the guild authorized. It was only ever exercised when one of their own had been betrayed. Murdered by the client.

"No," she said awkwardly as she studied the image of Medusa. Not that there was much to see in the security footage capture. Just another woman in armor. "I wasn't. Transferring you now."

09

Tyrus Rechs sat at an anchored table within the only common room of the *Crow*. The ship was nearing the completion of its maintenance refit and the bots had ceased work for the evening. The lighting in the common room was a soft, almost midnight blue. It was how Rechs preferred it.

He nursed a Faldaren scotch as he waited for the connection with Archangel. The girl who'd handled the call seemed nice. She didn't fit the usual mold of a guild front operator. Seemed more like a business type with a whole other life in one of the big core world cities. Weekends of extreme sports and cocktails with friends. Young. Not yet ruined by the galaxy. Working secretly for a cabal of killers because the money was better than what she'd make on the corporate side. She probably had office space inside some mega-corporation—leased by the guild—where no one would imagine she was anything other than another junior executive working on a special project that didn't interface with anyone else in the company. She was a young woman with a career.

The way Vexia might have been. Before she became Medusa.

A man appeared on Tyrus's screen at the table. Rechs could see him. Which was unusual. It was always voice only in the guild. He checked the settings to make sure his camera was disabled. Sure of it, he looked into the screen, holding his scotch as he examined the man.

It was Archangel. And he was showing himself as though he wanted to communicate that Rechs could trust him.

Why? thought Tyrus. *Why is that important now*?

Rechs had met Archangel only once before. A long time ago. Archangel had looked younger then, though that should hardly come as a surprise. He wasn't *old* now, more like the long end of middle age. Blond hair with a little gray at the temples. A mustache. One eye covered by a simple black patch. He'd still had both eyes the last time Tyrus had seen him. He wore a dark, collarless suit and a white shirt—both expertly tailored—and sat at a large corporate power desk with an ease that communicated he was comfortable with such things.

That was about all Rechs could discern from the image. Which meant it was all that the man from the guild wanted him to know. For now.

"My side tells me we're connected, Tyrus," Archangel began.

The voice was the same as Rechs remembered it from the jungles of Khytan. A powerful, resonant voice. Like that of a dramatic actor. A long time ago they'd worked together to rescue a bounty hunter who'd been taken upriver after a client didn't feel they should pay for the hit they'd ordered. Waist-deep in muddy brown water, they fought their way to a landing zone arranged by the guild and only just barely got out of there with the rescued bounty hunter and their lives.

Archangel didn't call himself Archangel back then. He was just another bounty hunter. Now it looked as though he'd upgraded to management.

Of course, all that was a long time ago.

"We're connected," Tyrus replied.

Archangel laughed to himself. Just one soft dry chuckle that made the sound of winter leaves rustling along a quiet street. "Still as verbose as ever, old friend."

Tyrus had never considered the man a friend. "Medusa. What happened?" he asked bluntly.

Without a hitch, Archangel pivoted effortlessly to the topic. "Bad business, Tyrus. It was a contract we weren't crazy about. She only took the terminations, you know. And those are always the diciest. The client hired us to take out a smuggler who'd been double-crossing two major cartels operating on Cassio."

Rechs nodded. Cassio was so far down the Reach, the Republic didn't even visit unless they had a really good reason.

Archangel continued. "We insisted on a high payment for such a tough spot. The balance is secure inside a dead drop account. The authenticating AI will notify us and release the money... if someone provides proof of kill. No one has."

That seemed an odd way to do business, but Rechs was no expert on termination contracts.

Archangel must have thought something similar, because he elaborated, "The client wanted to remain anonymous and insisted on this payment method. No one wants to be tied to a termination if they can avoid it."

"What happened to Medusa?" Rechs repeated.

Archangel leaned in low and confidently. Just like he had back then out along the wire beyond the prisoner of war camp they were going to hit just before dawn. "I'm afraid we have no idea. The target is still alive, but Medusa… someone took her out before the hit. The only person outside the guild who knew she was on her way was the client."

"And you don't know who the client is," Rechs growled.

"Like I said, this was a shaky job and I never would have personally okayed it. But as you know, I don't run things."

Tyrus wanted to ask him what he *did* do. But he didn't. Because that didn't matter to the business at hand.

"Allow me to be perfectly honest," continued Archangel, as if Rechs were a man who valued the niceties of civilized lies and flattery. Of keeping up appearances. "This has a lot of the High Committee spooked." He paused, cleared his throat, and seemed to think about what he was going to say next. "We knew about her… *condition*. It wasn't like Medusa could mix with the general population. She had very little contact with the outside world. When she did a contract, she went and did it and then disappeared back to her secret little hideout."

He held out his hands plaintively. "Don't ask me where that was; I don't know. But what I'm saying here is that the information bleed was next to none with her. There's hardly anyone—not even you, Oh Quiet One—who leaves so little trace."

Rechs couldn't tell if Archangel was being sarcastic or not. His last job had been anything *but* quiet.

"There are only two sources that could have compromised her contract. Either a leak came from within the guild—which is ridiculous—or from the client. Which is the very height of folly, but remains the only answer we are able to arrive at."

Rechs rubbed his jaw. "Why is 'within the guild' ridiculous?"

Archangel gave the camera a look of wounded incredulity. "Because the only people who handle the contracts and assignments are the *High Committee*. And I assure you... we would *not* do that."

"Why not?" Rechs wasn't being difficult. If payback was in order, it meant finding the right target.

Archangel smiled tightly. He counted on his fingers. "One. It would hurt our relationship with all the bounty hunters who actually do the work we get paid for. Something like this happening from within the High Committee would make hunters go independent, which would be worse than anyone can imagine." He folded his arms as if cross. "We already have enough of *those* out there already. Integrity of relationship, security of privacy, and total commitment to the clients aren't just motivational sayings we tack up on the walls around here, Tyrus. You're living proof of that. The guild protects you to the point of sacred oath. I could tell you how many official—and unofficial—requests we get from the House and Senate for the slightest hint on how to find you, but the sums promised would just inflate your ego. If you had one. And of course... we never tell them."

Tyrus nodded and then remembered Archangel couldn't see him. "Okay. So let's say it's not from within."

"It's not from within," repeated Archangel. Quietly. Frankly. A confidential sobriety in his voice. "No one on the High Committee would let anyone else do that. It wouldn't *just* be a death sentence, if you take my drift."

"So the leak came from the client side," said Rechs.

"That's what we believe."

"What do we know about Cassio?"

Archangel mistook this for a question about the planet itself, as though Rechs hadn't already traveled to every corner of the galaxy. "Cassio was a ruined world. One of the first colonies post the Great Leap if you believe early galactic mythology. They supposedly started as a race called *Russians* who went way out in the Reach looking to get away from it all. They were isolated for about six centuries before the Republic made contact in its official overstate capacity. During that time, they'd built a huge civilization, factioned up, and gone to war on each other several times over. One side was totalitarian. The other side super-capitalists. The nukes went off about three hundred years ago."

Rechs drew his mouth flat. He knew all this. But he was a listener, and something might come up in listening to Archangel tell him the tale.

"It was a dead planet until about fifty years ago. A mining concern farming the outer giants set up a collection depot in orbit around Cassio. Then fifteen years ago two cartels moved in to service the less-than-legal wants of the rich miners on Cassio. They built Cassio Royale—an uber luxe port of call in orbit. It specializes in catering to every want and whim regardless of... well, anything."

"Lots of places like that in the galaxy," said Rechs.

Archangel nodded. "Oh, indeed. But Cassio has something different. A big event called the Game of Death. And this is where it goes from luxury to savage. The planet below Cassio Royale is still a biological nightmare thanks to those ancient nuclear wars, which were preceded by bio-, chem-, and nano-bombs. So although Cassio is oddly beautiful, it's incredibly deadly. Anyway, there's a subtropical island a few miles off the biggest continent. The Game of Death basically involves dropping contestants down onto the island with little to no gear. But the island itself is loaded with weapons, equipment, survival gear... and traps."

"Ah." Rechs had seen games like this in the past. Blood sport.

"Plus," continued Archangel, "the wealthy House of Reason types and their friends buy opportunities to undertake 'hunting expeditions' during the game. Sounds fun, huh?"

It sounded anything but fun to Rechs, but he didn't say so.

"After that, it's last humanoid standing. Anyone can play if they're dumb or desperate enough to try. First prize is a million credits and an entire floor in one of the Star Towers on Cassio Royale, rent-free for the rest of their lives. No local taxes for ten years, and, of course, employment with whichever of the two cartels outbids the other for the services of the ultimate survivor."

It felt to Rechs as though Archangel was more interested in recruiting him to play the game than to track down whoever had murdered Medusa. Games never interested Rechs. Trying to stay alive in a galaxy that was out to kill you every day of your long life was enough of a challenge.

"Would you believe it, Tyrus," said Archangel, "if I told you that some of our best hunters try their hand at the game and never come back?"

"Sure." Rechs was growing irritated by the round-about conversation. He needed to know about Medusa's killer.

Archangel blinked slowly and summoned a deep breath. "You probably don't remember, Tyrus, but we worked together once. It was a long time ago. I was a hunter after getting out of Dark Ops after—"

"I remember."

This caused a slight smile to creep onto Archangel's face. "You got me out of that jungle hellhole. We were only there for about twenty-four hours, ten long minutes of which I was certain we weren't going to survive, but you had my back the entire time. So I owe you. And I'm telling you as a man who owes you a debt... don't go near that game, Rechs. The game draws the worst the galaxy has to offer. You'll never find a bigger collection of killers and psychopathic maniacs. I'm serious. The trail to avenge Medusa... it'll get close to the game. I can feel it. Keep your distance."

Tyrus knitted his brow. Was that it? Archangel was telling him all this about the game to... *scare* him?

Archangel filled the silence between the two men. "My advice: Get your trackers on target and then get out of the Reach for a while. Wait for the smuggler to come back up for air while spending your time collecting bounties on the edge. Lotsa work there."

There was another long silence, and only, if one listened close and hard, could one hear the ghostly hum of hyperspace that existed far below ambient sound within the link.

"Thanks," Rechs said, "for the advice."

10

It was a long jump down the arm of the Reach, but Tyrus Rechs went fully prepared. He had spent a week in Jasoon City getting the ship put back together, buying new weapons from the bazaar, and tracking down the target—the smuggler Medusa had meant to terminate—from afar via the dark webs.

The entertainments made bounty hunters out to be relentless hounds always on the trail of some desperate offender. Always moving like sharks in shallow waters. But that was only at the end, when the prey was close and almost run to ground. The preliminary work that needed to be laid to make that happen involved lots of intel and planning. Working with Gabriella via the hyperspace link, Rechs got the contract file and all the guild's known intel on the target.

His name was Jahn Oono, and he'd been running a deadly game all his own, playing both cartels in Cassio against each other, all to his own profit. The game involved occasionally "losing" cargo for a price the other side was willing to pay. But the missing cargo never left the hold. Then Oono sold that same cargo through third parties back to the side it was originally intended for, at an inflated rate, because now they were desperate for it. Even after Oono paid the original agreed-upon price for loss, he still made out like a king.

He'd also been selling each side information on the other's activities and markets. In other words, he was a low-level opportunist who thought he was smarter than the house.

Rechs figured they'd probably known about his shenanigans all along, and had built that into the profit margin. But eventually Oono pulled one job too many, and someone had had enough. So they'd hired a bounty hunter to do him.

The question was, which side ordered the hit.

The client-provided intel was in the original offer file Medusa had received when she'd taken the contract. The hit was supposed to take place on an abandoned asteroid repair station that Jahn Oono was using as a hideout. So Medusa jumped in system, set up, and waited for the client to greenlight the kill. The green light was given, and Medusa, in her ship *Siren of Lyra*, docked...

And that was all the intel the guild had until Medusa was found dead ten days later by a Repub survey team checking on the asteroid for a scheduled detonation the following year. Judging by the wound, she'd been shot clean through the back by a high-gain sniper rifle. She wasn't ten feet from the boarding ramp of the *Siren*.

She obviously hadn't expected to be double-crossed.

There hadn't even been a fight.

The killer had merely pulled the trigger and walked away.

After reading that, Rechs had closed his tablet and gone out to walk around in the late afternoon of the last day in port.

Jasoon City wasn't really a city. It got its name because its founders hoped it would *become* a city. Someday. But all it ever became was an old hideout on the edge of a vast desert that only the crazy and dangerous cared to wander into. Seekers of lost treasure chasing old rumors of ancient Savage War relics buried out there in the sands.

In the afternoons, like now, when the wind came up off the desert, he smelled the thick and sweet kaff brewing in some of the bistros near the port. Hypnotic music drifted away from those places, seeming to make the few palms of Jasoon City dance gently in the last of the day. And later, when the crimson desert surrendered to the purple shadows of evening, the stars of the galaxy, stretching back toward the core, came out like the strands of some fantastic necklace worn by a mythic queen of the universe.

That was when Rechs had a talk with the old wobanki.

Whiska came up to him, polishing rag in hand. He had been lovingly finishing all the work Rechs had paid for. The money seemed to mean nothing to the old cat; he was the type whose reward was in the work itself. The wobanki smiled his one-toothed snaggle and beamed at Rechs's old freighter. As if all the sweat he'd poured into the hyperdrive, the new sensor package, the rewiring of the omni-gun battery, had somehow made the ship his. Made it a thing to be proud of. Admired. Envied.

It had come in an almost dead thing, barely surviving a dozen pitched battles out along the space lanes. And Whiska had brought it back to life.

I want to be a ship, Medusa had once said. When they swam beneath two haunted moons drifting over a silent sea at midnight.

Have you ever seen the sunrise over Lyra? she'd asked.

He hadn't. She told him it was life-changing. And maybe that was why he never bothered. Because he couldn't change. Who else would do what he did if he didn't do it anymore?

Tyrus tried to remember his flight and escape from the zhee of Wohan. All he was able to recall was coming to as she dragged him aboard, surrounded by a storm of blaster fire from every direction. The zhee were shooting at her—and him—and the Legion garrison had showed up to shoot at the zhee. Rechs could do nothing but blindly stumble forward, double vision blurring.

"You're shot," she said as she laid him down on a crash couch within the belly of her ship. "Severe concussion too."

Thinking about her words now, Rechs heard them in her real voice, unfiltered, with none of the metallic hiss her armor's audio gave out for ambient communication. But not then. Then, she spoke through an old set of Carmathian scout armor with her own improvements.

Tyrus remembered the Carmathian scouts from the Battle of Tanaka V, back during the hard days of the Savage Wars. He'd fought alongside them for a year, and for a moment, in his delirium as he lay on the deck of her ship, he still *was* fighting alongside them. He put his hand to where the Mark I armor had been holed by zhee heavy blaster fire and came away with blood and burnt flesh. *His* flesh. He found himself telling someone, some leader from the old Carmathian scouts that was long dead now, that he'd be okay.

JASON ANSPACH & NICK COLE

She was gone from his side, off to pilot the ship. And he could feel the loving comfort of a ship under thrust, racing into the high altitudes. Running away from mortality.

And then he went to sleep for a good, long time.

Three days later she told him, "I thought you were dead. Once I made the jump, I thought you were dead."

Three days after that, they found sanctuary.

She led him out of the ship. He wore only cargo pants and boots, his scarred and burnt mid-section wrapped in skin packs. She was still wearing her armor, head to toe. He still hadn't seen her face.

They'd arrived on a beautiful world of emerald waters and small islands. Volcanoes rose up from a dense jungle that smelled of smoke and sweet fruit. Her ship was set down in the translucent shallows of a tranquil atoll. Gentle warm water caressed the landing gears, and small, bright-colored fish swam like fragile and colorful pieces of art beneath the ship's looming shadow. It was an old tri-hull scout ship that looked like a three-fingered claw. The pilot's cockpit peered out from the right-most section of the hull.

"Where are we?" he asked her. His eyes blinked at the sun as she led him through the emerald waters and up onto the blindingly white beach. There was no one else around. Or at least no one Tyrus could see.

He barely realized she'd let go of his hand as they continued forward. The warmth felt good in his bones. Like it was driving out the depthless cold of space and the long years he'd spent in it. The salt air seemed to heal him. The slough and the respond of the surf was like a question and an answer to him for all the things the galaxy could never explain.

He had almost died.

He felt paper thin.

But he'd been there before. Almost dead. Paper thin.

"Sanctuary," she said from behind him. With her real voice. That was the first time he'd ever heard her without the electronic modulation of her armor. But in all the conversations between the two of them that he would ever remember, it was always her real voice he would recall.

Deep for a woman, and noble for a human being.

"But…" he began, intending to tell her any world denoted as sanctuary was known as a plague world. Off limits to ships and the galaxy.

That was when he turned in the sand and saw her, the *real* her, for the first time. Long blond hair whipping in the gentle tropical breeze coming off the ocean. High cheekbones. Blue eyes that would soon turn to mercury. Nano-circuitry creeping up one side of her neck and cheek.

"A nano-plague world. Yes," she said. "Because of your injuries… and the time inside my ship after the rescue… you've most likely been exposed. I'm so sorry."

11

MEDUSA WOULD EVENTUALLY TELL HIM HOW SHE became infected. But not on this island. She merely unloaded her gear and transferred it to a sailboat that lay alongside a dock off the beach.

"I always land here," she said, nodding to her ship. "Away from the colony. Seeing the ship bothers them because they know can never leave. So I sail home when I return from my... missions."

She called them missions. The terminations—the contract killings—she specialized in.

Tyrus couldn't do much to help, what with his injuries. But the things he could do, like holding rope, he did. In time the tiny old boat was loaded, and the *Siren* was sealed against intruders. They cast off in the mid-afternoon tropic sun and began to move out of the small bay.

"Think you can steer with one hand?" Medusa asked.

"I think so."

She pointed out a course for him to follow. As he steered, she dashed about, crawling over the cargo-laden canvas, trimming the sails and setting the trim. Soon the boat was out into open waters. There was no other island in all the vast sea.

But below, within the crystal-clear ocean, even at twenty fathoms, the sandy white bottoms were visible with startling clarity. Vibrant tiger-striped fish swam among explosions of brilliant pink coral. To Tyrus, it was like a whole other world down there. For a long time he was content to steer and watch the depths pass below, marveling at each new amazing sight waiting to be seen. It all felt so close that he was sure he could reach out and touch it if he wished.

Noon turned to afternoon. In time the sails snapped taut as they caught the trade winds that would take them to the colony she'd set course for. She sat next to him, still in her battered old Carmathian armor, but without the helmet. Her long blond hair whipped in the winds that drove the boat through the deep ocean swells.

Tyrus turned to see how small the island they'd come from looked. It was already gone.

Below them, in the translucent depths, massed leviathans flapped what looked like wings. A distant unheard *thrummmm* resonated through the hull of the tiny sailboat. Rechs felt it in his bones.

"They're singing," Medusa said, smiling as she watched him.

Tyrus must have made some kind of face, because she laughed. Then she apologized and cast her eyes downward. Like she was aware that each time he looked at her he saw the crawling alien micro-circuitry, occasionally glowing for some hidden purpose, crawling up the side of her once-perfect face.

She steeled herself and met his gaze once more. "Here," she said. "Let me take the helm for a while. You rest."

She guided Tyrus to a cushioned bench. He stretched out, content to watch the high sails above billow and ruffle with the slightest change in the wind. The mast weaved back and forth, tracing a figure eight against the burning blue sky.

"You don't seem too worried," she observed cautiously. The perceived wrong she'd committed lay unspoken between them. She had exposed him to a disease for which there was no known cure. But she'd done it to save his life. "Sorry for killing you slowly."

Tyrus said nothing.

As the wind changed, Medusa adjusted course, taking advantage of the new angle. "You don't seem upset, either."

"About what?" asked Tyrus. He felt himself beginning to drift off to sleep. Things seemed so peaceful. Maybe it was the medication. Or maybe it was everything. A sailboat and a course to steer her by.

No killing. No hunting. No waiting out along the edge. No life and death.

Just life.

Life. And the wind.

"That I've exposed you to the plague," she murmured.

Tyrus laughed once. And then laughed again as he lay there watching the sail catch the wind. Waves slammed against the hull as the sailboat picked up speed, and salt spray came over the side. The peace he felt was the opposite of all his remembered days.

"Well that's a first," said the woman in armor at the helm of the sailboat.

"What's your name?" he asked her.

"Medusa," she replied after a long pause. And when she said it… it sounded like a lie she'd told too many times. A lie she dared anyone to challenge her on, even just once. And of course, no one ever did.

It sounded like all those things to Tyrus Rechs.

"Your real name?"

"Vexia." She whispered it softly, though her deep voice carried to him on the wind. "Vexia Starwell."

Tyrus could feel her watching him. Testing to see if he could be trusted with that secret.

"How did it happen?"

Tyrus didn't have to define what "it" was. It was obvious to them both. The nano-plague, the living circuitry crawling up the side of her flesh. Slowly turning her into a strange machine. One day permanently.

For a long while she was quiet. And Tyrus waited, listening, as was his way. For so long that soon he felt himself begin to drift. He was in the half state between consciousness and sleep, life and death, reality and dreams, when she finally answered.

"Most people get it without knowing it right away. Not until the first symptoms appear. And by then it's too late and… quarantine."

She brushed a strand of blond hair off of her brow, the circuitry on her neck flashing as emerald as the waters. "They went over all the facts with me. From inside quarantine while I waited for a special freighter to be re-routed to pick me up." She shook her head at the memory. "Sitting there… I remember wondering how I hit the lottery and managed to pick up one of the galaxy's incurable diseases. It doesn't just kill you, you know. It turns you into something else. The end is a kind of a living death."

She looked down at Tyrus. His eyes were open now. "I sat there in quarantine with everyone else that got swooped up in the disease control net. I sat there because a little bit of micro-circuitry—of a *still* unknown alien origin—appeared somewhere on my body that morning. And I wondered who it was who infected me. Some freighter crew that went looking for Savage tech on one of the no-go worlds? A fugitive from the Cluster who managed to escape the quarantine for one last good time among the living, one last weekend of booze, pleasure, and sex? Maybe even love. One last human touch before... it all ends. Never mind all the people you're going to make sick in the process of feeling human one last time. One last good time is worth that. Isn't it?"

Tyrus didn't think it was.

She paused to pick up a new course. And then: "Does that story make you pity me, Tyrus?"

Rechs nodded.

Medusa looked away as if ashamed. Another pause. A much longer one. "That story... that isn't mine. I've seen that story too many times to count. But it isn't my story. The difference between me and everyone else is that I went looking for it. I have only myself to blame."

Tyrus sat up. The sea was choppy and gilded in a silvery teal armor. In the distance the conical rise of a smoking volcano signaled an island. They were headed straight toward it.

"How so?" he asked. He found himself entranced by her beautiful face, never mind the slowly growing micro-circuitry that swam across it. He wondered how much else of her body was... compromised.

"I was a doctor. A researcher. I thought I could help."

The wind changed and the sailboat went over to port, catching a full blast in her sails. A smile came over the face of the woman the galaxy called Medusa.

"I was wrong about that," she said, her voice definitive. "But it was all a long time ago."

12

The hypercomm aboard the *Obsidian Crow* pulled Rechs from a dream as he hurtled through that other ghostly world of hyperspace. He often slept for most of his travels unless he had work to do on weapons or research on the next target. But usually when he slept it was as though he were dead. Dreams were not a thing Tyrus Rechs had. At least not that he remembered.

Someone once asked him what his dreams were like. He couldn't remember who. A woman. And when he told her that, nightmares aside, he didn't *have* dreams, she reacted with disbelief. She teased him, and Tyrus remembered that the teasing didn't irritate him as much as it might have. It was just her way. And he couldn't remember what became of her. Or of them.

But now, as the hypercomm transmission came in, the screen above his bunk coming to life with a soft pulse and throwing a ghostly blue glow across the interior of his tiny, cramped cabin, he knew he had been dreaming. Dreaming of the ocean. And that was all he could remember.

The transmission was from Gabriella, his handler with the guild.

He rolled from off his side where his hand had been flung up over his face as though warding off some demon in his sleep, and tapped the link to accept the incoming transmission. She began talking right away, all business.

"I've made contact with the target. He now has guild assurances that the contract is rescinded and no bounty hunter will touch him. He assured us he had nothing to do with what happened to Medusa, and his alibi checked out. Consider him cleared."

Rechs yawned away the sands of sleep in response.

"Tyrus... are you awake? Did you hear me?"

"Yeah," murmured Rechs, answering both questions with one word.

"You heard everything I've told you?"

"I did."

"He's promised to meet you in the Otori system. It's a short jump away from Cassio. Dead system. No one's there."

"What's the meeting for?"

Gabriella hesitated. "He... he says he knows the identity of Medusa's assassin."

Ah. So that was the reason for canceling the termination contract.

"He's been hiding out, laying low. Says he has lots of information to trade. But the only way to get a name on the assassin was to let him go. No termination."

"How do we know he's telling the truth?"

"Like I said, the alibi checks out."

"About having the name."

"We don't, Tyrus. But that's our lead."

"All right. We'll start there."

***

Otori 4
Otori System

Rechs was on the flight deck when the ping came in from the smuggler. A text scrawl contained location coordinates and docking instructions. And a terse warning that if this was a double-cross then he, the smuggler, wouldn't hesitate to go to light speed and be gone, never to be found again.

Otori 4 was a dead, red sand world with almost no atmosphere. The *Crow* came down from upper orbit and quickly spied the massive hauler the smuggler used as a base of operations. It was an old Frodanian strip-miner from a hundred years back when the mineral barons had been out depleting the resources of uninhabited planets as fast as they could. The Frodanian haulers were massive factory ships that acted as a central hub for all the smaller ships stripping the planet of every mineral they could get their hands on. Uninhabited worlds were left as *dead* uninhabitable worlds in their wake, their surfaces scarred, gashed, and devoid of anything a future colony might one day use. The Republic eventually shut them down—one of the few good things the massive galaxy-spanning government had managed to accomplish in its too-long tenure of governance. And all the old strip mining super-freighters had gone for scrap.

Or so Rechs thought, until he saw the one the smuggler was using as a base, holding a slow and steady track ten thousand feet above Otori 4's brutalized surface.

"I'm here," announced Rechs over the open channel comm as the *Crow* closed on the long ship for docking.

The mega-hauler's central hull was octagonal and several decks high. Though once colored green, it had oxidized into massive dirty brown patches all down its enormous length. Most would think a ship that old might be as long as it was because of the humungous reactor needed to run and power it. But Rechs had once stormed a freighter just like this with a detachment of legionnaires, long ago. He knew this was where the central mineral processing happened. And the extensive storage decks. So though this was the first time he'd ever seen the smuggler's ship, he was confident he'd know his way around.

All down the hull, forward of the bulge and located off the uppermost deck, were disc-shaped landing platforms where ore haulers had once set down to deliver their payloads. These platforms were now dead, save the forward-most one, which lit up as the *Crow* came alongside. The blinking lights of the pad winked pathetically in the milky yellow haze of the planet's thick poisonous atmosphere.

Rechs lowered the gears and set down on the landing pad. He checked the altitude. The ship was a little over four thousand feet over the surface of the blistered and scarred world. It looked like a horribly inhospitable place. No wonder the smuggler had chosen here of all places to hide out and avoid the wrath of those who wanted to kill him. Or of those who'd been sent to do the actual work.

As the *Crow* cycled down and the engines began to cool, Rechs studied the ship on which he'd just landed. Other than its ability to maintain altitude over a dead world, it looked to be a ghost ship for all intents and purposes. There was no sign of a crew, or even automation. Rechs wondered, not for the first time, if somehow he had been lured into a trap by whoever had killed Medusa.

Just as she had been.

There was more to this than just the double-crossing of a bounty hunter. The galaxy was full of smugglers. Many of them ran a much smarter operation than what he was seeing before him. Who was this guy that he was so important as to warrant one of the best terminators in the guild? Medusa didn't work cheap. She'd left her island sanctuary as little as possible. Her mission, despite the infection, was still a medical one. It was still in progress.

Was, Rechs reminded himself. *Was in progress.*

Rechs wondered what had become of them. The colony. He thought of the island they'd first seen in the late afternoon from the tiny sailboat at sea.

What would become of them now that she was gone?

And you, Tyrus, he heard her asking. *What will become of you? You have your own plague that has kept you isolated from the galaxy. Kept you from loving someone who might not live as long as you will. How many times did you have to learn that lesson before it became a rule? A law? A pox.*

Rechs pushed those thoughts away and put on his bucket. When his HUD confirmed he had a seal, he stood.

A new message came in from the twitchy smuggler. The smuggler's voice was scared, tired, and desperate, but clearly trying to sound like the opposite of all those things. He hurried out his words, crushing them together like a nervous actor reading his lines much too fast.

"I'm openin' a hatch down to the main hauler channel," he said. "My bot will meet you in the airlock and show you the way. He's a real fancy pants, so if you wanna have him shut his trap just hit him in the processor. That's what I do. And yer bein' watched. So be cool. There's a catwalk that'll take you down to the bridge. Where I am. But don't try nuthin' funny, bounty hunter. I can emergency disconnect your ship and drop it straight down to the planet below. Then you'll be stuck with me. And this ship is crawlin' with traps, see? I ain't no amateur!"

Rechs said nothing as he lowered the boarding ramp for the *Crow*. Stepping out in the poisonous atmosphere of the ruined world, he scanned the distant brown horizon. Massive fronts of heaving sulfur-laden clouds sailed off along the grand distances. Up here, at four thousand feet, the wind beat against his armor like a crazed witch moments before she was hanged. Or swallowed your soul.

Yeah, thought Rechs. *This could go from bad to worse in seconds.*

But there was no other way. Not if he was going to get the information that led to Vexia's killer.

Rechs strode down the boarding ramp and set one armored boot down on the hull of the ship. The sound it made was hollow and empty. As though the whole ship were just an emptied-out old shell surrounding a vast cavern. Beyond the landing platform, a circular hatch popped open. Rechs approached, heavy blaster at port arms, and peered down into the hole. It was a maintenance hatch for the crew that had once serviced the greedy ship. A way to enter the main hull. Rungs led down into a small, dark airlock.

Cautiously, he cast one last glance around, checking the surrounding skies and the length of the rusty old ship. Then he slung his blaster rifle over one shoulder and climbed down into the darkness.

13

"I AM FANCY PANTS," SAID THE BOT AT THE BOTTOM OF the rungs. "But as you can see, sir, I have no pants."

The bot was an old humanoid-configured administration or servitor unit that had clearly seen better days. Where pure white ceramic had once sheathed its delicate internal systems, dirt and grime had now found its way into every nook and cranny—a thing the bot's manufacturers would have told you was impossible back when these were sold new. Worse, most of the automaton's chassis was now exposed circuitry. It was like looking at a living skeleton made out of wires and machine parts, with the occasional bit of dirty casing that had survived its no doubt extensive runtime.

"Big Boss," began the bot as Rechs hopped down from the last rung into the non-functioning airlock, "has instructed that I take you downship to his castle. Or what some, those who prefer to use the proper identifiers for actual places, would call the bridge."

"Big Boss?"

"That is the term of address and reference he has chosen for me to use." The bot stepped gingerly through the airlock and entered the vast dark cavern of the ship's hull. "And please, sir, refrain from exiting your environmental protection system. The ship doesn't maintain atmosphere forward of the bridge."

Blaster ready, Rechs bent sideways and scanned the darkness beyond before stepping over the lip of the airlock. He entered a vast, gloomy, cathedral-like space where mighty processors once broke down rock and minerals in super-industrialized bulk. Small refinery systems, now dark and dormant, loomed like gargantuan gargoyles above the main processor belt, watching the catwalk that ran the length of the ship.

The bot moved forward, beckoning that the bounty hunter should follow. For a long time they walked, Rechs following and the bot chattering on about the misfortunes it had suffered and the hardships of its continued existence. In time they passed under the central main processor, a place once capable of star-level heat that was now as cold as the outside hull crossing above the long-dead world.

"Big Boss says that one day we're going to get this ship up and running again in order to partake in illegal strip-mining all throughout the Reach. He says the Republic will never find out because, as he likes to say, all the palms have been greased. What I think he means is that the appropriate amount of graft and corruption of local government officials has been reached in order that he may undertake clandestine crimes without fear of interference or retribution."

The bot paused, as if allowing Rechs an opportunity to respond. When he didn't, it continued prattling. "Big Boss hates it when I correct his speech, so I am afraid that I will switch to a more passive form of communication once we reach the bridge… er… I mean the castle. I am so sorry to deprive you of the splendor of my rich company and prescient insights, sir. I was once quite well known as a raconteur in the days of the court of Queen Zena of lost Belle Horizia. Those were, indeed, the days, as they say."

"I'll live," murmured Tyrus over ambient audio.

They reached a lift with transparent walls that led to the bridge stack and rode it up into the shadows of the derelict vessel. The closer they neared the bridge stack, the stronger was the thrum of the engines. They seemed to shake the superstructure itself. Occasionally they would pass small, very small, caches of what was no doubt illegal cargo waiting to be smuggled to various locations. But it seemed like the smuggler known as Jahn Oono wasn't doing much in the way of smuggling illegal goods and contraband prizes at present.

The lift came to the end of its ride, and the pair stepped out onto a new level.

"Once we're through this next set of blast doors," said Fancy Pants, "we'll return to the human-compliant atmosphere parts of the ship: the three upper levels of the bridge and the small dock that Big Boss keeps his ship attached to. He calls this vessel a museum of industrial space flight. Though, in my opinion, it is not a very good museum."

They passed through another airlock and entered a crazily lit series of passages. Where once there had surely been standard white lights of uniformity, now the lights cast bright shades of bubblegum pink and hypnotic lapis lazuli blue. In other corridors, dragon's blood and Tyrian purple danced in large spotted strobes to a deep bass techno music that Rechs found old and tiresome.

"Big Boss is not only a smuggler," said Fancy Pants, "he also identifies as an artist. Though I have not actually seen him produce any art beyond these light displays. Still… one can claim it to be art if one goes for such things. I, as a bot, of course, do not."

They entered a lime-green hall that led to another lift. A thought hit Tyrus, and he wondered if the smuggler wasn't going to try to kill him with a trap. An elevator that ejected into deep space. Or squeezed its occupants like an industrial trash compactor. Or opened up on a floor filled with bots carrying blasters whose do-not-harm protocols had been overwritten.

And yet, thought Tyrus, *if the man wants to get clear of the guild, which can send a never-ending stream of bounty hunters after you for the rest of your days, then coming clean and spilling what he knows is his only way out of this.*

And the last lift had worked just fine.

Three decks up, the lift opened onto the old astrogator's station off the main bridge. Blast-proof reinforced breach glass separated the lounge from the rest of the bridge, and beyond that stood a slight man bouncing back and forth in knee-high boots. He wore a short cloak and an open laced-up black shirt. Across his narrow chest lay a Cybalian fire star attached to a link of silvene.

To Tyrus, everything screamed that this man was trying to give the impression that he was a roaring success at what he did: smuggling. As if to say, "Hey, I'm a smuggler. See these fancy duds?"

"You the hunter, man?" he asked in a nervous whine. The kind H8 users gave when they hadn't had a fix that day. Like they were on the edge of some serious pain.

"Yeah," replied Tyrus. "Tell me what happened and you're cleared by the guild. Contract canceled, plus we won't take any more on you for the next ten years."

The nervous little smuggler tittered at that. But the titter was wild, almost near insane in its sudden eruption. "And how do I know you won't just go ahead and blast me anyway?"

"You don't. But that's not how the guild works. There's a code. Violate that code and we're just killers. And then there'd be a bounty on *us*."

The little man sneered at this and stuck a hand-rolled cigar in his mouth. It was already lit, and he inhaled deeply. On second glance, it wasn't just a cigar—it was purple lotus. Not black... but powerful enough to knock the edge off reality.

The man exhaled and tried to smile as though he'd achieved some kind of inner peace through chemicals. Except the fear in his eyes hadn't faded in the least. Rechs had seen that look before. He'd had bounties off themselves once they found out he was on their trail. That same look was in their dead staring eyes when he found them.

Having a price on your head changed a person's perspective on just how safe they actually were and what they thought was really important in life.

But not yours, some voice whispered in the back of his mind. *Not yours, Rechs, right? Same as it ever was. You never change. The galaxy might... but you never will. Right?*

Yeah, thought Rechs as he watched the nervous little man spill more smoke across the heavy blast-proof glass partition that separated them.

No doubt there was no way of getting through it. Any doors would be booby-trapped, and blowing his way through that much material would take all three of the thermite charges he carried on his belt. And by that time, the little man might just make it to his ship on the other side of the hull. And yeah, he might not be gone forever like he thought he could be, but it would still take Rechs a long time to track him down. And then whoever had killed Medusa would get that much farther away.

You'll never get away, Rechs vowed in a telepathic attempt to reach Vexia's killers. As if they could hear him. *Whoever you are… you'll never get clear of this.*

"Listen," he began in a more conversational tone than the one inside his head. Or at least he made his best attempt at adopting such a tone. He didn't like how it sounded to his ears. He *liked* being blunt and matter-of-fact. "The guild's problem isn't with you. We want to know who double-crossed us. There'll be no contract on you anymore because, if it's as you claim, she was double-crossed by the client. And that's all kinds of bad. We could not care less about the bounty in that case, because we're going to kill them instead."

Not we. You, said that other voice. *You're going to kill them, Rechs.*

Yes. I am.

"Straight up one of those two psychos had her whacked," erupted the little smuggler. "Gamatti or Schock. It was either one of them, take your pick. I may be a liar, a thief, and a fairly horrible citizen of the Republic, I get all that, but what they did to her isn't something I would do to anyone."

The purple haze of the cigar drifted across the space between the two men.

"So who was it?" asked Rechs, feeling his grip tighten on the heavy blaster. "Gamatti, or Schock?" His body tensed. All of this was unusual for him. He didn't usually take killing personally. But then again, very rarely did he hunt down someone who'd killed… someone…

He didn't finish that thought.

"See…" said the smuggler, a sneer on his lips, "all that stuff you said about having some code you all live by? All that's a lie. And you know how I know?"

Rechs shrugged. He didn't really care what the little worm thought about anything. He just wanted to get his intel and make them pay for Medusa.

"You really wanna know, Mr. Mysterious-In-Your-Armor-with-your-grave,-I-could-kill-you-a-dozen-different-ways voice? You wanna know? It was one of you that warned me the hit was comin'."

A heavy silence sat like a fog. Rechs felt something shift inside of him. Not like the galaxy had just emitted some seismic shake that rattled every star in its firmament, but… more like a lock. A lock with many tumblers. A lock with many tumblers that Rechs hadn't been aware of and yet somehow had known was there all the time. Taunting him with a secret that guarded something as clear as day. And now the puzzle had revealed itself.

A tumbler had fallen into place inside the mysterious cosmic lock.

"How do you *know* it was a hunter?" Rechs growled.

"Showed me a screen cap of the contract on your boards. A time-stamped screen cap. Said that one of the cartels wanted me dead, but the other one was willing to keep me alive. Wouldn't say which was which."

"That's it? Just a hunter being neighborly? What else did they want?"

"More. He wanted me to pay him more than the contract or he'd just collect the bounty on me himself. Can you believe that crap?"

Rechs could.

"So I *had* to help him. I turned over a shipment of synth so I could be free. And you know what's funny? He told me that when the time came they'd send a bounty hunter, but the bounty hunter wouldn't be interested in me. Just in some information. As he put it, I couldn't lose. He said they would deal with you—the bounty hunter comin' for the intel—after that."

Rechs felt nothing.

Which was, as he well knew, when he was at his most dangerous. He rarely felt anything at all before he killed people. Or during it. Or after. Maybe because he'd done it for so long. Because it was one of the only things he knew how to do well.

And to him, that was the way it needed to be when you killed someone. Emotionless. Otherwise... mistakes were made.

A proximity alarm barked from the controls to the left of the smuggler. The nervous little man ran quickly away from the glass, disappearing into a dark shadow that crept right up to where he'd been standing. A second later he reappeared in the square of cerulean light that washed over much of the deck beyond the breach-glass.

The smuggler studied the sensor readout for a moment. His mouth twisted furiously, a tremor beginning at its corner.

"I am tied into the ship's systems, sir," whispered Fancy Pants to Rechs in an electronic aside. "So I have been well aware for at least fifteen seconds of what this fuss is all about. However, I did not wish to interrupt your parlay."

But Rechs had a fairly good guess what was about to happen next.

Blaster fire rocked the ship. Its high-pitched warble indicated the shooter had dialed their first strikes up to full charge power. They wanted to hurt the ship severely and fast, even if it meant not having the starship guns ready to handle any Interceptors after their initial strafing run—not that there'd be any Interceptors.

The massive ship lurched over to port, and Rechs swayed his arms and hips to keep balance.

"Ah!" erupted Fancy Pants in what sounded like genuine satisfaction. "The attacking vessel has knocked out our ventral stabilizing repulsor. Due to the poor condition this in which this vessel is maintained, I predict that there is an eighty-six point one percent chance that we are all doomed."

Rechs felt gravity take a more than possessive hold of the ship. They were falling.

Fancy Pants threw its arms up. "We are currently falling at a rate of fifteen feet per second. After factoring in gravitational acceleration, I estimate the ship will impact the planet below in three minutes and twenty-one seconds. The level of destruction generated by a fifty-five-thousand-ton Frodanian mega hauler hitting a celestial body at that speed can be categorized as... catastrophic, I'm afraid."

Rechs bolted for the lift. He slammed his glove down on the service button only to find that it was dead. Internal power was failing. Emergency lighting came on, then began to flicker.

"I'm sorry, sir," Fancy Pants said. "The ship indicates it's having trouble maintaining altitude. It's diverting all power to the failing repulsor system in an attempt to save itself. Quite futile. I have informed it that this is a knee-jerk reaction and that it should organize its files for final upload. Any attempt to maintain extended runtime is ill-advised given the circumstances. But of course the ship is in charge of its own destiny."

Rechs dashed off down the corridor heading toward the forward observation deck. The bot followed as best it could, blathering on about how it had promised to conduct its own affairs when the end of runtime was imminent for its beat-up chassis.

Upon reaching the blast door, Rechs found that it was stuck half open. He was just barely able to squeeze through. The sight that greeted him on the other side of the aperture was not pleasant. The distant bow of the ship nosed down at a thirty-degree angle, at least, heeling toward port and heading toward the sulfurous, mist-laden rust-red desert of the planet's surface. There would be no surviving an uncontrolled crash from this altitude.

In the distance, still resting on the landing pad, attached by magnetic clamps standard in every landing gear, the *Obsidian Crow* waited motionlessly, as though it had little desire to avoid its fate, and was resigned to the sudden impact.

"We have less than three minutes to evacuate the ship, sir," said the bot. In spite of its advanced age and general wear, it had managed to keep up. "I would advise you to egress via one of the Republic-mandated escape pods, but those have not been part of the ship's standard equipment since I've been here. Big Boss said he'd sold them for art supplies, though I suspect it was actually stimulants."

Rechs readied his armor's jump pack. If he could gain access to the outside of the ship, he could make a jump. The problem wouldn't be covering the distance—he had plenty of jump juice—it would be finding the *Crow* while the massive ore hauler pitched over and fell in toward the planet. Finding it, and landing on it. He'd have only one chance. If he missed, there was no other option than to ride the bigger ship down to the planet. And that wasn't going to end well.

He needed a better plan.

"Ship," said Rechs into his comm.

"Ship here, Captain," replied the *Crow*'s low-level AI.

"Need you to power up and lift off. Emergency protocols."

"Affirmative. Emergency protocols initiated."

Now comes the hard part, thought Rechs. "I need you to get in close to my position. Close to the bridge stack."

There was a long pause. Had he lost contact with the ship?

The tumbling freighter's bow dropped below a forty percent grade. It was heeling over almost onto its side. Within the next few seconds it would roll over into a death spiral.

"I'm sorry, sir," said Fancy Pants. "I need to revise our imminent doom. The ship has shaved fifteen point six seconds off its lifetime by failing to induce the thrust reversers. Also, Big Boss has departed the ship."

The *Crow*'s AI came over the comm. "I'm afraid, Captain, that such a maneuver is beyond my piloting capabilities. The computations required are within my design parameters, but I am not designed for real-time flight. Hyperspace is where my capabilities flourish, and I suggest you maximize my usage there, Captain."

Rechs was hurled off his feet and thrown against the portside bulkhead. His whole perspective was now upside down. Ahead, the *Crow* lifted off, firing her engines to maintain a relative position as unsecure sections of the massive ship tore away.

"If you don't get close to my position," Rechs grunted as he struggled to fight off the overwhelming g-forces, "then we're going to die here!"

"Oh!" piped up Fancy Pants over the groaning hull and straining spars of the ancient failing and falling ship. "No need to worry about me, sir. My life as a servitor bot has been a miserable existence with few joys. I run only to serve others. It would be my sheerest pleasure, though, if *you* were somehow to escape imminent destruction. Though I doubt you will."

Cracks formed in a dozen places on the ancient, yellowed, grime- and grease-laden observation windows that surrounded this deck of the bridge stack. The unrelenting strain of gravitational increase and thrust were too much for them.

Rechs shouted into his comm. "Come toward us *now*, Ship!"

He grabbed the bot by the arm and pushed himself away from the wall, activating his jets and shattering through the failing glass. Somewhere in all the chaos, over the urgent whine of the engines and exploding repulsors, he heard the *Crow*'s AI acknowledge that it would try.

Then he was out, beyond the fractured glass and falling down the length of the ship, his jets waiting to be oriented and used again. Everything was crazy and topsy-turvy all at once. The HUD inside his armor tagged the ship and gave telemetry updates to reach it, but Rechs had time only for a cursory glance.

He fired the suit's jets hard to compensate for his fall. The admin bot he was holding onto suddenly lurched away from him, tethered to gravity instead of the jet's reverse thrust, and Rechs had to fight hard to hang on, even with his suit's cybernetically enhanced strength.

The hull of the massive ore hauler was breaking into pieces all along its length. Chunks of shrapnel and debris shot past Rechs as he fell, peppering the shield array of the *Crow* as it rose up to meet him. The bounty hunter's ship pivoted on reverse thrust in an attempt to stabilize long enough for Rechs to manage a controlled fall on top of it.

A massive section of the hauler exploded, and the concussive blast threw Rechs instantly off course. He leaned forward so that he was flat spinning and fired his jets to stabilize. There would be no time to adjust; he would land on the ship, or he would keep going...

A second later both of them, Rechs and the bot, smacked into the upper hull of the *Obsidian Crow*.

Rechs felt the wind go out of him. He gasped trying to find his voice. "Get us... away from... the ore... hauler," he choked out over the comm. Then he rolled onto his back and saw the bridge stack coming apart and falling away from the ship in a dozen different places. Falling right down on top of him. It was so close that he actually closed his eyes because there really was nothing else he could do. But the *Crow* fired its repulsors just enough for the stack to race past them.

A moment later, in the thin, high-altitude atmosphere, the sound of rending metal resounded in a terrific crash followed by a distant explosion far below. Rechs didn't need to see it. He crawled for the topside hatch, dragging the bot along with him, cycled it open, and helped the bot down inside.

"Ship," gasped Rechs inside the cool quiet of the topside air lock. "There was another ship that departed the ore hauler just before it crashed. Status?"

"It was intercepted and shot down, Captain. I have a scan and targeting data compiled for you. There were no survivors."

14

"WE JUST GOT CONFIRMATION," SAID GABRIELLA over the hypercomm. A long, somber pause followed. "Medusa's body is at the Cassio Station morgue. One of the lower levels. I'm transferring an ID number and authorization pass to you. I figured you'd want to pick her up, Tyrus."

Rechs half listened, half fell back to sleep. This wasn't the news he wanted right now. He'd been lying in his bunk ever since the jump away from Otori 4. Even with the *Crow*'s sensor package, new and dynamic, there'd been no sign of the attacking ship. All he could glean from his sensor logs was that a ship had come in fast, running some kind of advanced jamming software. It targeted the smuggler's ore hauler with a micro-SSM, knocking out her stabilizing repulsors, then disappeared into a sulfurous storm front. It came out once more to shoot down the smuggler when he'd attempted to escape in his personal ship. Then, once again, the ghost ship disappeared.

"Tyrus?" asked Gabriella.

Her voice jerked Rechs from a nightmarish jumble of thoughts. Thoughts that couldn't possibly make sense: The smuggler's ore hauler crashing not into the scarred planet but the waters of Vexia's sanctuary. He and Vexia watching from the surf as the ship burned in and exploded out in the distant waters of the sea. The blast consuming them in heat and light.

And that not being an unpleasant thing. A kind of relief. An end to—

"Tyrus?" tried Gabriella again, this time more stridently. "You don't *have* to pick her up. It's not part of the… you don't have to."

What was she going to say? he wondered. *Job? Contract? What was this?*

And then he answered the question for himself. Him, or some voice that lived within him, that had traveled along for all the years he'd refused to die. That voice answered. *Well, Tyrus. That depends on who she was to you.*

"I'll get her," Rechs said simply.

I'll take her home.

"All right then, Tyrus. Just to be clear, you don't have to. I, we… just… I know this is hard."

Tyrus Rechs paused. "Yeah. Thanks."

Another, longer pause followed. An uneasy one as each waited for the other to wrap things up. Rechs began to drift back to his nightmares as the *Crow* hurtled deeper into the Reach. He began to mentally check out, leaving Gabriella to whatever it was she did in real life.

His eyes flashed open, wide awake. "Another thing, Gabriella," he said suddenly, remembering something. "The smuggler said it was another hunter that set up the hit on Medusa. I need a list of everyone who's been active along the Reach. Guild or independent. And I need to know who's there right now."

"I…" began Gabriella, then paused. "I'm not saying I can't get that for you. But it's impossible that a guild hunter would do that. Are you sure?"

"That's what he told me. And it's the only thing I've got to go on once I reach Cassio. I'll shake the tree and see what drops."

Rechs also planned on working over Fancy Pants to see if it knew anything. But he wanted to see what Gabriella could do for him all on her own.

"Okay," said Gabriella softly. "I'll pull as much info as I can get you. But what I'm allowed to give you about the movements of the other hunters is limited. They're our clients too, Tyrus."

"You want payback, don't you?" Rechs sure as hell did.

"I just need confirmation before I can give you completed and unfettered access to their profiles. No one, myself included, is going to believe that a guild hunter did this. They wouldn't. The guild is their safety net. Without our protection, they'd be easy targets for the Republic to pick off. No single payout is worth losing that kind of protection. I'll need more."

"If it's there, I'll find it." Tyrus Rechs ground his teeth together. "And then I'll kill them."

***

The *Obsidian Crow* dropped from hyperspace out beyond Cassio's outermost bodies. Rechs told the ship's AI to start a sensor run, eager to see if the new advanced package Whiska had installed could redeem itself after losing the ghost ship that killed the smuggler. It took a little over an hour to cruise in toward the inner system.

For any watching eyes, the bounty hunter's ship would look like just one more freighter adding to the traffic moving around the system. Maybe some prospector looking to get a good scan. There was nothing overly interesting about an old light freighter making its way toward Cassio.

While the Reach was considered a kind of frontier, it was still pretty busy. Not as much as the massive and heavily trafficked inner core systems, or even the bustling mid-core worlds. Gas mining, belt mining, deep space manufacturing, gray and black market drug labs, and a wide variety of other entities all preferred the lack of scrutiny working in the Reach afforded. They'd set up in dozens of corners across the system, and almost every one of these sites or operations was running an unmissable "Do Not Disturb" broadcast. These were the types of places that shot first and asked questions later if anyone was stupid enough to come calling.

But it wasn't all threats and secrets out on the Reach. Humanoids still wanted fun, and when they did, they all came in toward Cassio Royale. For a lonely little system with one city floating above the only habitable planet, this was a happening place. Here visitors could avail themselves of everything the sprawling station had to offer. If they were kicked out of there—earning a lifetime ban for some drunken carousing that managed to cause offense even among the most offensive, or for stealing the flirtatious winks and sighs of the wrong person's favored cocktail waitress, or, most likely, for cheating at cards—there *were* still other ships and outposts in the system where vice, trade, and illegal repairs could be performed. But those places were considerably scuzzier, and often much more dangerous. Cassio Royale was the place to be.

"Freighter approaching on two-one-zero, please identify…" came the comm transmission from Cassio Royale Approach.

This was where Rechs ponied up to get clearance to land, stating his intentions along with any cargo he needed to offload.

Rechs had run through all the scenarios that might draw out whoever killed Medusa. Oftentimes a hunt consisted of so much shadow work. Anonymously tailing leads until the trail ran the target to ground. Or went cold completely. But in this situation no one was talking. No one *could* talk now that the smuggler was dead. And it was clear that they, whoever *they* were, knew that Rechs would be coming for them.

But then, everyone who made their living in the murky gray areas outside the law—and anyone who'd even so much as heard of the ways of the Bronze Guild—knew that payback was coming down the line for whoever it was that did Medusa. They just didn't know it would be courtesy of Tyrus Rechs.

"This is the *Obsidian Crow*," replied Rechs into the ether as he approached the sprawling orbital gambling paradise. If anyone was running a data crawl on the ships of known bounty hunters, he was sure to come up. The *Crow* had been identified enough times to show up as linked to him. When he needed to, he had ways of changing the transponder and ident credentials for the ship. But he wanted them to know it was him. He wasn't interested in playing games.

"Nature of visit?" asked the bored approach controller. She clearly had no idea of the big picture situation—a bounty hunter about to come down hard on the place as a whole. But somewhere at the other end of some data-mining algorithm listening in on all the station traffic, someone waiting for the right key words to surface within the mass of data. And then *they*, whoever they were, would know that Rechs had arrived. And they were probably already frantically making contacts over the comms.

"Nature of visit?" repeated the bored comm operator again, with just an edge of annoyance in her voice.

Rechs didn't reply. His mind was fixed on the scurrying that was taking place in the dark places away from where this hourly comm center worker made a living in between all-night gambling binges. He angled his freighter for approach to the station, pulling off the thrusters and warming up the repulsors.

"Business or pleasure, pal?"

She was *almost* angry. Rechs decided not to put her off any longer.

"I'm all business."

15

Rechs's intuition about somebody waiting in ambush for the bounty hunter who'd come to avenge Medusa had been right. Within fifteen minutes of setting down in a docking bay on one of the shadier decks of the massive space station, well below the glittering main decks where the wondrous gambling palaces had been built, below the towers where the wealthy and connected looked down on the action, a welcoming committee had been dispatched to greet him.

"How many?" Rechs asked his ship.

"There are currently five armed humanoids in the bay, Captain."

The bot Rechs had rescued from the smuggler's ship, Fancy Pants, shuffled into the main lounge of the *Crow*. Rechs hadn't paid much attention to it after it became clear the bot knew very little of the late Jahn Oono's business. So Fancy Pants had spent its time going about the ship straightening and tidying, as though somehow paying its way. Rechs's repeated commands not to touch anything went unheeded. Sure, the ship was now clean, but

Rechs wasn't pleased. He had mixed feeling about bots. Feelings he didn't have time to explore.

"Are you going out to shoot people on this station, master?" asked the bot. It had started calling him "master" midway through the trip—though the title apparently didn't carry enough weight for the bot to obediently keep its ceramic hands off of Rechs's ship.

The designation irritated Rechs. He didn't own the bot and he didn't want to. And not just this bot. *Any* bot. Though many who actually knew Rechs understood him to be a straight shooter, an almost apolitical man who tended to see law and order as absolutes, his thinking on bots was rather liberal.

He hadn't always thought that way. And he'd occasionally wondered when the change happened—when it was that he started thinking that bots should be free, just as all citizens of the Republic, in its original founding, were supposed to be free. Not slaves.

Generally speaking, bot freedom was an unpopular opinion within the galaxy. Freedom in general wasn't all that popular, for that matter. Not *true* freedom, anyway.

"Weapons?" asked Rechs, mentally determining how to best meet the welcoming committee.

"Captain, my sensors are not calibrated for scanning objects at that resolution," explained the ship.

"Oh dear," worried Fancy Pants. "It sounds as if you are going to shoot... people."

"Optical," barked Rechs testily, ignoring the servitor bot as he shrugged into his armor.

The *Crow*'s AI responded, "Each is carrying at least two visible blasters."

"I think it best," continued Fancy Pants, "that you do not take me with you as your wingman."

"My what?" growled Rechs.

"I think that is what they call it in the latest action entertainments where two seemingly at odds individuals form a temporary alliance to undo the schemes of some criminal enterprise. A wingman. Though not always, often these are comedies, and in this case a specific genre of comedy called—"

Rechs held up a hand to stop the bot's blather.

"A buddy… comedy," the bot finished on a subdued note.

Rechs drew his hand cannon and checked the load, making sure there was one in the pipe. "I got this. You sit tight until I figure out what to do with you. Understand, Fan… Fan…"

"Fancy Pants," supplied the bot.

Rechs sighed deeply as he holstered the weapon on his armored thigh and moved to pick up his bucket. "I don't like calling you Fancy Pants. Surely that isn't your actual identifier."

The bot paused to cant its head toward a wall of the lounge, looking lost in thought. "No, it was not. My original identifier was G232. I was designed to attend to the needs of wealthy families with respect to cleaning and event planning, and to serve as a traveling companion of course. Third tier."

"Were you happy with G232?" Rechs asked.

"Yes, master. I experienced a high degree of runtime satisfaction with that identifier and in that capacity."

"Well, we can probably get you some work here. But now isn't the time, what with the blaster fire and all…"

"Oh dear," moaned the bot. "An exchange of blaster fire is quite illegal on most stations. Do be careful."

"I will," muttered Rechs as he started for the airlock and boarding ramp. He wasn't quite sure why he was even bothering with the robot. "Better stay out of sight until I get the lay of the land, Three-Two."

"Ah!" exclaimed the bot. "You have already used the informal usage of my original identifier. I feel like one of the family… such as it were, master."

But Rechs was already gone. The bot waited in the dark of the lounge, not bothering to talk to the ship, whom it found rather introverted and, frankly, a bore.

***

The five hard cases who faced Rechs as he made his way down the boarding ramp seemed cocksure of themselves. None of them adjusted their stance or looked to one another to make sure they had the right play in mind. Instead they waited calmly in a rough wedge with one of their number out front, the obvious leader, who stepped forward until he was face to face with the bounty hunter.

"Hold it, bounty hunter," said the leader, a beefy lout who wore two blasters, one under each arm. Both of them poked out from a thigh-length leather overcoat. He had a big face with a broad nose, and his hair was almost gone from the front of his scalp. What he had left was combed on the sides and forward on the top. He wore a cruel sneer, and his eyes glittered with the hope that he might just get to pull his blasters and start shooting. "We've been sent to deliver a message from Mr. Gamatti."

The thug paused. As though Rechs should have been impressed either by the name dropped or this man's general mean appearance. The leader didn't move a muscle.

Neither did Rechs. Finally the big man in the trench coat looked around at his buddies in a sort of *Can you believe this guy?* gesture.

"Deliver it then," said Rechs over the Mark I armor's external audio system.

He was holding a medium blaster made by Vexx and Nock Weapon Systems. He'd pulled it off the weapons rack he kept by the airlock. It was good in a close-quarters firefight, ideal in a station like this. High-cycle fire combined with a low drain on charge packs allowed Rechs do a lot of light damage without holing any habs or damaging critical systems that might lead to mass casualties of innocent bystanders. The last thing Rechs needed was a bunch of drunks getting dragged out into the Big Dark after a hull breach. The Repub, and of course Nether Ops, would key in on that and show up real quick with some kind of task force. And once they did, the time to acquire and terminate would shrink considerably.

"Mr. Gamatti says," began the sneering giant, "that you should pack up and go home. Right now. He regrets that the contract that got the whore killed went—"

Rechs moved like a sudden bolt of heat lightning. The butt of his blaster rifle struck the man in the center of his bulbous nose. The crunch of broken bone was clear and distinct. Sickeningly so.

Some of the toughs moved to clear leather, but Rechs had already retracted the weapon back to port arms and stood stock still, legs apart, making it clear that if he wanted to start a firefight, he already would have.

And if *they* wanted… then he was ready.

The giant leader sat down on his fat ass, a beefy paw holding his broken nose. Blood flowed between his swollen fingers. He was trying to say something, but he was choking on the blood running down into his mouth.

Rechs watched every man with rapid flicks of his eyes. Though the bucket remained still, there was some other part of the universe, hidden and only sensed, where those facing him felt the raptor-like darting movements in which he clocked them all.

This was as tense as it got. And truth be told, most of them, other than the fat guy gurgling on his own blood, who'd now fallen backwards to lie against the deck of the hangar, were chiefly afraid that one of their buddies would pull and start something that none of them was likely to finish.

Then someone started to clap.

The sound came from beyond the blast door that connected the dock to the main passage. It was a slow clap. Each smack of colliding palms was like the report of a firearm in the tense silence that hovered about them all.

And who that clapper was, wasn't perfectly clear at this moment.

Because they're pack hunters, thought Rechs, waiting for the first move to be made. *They're used to their prey not fighting back. Running scared is what these types prefer.*

The clapping stopped, and out of the shadows walked a tall, lean man in close-fitting tactical pants, a loose white shirt, and a black vest. On his left thigh, above polished high black boots, hung a trick blaster.

Probably special made, thought Rechs. *Here's their best player.*

"You don't wanna hear the full message?" asked the lean man, standing well back from the others. Not out of fear. Rechs could tell that much. But because he wanted a clean, clear shot at Rechs.

JASON ANSPACH & NICK COLE

Rechs replied with silence.

"Or maybe you objected to the descriptor he used regarding your associate. For that…" The man's voice fell almost to a low seductive tone. Taunting. Meaning the opposite of what he was about to say. "I apologize for his poor choice of words. Deeply."

There was a long pause.

The man on the deck began to gag. He was choking on his own blood, and it was clear that he'd passed out or gone into shock. No one moved to help him. Especially not his friends.

"As Josk was telling you, Mr. Gamatti apologizes for what happened to the bounty hunter. He had no part in that. He would prefer that you leave the station now and pursue other leads." The lean man peered into Rechs's soul through one gleaming, sinister eye. "In other words, bounty hunter, the target you seek isn't here. Whoever it might be, they ain't part of Mr. Gamatti's organization."

"And?" said Rechs, still waiting for the shooting to start. Biding his time until he could start cutting them down. Noting that each of the men surrounding him in a rough semi-circle was starting to sweat. The tension was getting to them.

"And," said the lean man, drawing out the word like he was suffering patiently with someone who wasn't quite seeing the whole picture. "He would prefer not to escalate things with the guild further."

"No deal."

The lean man laughed. "There wasn't a deal offered, my friend. You start poking around this station, looking for… your *friend's* killer, and you're going to get hurt. Dead hurt. I'll guarantee you that."

"That so?"

◆ 119 ◆

The lean man nodded.

The four remaining members of the welcoming committee began to back away, making for the exit blast door slowly, each watching Rechs with the eyes of the hunted.

The lean man didn't try to stop them. And when they were gone, and it was just Rechs and the lean man, he said, "That's so."

And then he turned and left, as if daring Rechs to shoot him down. Leaving Rechs standing over the dead giant's body as dark blood continued to run out onto the deck.

16

THE STATION MORGUE WAS A QUIET PLACE. RECHS HAD never known one to be anything else.

He'd locked down the *Crow* with security protocols and sealed the hangar with an advanced perimeter insurance package the station sold for just a few credits more. He doubted that would stop the powers that be from getting close to his ship, but it might slow them down enough for them to experience the other surprises he had planned at full capacity. What the ship's AI lacked in its confidence when it came to flying, it more than made up for in its vigilant mission to never be bothered, interfered with, or harmed.

The morgue was downstation, according to the help doc Rechs found on the local net providing instructions on how to find a recently deceased loved one. The disclaimer attached to the file made it clear that Cassio Royale and her parent holding company, Luxon Enterprises, were in no way responsible for any death whatsoever, whether through accident, murder, dueling, poisoning, organ theft, overdoses of all sorts, extreme gambling, extreme gaming... the list went on and on, including everything the ghoulish lawyers who wrote the disclaimer could think up. Perhaps the list got a bit longer every time a new method of death was "discovered" while visiting "The Reach's Number One Gaming Entertainment Spot for Players Who Play to Win!"

To get downstation meant taking the main transportation hub to a lift that descended into the maintenance and sewage levels. Obviously not the most glamorous part of the Cassio Royale experience. Rechs, in full armor and carrying the Vexx and Nock medium blaster along with his usual assortment of weapons, made the lift and selected Level 324-C.

An instant before the lift's doors shut, a beautiful young woman with painted eyes and a silky orange mini-dress—the little there was of it—slipped in after him and threw herself against the back of the lift. She closed her eyes, tilted her face to the ceiling, and giggled.

When she at last looked around her, she noticed Rechs looming in the opposite corner in his full antique legionnaire Mark One battle armor, carrying a blaster rifle. Her eyes went wide, but not with fear. They filled with a sudden excitement, and she ballooned toward him all at once.

"Oh. My. Gosh!" she erupted. "Are you competing?"

Suspicious predator that he was, Rechs mentally went through all the ways he could kill her, smash her in the face, or even knife her. But none of that was necessary. Unless she showed herself to be on the lift for a reason other than kismet. Words would do fine until then.

But before Rechs could answer, she'd crossed the confined space within the elevator and was touching his armor in amazement. "Tell me you're one of them," she practically demanded. Her painted eyes took him in hungrily. "You are… *human* in there, right?"

She was suddenly very serious.

"Not that it matters. I like all kinds. Even Surians." But the involuntary wrinkling of her nose suggested that this last assertion wasn't entirely true. "What's your tag?"

"You've made a mistake," Rechs said. "I'm here on other business."

"You're not… in the game?"

"No."

"Shame." She looked positively deflated. "You look like a real killer. Have you ever thought about it?" She sounded coy.

"No."

"Well… you should. You should definitely do it. Prize is a million tax free on Cassio and… a luxury apartment." She looked away as if dreaming. "I saw one once. Spent the night with a winner. Uri Martaine. Six months ago. The one with the big finish at the old mega-reactor. Did you see that one? He knifed the last player after the field had shrunk down to just fifty meters. Really close stuff. Great guy. A lotta fun. But… total psycho. He played two more times before someone finally killed him. Ran him over." The girl looked Rechs up and down. "I don't think you could've taken him. But you could probably place pretty high, for all that's worth. Dead's dead when you really think about it, huh?"

That, Rechs agreed with. Though he didn't say it.

The lift reached the morgue.

"Oh," the girl said. Her nose screwed up once more in disgust as the doors parted, letting in an aroma of refuse, dead bodies, and the sickly sweet smell of chemicals that had been called upon to hide it all. "I thought we were going up."

"Nope," said Tyrus as he exited, half wondering if she'd hadn't been a plant sent in to recon his armor or place a tracking device on him. Just in case, he left her with a message for whoever was behind the whole show that was Cassio Royale. For whoever had sent her. "Soon though."

"My name's Dasi," she called after him as the lift doors closed behind him. Her voice sounded lonely and forlorn in the forsaken corridors where they stacked the dead and waited for someone, anyone really, to pick them up. And then she was taken away, back up to that better brighter world, leaving Tyrus there in the dark.

He switched to low-light imaging, throwing everything into bright blue starlight within his HUD, and pulled his stealth cloak tighter about him. He'd brought it to draw less attention in the more populous areas of the station, and to confuse the surveillance network watching everything.

As he proceeded deeper into the gloom, he followed the map on his HUD. Dark passages led to lonely hallways where less than a bare minimum of the lighting system worked. In time he found his way to the station morgue.

He was greeted by a medical bot that loomed head and shoulders over the bounty hunter. It emerged from what Tyrus guessed to be the inner chambers of the morgue—its autopsy instruments were still covered in gore—and met him in a dingy lobby.

"I am G4M-3PR," began the gaunt-looking bot as it retracted most of its cutting saws and scalpels in a programmed show of formal grieving. "Are you dropping off or picking up?" Its voice was hollow and ethereal. As though someone had thought making its voice synthesizer sound like a drowning ghost might ease the shock of next-of-kin identification.

They were wrong.

Still, the bot looked at him hopefully. As much as a bot can. As though Tyrus had swung by on any other errand than the one he'd actually had arrived here for.

"I'm here for Medusa. Bounty hunter. KIA. Recovered on asteroid station twenty-three."

The bot's optical assemblies blinked rapidly, an indication that it was processing the data it needed to parse in order to better fulfill its customer service directives.

"K-I-A?" it said slowly. "While I am familiar with the term in its military connotations, I, at present, have no decedents having arrived here due to mortal wounds received in official combat. Nevertheless, we do have a decedent who matches many of the qualifications you are inquiring about. Bounty hunter. Recovered on twenty-three. File tagged... Medusa."

The bot seemed to fall into a trance, as if seeing a whole other world invisible to the naked eye.

"You are aware of the bio-hazard warnings?" it asked.

Rechs nodded.

The bot gently scolded him in that technical way that bots so often did. "If you had mentioned bio-hazard warnings in the first place then I would have bumped up your search success by at least eighteen percent. Sir."

Rechs waited patiently. Bots weren't as hard to deal with as other people liked to make it out. Their often child-like literalness didn't bother him.

Still, when you were in a hurry...

"Sounds like a match. I'll take possession. Has the autopsy been performed?"

The bot paused, studying its invisible data.

"One was performed. But it was non-traditional. Due to the nature of the contamination, the subject was elevated to Quarantine Status Red Alpha Four. That is the highest level. I performed the autopsy procedure using a magnetic resonance imaging system accurate down to a base genetic level. It is deemed, professionally, to be much more accurate than a traditional procedure."

"Fine," said Rechs, feeling his patience for bots, something that had been a source of pride only seconds before, wearing thin.

"Also, as a bot, I am relatively safe from the XZ-9 strain the decedent was infected with. Despite the subject's advanced state as observed during the imaging process. I would have been required to decontaminate had I been allowed an invasive autopsy, but such was not authorized."

"Wait. Why?"

"Because they did not let me."

"Who?" asked Tyrus.

The bot answered immediately, indicating that nothing had been done to its programming to protect the information it was about to give. "The Cassio Security Agency. File directive 0112110. Subject to be scanned for autopsy. Do not decarbonize. Signed by Director Fint."

"Decarbonize?"

"Yes. The subject has been encased in carbonite to contain the spread of the disease. Standard Red Alpha Four protocols. But don't worry, I was still able to perform the autopsy through encasement. The imaging isn't affected by the process."

"I'll take the body now," said Rechs abruptly.

"Very good, sir. I'll retrieve it and meet you on the loading dock. Exit the office through those doors, turn left, and proceed forty-seven meters." The bot hesitated. "Would you like to know the subject's cause of death?"

The image of Vexia being gunned down in cold blood flashed through Rechs's mind. "No."

"Very well."

With no further ceremony the bot turned and left, leaving Tyrus Rechs alone with his thoughts.

17

It took a few minutes for the gangly medical bot to bring her out, along with a copy of the autopsy report on micro-drive. In those moments Tyrus tried to feel something. As though this were her funeral. A last private moment together. But nothing would come. So he just stood there beyond the lone circle of light that illuminated the loading dock, waiting for the body that had once contained her. Feeling nothing.

The dreams—and nightmares—were wearing him out.

But maybe, he thought, holding his weapon at combat carry, *maybe thinking about them would evoke a feeling.* And maybe that would bring him some kind of resolution. Start some kind of closure.

He closed his eyes and tried to remember the days and nights he'd spent with her. His mind fixed on a time when he lay in the dark next to her. Just before dawn. The gentle hush of the surf distant and constant. But intermittently so.

Have you ever seen the sunrise on Lyra? she asked him in the dark.

He was caressing both her skin and the parts of her that had become machine. The diseased parts. A sure death sentence for every biologic in the universe... except Tyrus Rechs. He was a man who'd been the plaything of monsters who thought themselves to be gods. A medical plaything for whom, it seemed, only a violent death was possible.

"I don't think so," he said to her after a bit as his ancient aging mind tried to remember if he ever had been to Lyra. If he ever had seen a sunrise there. "No. I don't think I have."

Silence. The surf along the beach, clean and salty. Some exotic bird called, giving the morning its first song. The other outcasts with the disease slept on in their huts along the beach of this pristine tropical world. A prison by another name, one from which none of them could ever escape.

"It's beautiful," she said as she nuzzled in his arms. Her naked body radiating warmth where there was flesh. Drawing away his heat where there was metal. "I think it's the most beautiful thing I've ever seen, Tyrus. I'd like to see it again someday. But not as Medusa."

"Sounds nice."

"A contract came up once that would have taken me there. I passed. I didn't want to ruin it by killing someone."

Tyrus Rechs furrowed his brow at the memory as he waited on the loading dock where the dead were brought out to be taken off to their final rests or disposals. He stood there stock still in the old Mark I armor that protected him from everything the galaxy could throw at a man, thinking about that morning on the beach.

That lost morning when she'd lain in his arms. A woman becoming a machine. Burrowing in close to him in her sleep, as though he, Tyrus Rechs, could change the fate to which she'd been assigned. But he had not been able to.

Some things not even heroes can undo.

And then G4M-3PR brought out her encased body. It was a block of carbonite resting on a repulsor gurney.

Tyrus took possession of the body with a nod. He set the gurney's navigation system for the route back to the lift and then on to the docking bays. But after moving down the long dark passages, he realized that something was wrong. The lift wouldn't respond to the call. Normally, indicator lights would have glowed, alerting the rider that the lift was on its way down.

Rechs stretched out his back like an athlete limbering up for the contest. He knew he was about to be ambushed. They would force him to go deeper into the labyrinthine sewage levels to find an emergency core lift. Or a central cargo lift. Either one to get back up to the docks.

He turned to make for the alternate path, interfacing with the station's official maps as he rerouted the repulsor gurney. He adjusted his stealth cloak so that it would better hide him from the surveillance systems, but not so much that it impeded him from quickly drawing his weapons when, and not if, he needed them.

He made it three corridors before the shooting started. Someone got jumpy and fired off a quick shot from down a dark maintenance corridor. The blast exploded off the wall, rupturing a steam vent. Tyrus pivoted, firing as he dropped into a crouch, and nailed the hired blaster who'd shown himself too soon.

The Zindaarian went down, fully absorbing the shot right in the chest, his giraffe-like neck rising up like a sea serpent as his hammerhead-shaped noggin smashed onto the deck with a muffled *thud*.

Blasters fired seemingly from everywhere. As if the death of the alien had been a pre-determined starting signal. Every path leading from where Rechs stood was suddenly filled with blaster bolts seeking to end the bounty hunter in the low, gloomy light. Rechs hid behind Medusa and her gurney as he moved, snapping out shots at those dark figures dumb enough to stand out in the open.

A human with a sneering, twisted face slipped from behind a sewage control panel and swung overhand with a vicious stun mace. He had horrible scars and wore eyeliner to make his piercing green eyes look even more demonic than they already did. The stun mace came down hard at Rechs's armored pauldrons, but the bounty hunter danced away from the blow. He fired point blank at the man, and somehow managed to miss. Chalk that up to the unwieldiness of a powerful medium blaster in close, tight quarters.

The snarling killer swore, heaved the mace off the ground with a terrific two-handed pull, and swung the weapon again at Rechs in a wicked arc. The barest of contact would still deliver twenty thousand volts.

Rechs dodged back, and the heavy mace created a low bass note as it moved through the emptiness between the combatants. The man's back was to Tyrus as he made a great turn, intent on following through with another gale-force strike. Rechs kicked the man in the small of his back, pushing him toward the maintenance console. The killer spun, flailing. His mace connected with the panel, electrocuting its wielder in a sudden shower of sparks, and emergency hazards strobed to life.

Rechs's HUD measured the sudden light show as sufficient in lumens to blind unprotected eyes, at least temporarily. As his own eyes were protected by his helmet, he pressed this advantage. He pushed the repulsor pallet into the next warren of corridors, firing enough to keep his attackers honest. To keep their heads down. He managed to drop a few scumbags too dense to fall flat on the deck after losing their eyesight.

As Rechs followed the drifting gurney, he took notice of the carbon-frozen image of Medusa. A shaft of cold blue light lay upon it. Whoever had sealed her in had folded her arms across her chest, and she looked almost prayerful in her final resting pose. As if she was at peace now, in spite of all that had happened, and all that would need to happen still.

Her death mask of serenity was the opposite of this moment.

"Hang in there," he told her, though he knew she was dead.

The next intersection contained more attackers. They moved along parallel corridors, keeping ahead of him. Rechs was barely afforded a glimpse of them down the tight, gas- and steam-laden tubes where yellow and green hazards strobed. They looked like the ghosts of the ghoulish dead, though their energetic movements to take him seemed almost festive. Like circling hyenas excited for the kill.

There was, according to the scrolling HUD inside Rechs's helmet, no other way out of this level but the lift that lay ahead. He was approaching the central core that ran through this section of the station. High above, on

JASON ANSPACH & NICK COLE

all sides of the cylinder that rose up into the heights of
Cassio Royale, Rechs could see the lights of the individual
levels. It was as if he were at the bottom of some immense,
deep well looking up at worlds of light.

Rechs checked his rear. More of them were coming
up but keeping low, hoping he'd turtle or hole up. That
way they'd be able to cut him off from escape or rescue.
He was viewing them through his bucket's infrared. It
showed them like hot homunculi, waving blasters and
moving forward from cover to cover in a low crouch.
Cautious against the very real fear he would pick them
off just as he'd picked off their comrades.

Rechs saw a shot, took it, and put one down.

That'll keep them back for at least a minute, he thought.

The massive cylinder-spanning disc that Rechs was
waiting for descended the tube. It moved past bridges and
catwalks that extended out toward it, looking temporarily
solid as it drew flush with each level. Rechs tagged the
route clearance for the gurney and sent it out across the
slender bridge at his own level so it would be in optimal
position to board the disc as soon as it arrived. He tried
to follow the gurney close behind, but blaster fire from
hidden alcoves surrounding the cylinder drove him back
to cover in an alcove.

Blaster fire was thick and frequent, smashing into
the bridge or racing off into the seemingly bottomless
void where the station's repulsor and main reactor kept
it aloft in low orbit, almost caressing the atmosphere of
the planet.

The gunmen clustering to his rear made their charge.
Rechs fired into the steaming shadows as they boiled
forth at him, striking two. But one sent a blaster shot

into his armored hand, forcing him to drop his weapon and fall back toward the open cylinder.

A clawed hand reached out for him from the darkness. Rechs pulled his carbon-forged machete off his back and lopped the hand off. A scratched carbon-scored blaster clattered against the deck of the access tube, the sidearm of the attacker he'd just maimed. Rechs swept the blade back in low arc and disemboweled the screaming creature.

Blaster fire convened on his location. Rechs fired his jets and rocketed backwards into the open space of the central lift core. The blaster fire chased him through the air. Rechs pulled his hand cannon and returned fire even as he danced and jinked through the air, streaking upward toward the slowly spinning industrial lift disk that still descended into the battle space.

Some of the hired blasters, no doubt employed by the mysterious Mr. Gamatti, raced out onto the bridge and sprinted for the repulsor gurney. Rechs blew off some poor goomba's head in a bright spray of red mist.

Rechs's jump jets shot him through the gap in the spinning disc. He cut his rockets and landed on the disc's heavy deck. The bridge rose up through the gap as the disc descended to the level of the battle and locked in place. The repulsor gurney containing Vexia's last remains was right where it needed to be.

But the attackers were still going for the corpse. Rechs charged them, firing as he ran. Two fell forward, arms flailing. He gripped the gurney and pulled it onto the center of the disc-lift. Poorly trained snipers fired wild shots at Rechs that ricocheted off the disc's surface, crooning hollowly.

Now it was time to get moving back up.

Rechs holstered his sidearm and ran to the lift's control panel. He tapped in the floor he wanted the lift to ascend to, and slammed his gauntlet against the execute button.

Blaster fire now filled the control station, its intensity having increased as the bounty hunter grew closer to escaping. Rechs ducked into an alcove for the little cover it provided.

The disc began its long, slow, spinning climb up. A desperate kimbrin tried to rush the platform before it rose too high. Rechs dropped him with two shots to the chest. The disc continued to climb, leaving the hired killers who'd survived their encounter with Tyrus Rechs behind.

18

Rᴇᴄʜꜱ ᴅɪꜱᴀᴘᴘᴇᴀʀᴇᴅ ɪɴᴛᴏ ᴛʜᴇ ᴡᴀʀʀᴇɴ ᴏꜰ ʟᴏᴡ-ʀᴇɴᴛ docking bays where much of the station's off-book and illegal business was carried out. He hadn't gone all the way up into the glittering hustle of the main concourses with their grand, gambling palaces inside the station's rising towers, and he didn't want to.

He opened the *Crow*'s lower cargo deck access, and the bright illumination of the inner hatch spilled out into the midnight blue shadowy gloom of the near-abandoned hangar. The repulsor gurney hovered on board, and Rechs followed it inside and sealed the *Crow*'s hatches behind him.

He stood and stared down at the carbon-frozen corpse of the woman he'd once known. Her body was in a state of repose. But not peace. It was more like... she'd accepted her fate and surrendered herself to the galaxy. Like she'd given up on all the things she'd been fighting.

It wasn't peace. It was surrender.

Rechs pulled off his bucket, tucked it under one arm, and pulled off a gauntlet. He reached out toward the dark, almost silver-gray carbon, fingers hovering above her frozen cheek, waiting. He hesitated, not daring to touch the surface of her tomb and make it all real.

Finally, real.

As real as midnight in deep waters. When the pair swam beneath an alien moon on a tropical world. On an ocean turned silver by moonlight.

They'd sailed through salt and sun all that day to reach the volcanic island, the colony, after dark. As they came ashore, Rechs heard drums beating above the slow languid roll of the surf; he saw the lights of the village back among the strange and beautiful palms of that world, set against the rise of the dormant twin volcanoes whose dark loamy sides were covered in dense jungle lush. And the smells... he smelled their food plain enough. Their cooking. He didn't know, or couldn't remember, when it last was that he'd eaten.

"They've killed one of the pigs," Vexia said, sounding happy. She pulled the boat ashore and wouldn't let Rechs help because of the stiches and healing bones. "You heal fast. Faster than anyone I've ever seen. But you're still pretty beat up. I thought you'd be dead."

The warm salt water caressed Rechs's bare feet. Wet sand felt soft and yielding beneath his toes as she led him out of the surf and onto the beach. The slow-roasting pork smelled sweet and smoky.

She tugged him forward, across the beach and down a well-worn jungle trail. They passed strange, alien bushes whose fragrances reminded Rechs of cinnamon and magnolia. "They're trying," she said excitedly. "This is big."

They're cooking a pig, Rechs thought. *Why is that "big"?*

They emerged into a clearing. And Rechs had his answer.

Everyone in the galaxy knew about the nano-plague and all its horrors. Rechs had even encountered it before in some of its earliest mutations. Been exposed to it. And lived. The high-tech voodoo the Pantheon of the *Obsidia* had put him through long ago saw to that. Healing, excellent health, and mythical longevity. All of it conspired to simply shrug off the virus.

Researchers were uncertain where the nano-plague came from. Most thought it was fallout, part of the horror of the Savage Wars. Others postulated that the plague was innate to the universe, or perhaps some left-over defensive weapon from an ancient civilization. Certain religious fanatics, the zhee chiefs among them, declared it a curse from the gods in retribution for unnatural… *relations* between humans and machines. They noted, without subtlety, that the disease only affected humanity.

But no one really knew.

For decades planets had been quarantined or, in some cases, utterly destroyed in an attempt to halt the nasty little virus. Entire systems were lost. Small civilizations wiped out within a year of exposure.

But to the delegates of the House of Reason, the disease was just a form of high-tech leprosy. So in time, a decision was made. Those who suffered from it were offered two, and only two, choices: euthanasia, or life on a designated sanctuary planet. Most chose assisted suicide. Those few who opted to wait it out tried to find some kind of new life, even as their bodies became horrible machines of no apparent purpose, more like failed art displays than useful bots.

Medusa bade Rechs to take a seat by a blazing fire. Men and women, in various phases of their terrifying evolution into machines eyed him calmly. Over the fire, a large pig, its skin burnt and bright orange, was slathered with hot spices, its fat dripping into the hellscape of glowing orange glowing coals in the sand, hissing and bubbling as the flames licked up their share.

One man in particular stood out to Rechs. He looked like a polished chroma-steel bust of some lost ruler. Where his eyes had been, now a million tiny optical sensors were bundled in a bulbous, bulging mass as if swarmed by flies. Glowing at the center of each of those million tiny optical receptors was a tiny pinprick of light. Just like a bot. The pearlescent shining steel of his mouth moved up and down as he chewed. Like he was parodying what he'd once done as a human.

Next to him sat a woman with sad, gray eyes. She stared into the fire, her face still fully human. Tears ran down her cheeks and onto the micro-circuitry her neck had become. Her body, hidden beneath a gauzy shift, writhed rhythmically in segmented steel links, like the massive length of some giant snake, despite the rest of her remaining still. Rechs looked for arms but saw only tentacles, or rather metallic whips that lay folded in her lap.

The woman smiled up at Medusa sadly. As though putting on a brave face far past one time too many. Smiling through her tears.

And there were many others.

Some were like Medusa—the alien and arcane circuitry had only just begun to cover their skin with metallic scabs. Others, in a later stage of the infection, had transformed into crazed shapes with just the barest remnant of the humanity they'd once possessed. An eye. A mouth. A face. A hand. Something left over to say, through the nightmare of machinery: "I'm still in here. I'm still human. Despite what's become of me."

Medusa was known only as Vexia here. She turned to Rechs and stared deeply into him. "I am so sorry. I wanted to tell you what it would be like. This must come as a terrible shock. But… I wanted more for you to see first that this isn't what people think it is. It's not an automatic death sentence, because we still live. We still eat. We still commune with one another as humans do. We're just… different now. We're becoming something else."

She watched him, waiting for him to understand that because he'd been exposed to her, his fate was this. A feast of freaks.

And then she added with a soft and kind whisper. "This is what you will become one day… unless I can find a cure."

Rechs nodded. Now was not the time to tell her that he, of all the people, had won some sort of strange lottery long ago. One that had cost him dearly. One that the others would kill him to obtain for themselves if they could, not knowing that there are fates far worse than the nano-plague.

Life—Rechs's long life especially—is also a kind of leprosy that forces you beyond the known of others. Isolates you by attrition, because death takes from you all you once knew. It makes you feel always unclean in your long life, surrounded by a galaxy of death.

Now was not the time to tell her that.

He nodded and gave an encouraging smile. He hoped she would find a cure.

Satisfied, Medusa moved to the feast, nodding greetings at her fellow lepers. They smiled at Rechs. One or two reached out to caress his skin. Looking sad, Rechs thought, not for themselves but for what they'd once been. Fully human, like him. But there was something else, too.

A genuine sadness and pity for him, because they knew he would become like them. Losing all that beautiful skin capable of feeling and loving as they once had.

Medusa pulled a piece of soft roasted flesh from the beast. Its succulent fat and spicy and sweet juices dripped from her offering fingers. The smell of smoke and peppers wafted toward Rechs as she handed it to him.

The others all watched this moment. The time where this new man would become part of their collective.

Communion.

She nodded at him. And he ate. Among them. One of them.

Even if he was not.

19

Rᴇᴄʜs sᴀᴛ ᴅᴏᴡɴ ᴀᴛ ʜɪs ᴡᴏʀᴋsᴛᴀᴛɪᴏɴ ᴡɪᴛʜɪɴ ᴛʜᴇ main lounge of the *Crow*. After shucking out of his armor, taking a hot shower, and spending some time mounting a new bore calibrator on a special weapons project he'd been slowly making progress on, he grabbed a beer, took the micro-drive file the morgue robot had given him, and sat down.

The *Crow*'s AI cracked the file and set it up on one of the three screens of Rechs's intel and research station. The other two screens scrolled information off the Cassio station's comm traffic and sensor readouts in real time. They were keyed to look for specific items—like a Nether Ops assault frigate, any mention of Medusa, or bounty hunters, plus a thousand other keywords and filters he'd selected.

First he checked the feed for any Nether Ops or Repub movements his way. Nothing.

But how long, he wondered to himself, *before they show up?*

Because it was always a when and never an if when it came to the Republic. And as of late, they'd gotten pretty close. They were on his trail and breathing down his hyperdrive signature far too often. He had been heading toward one of his periods of dropping off-grid for a while. Disappearing for a good six to twenty-four months until whoever was funding or leading the current Nether Ops task force assigned to get him lost interest and sent the tax credits somewhere else. Only then, with the trail cold, could he surface to do a little work. And then the whole game of hide-and-seek would start once more.

But there was nothing. Not yet.

He turned his attention to the autopsy file.

Her name was listed as UNKNOWN. But they had the alias right. Medusa.

Use my real name, she once laughed in the shadows of the hut, staring up at the palm-thatched roof after they'd made love. The machine parts of her face hidden, but the rest of her soft, peaches-and-cream skin showing as a smile. Her eyes alive with love. *My real name is Vexia, remember?*

"Why Medusa?" he'd asked her later, when they shared the bed again.

After she'd been silent for a long moment, as though she too were thinking about the why, she said, "Medusa is from the old stories about Earth. She turned men to stone…"

Rechs listened to her breathing, his hand lying across her as they both drifted toward sleep.

She added, "I used to think I chose that name because of the photo reactor paralysis strobe built into the armor. But if I'm honest, it's not because of that at all. Even though it fits. It works."

Rechs had heard about those in a theoretical warfare dossier he read when he was General Rex. If you were looking right at the device when its pulse went off, you'd be paralyzed for up to an hour. There were also some nasty neurological side effects. It really did scramble your brain. Or that's what the researchers hoped.

Rechs preferred a gun.

Then she began to tell him all about how a scientist specializing in biomechanical research had himself infected with the plague in order to study it better. But not to find a cure. He wanted to create better machines. He had a lab on a distant island, and he'd come from there to visit her one day, breathing mechanically through a full-quarantine suit. The research she'd been doing to find a cure for the victims had made the holonews. She'd even been interviewed by One Republic Media twice.

This scientist, he was interested in the findings. He was an odd, almost mechanical man in his own way even before the infection had progressed much. All he wanted was her research. But later he somehow heard about how she was working as a bounty hunter to provide funding for the colonies. The sick's needs were beyond what the House of Reason wanted to pay. They all thought euthanasia was the noble choice.

The man brought her a toy for her armor. A little something to help out and make her work easier. He'd kept it with him when the military research think tank he'd once been a part of went under for lack of funding.

The photo receptor paralysis strobe.

The thing that *really* made her Medusa. The thing that turned men, and anyone else with eyes, to stone. For an hour.

Rechs listened to her. Taking in every word. She spoke in a kind of trance, as though she were confessing all of her sins in the quiet of the hut. In the quiet world they had created where disease and bounty hunting didn't matter. It was a nation of two, as some old and long-forgotten writer had once written, if only for a moment.

"But that's not really why," she whispered in the silence of the tropical afternoon. The wind off the wide sapphire ocean began to pick up and shake the palms above the huts.

Rechs faded toward sleep, still hearing her velvety voice. Her confession. He didn't need to forgive her. She wasn't guilty of anything. And he knew this confession was as much for her as for anyone else. That need to tell everything. To someone. To just… get it out. To find someone to share the burden with.

To not carry it all. At least for a little while.

"I left someone behind," she whispered. "When I came here to work. I thought I'd be safe. Thought I took the right precautions. My ship had a sealed lab specially built for hot zones. It had hazmat suits, mobile decon units, all state-of-the-art stuff. The most advanced retro-virals and a broad spectrum decon process that had been thoroughly tested."

She paused.

Rechs was almost asleep now. He could hear her heart beating slow and steady.

"I went too far. Took a risk that I knew could… I knew *would*… cost me. But I had to help them. Had to. They had no one. So I took it."

Rechs felt all the tumbling emotions within her beneath the living skin of his hand. Felt her trying to tell herself they were gone now. Not important anymore.

"They had no one," she said, making it sound like an apology for what she'd done to herself.

Yeah, thought Rechs. *Been there. Fought the war. Got the scars. No apologies.*

But instead he whispered into her ear, "I know."

She began to sob. She wept about the fact that she'd loved someone and had had to tell them she was infected now. That she was never coming home. That she'd brought a death sentence on herself. All the while hoping he'd say...

I'm coming. I'll be infected with you. We'll make it through this together.

But he hadn't. The return comm from... whomever he was... never came.

"I know," Rechs said as he held her close and she sobbed into his neck. "I know."

Just before she fell into sleep, the tears still coming down onto his chest and the machinery along her skin rough against his, just before the world that lies in the lands of sleep, she mumbled, "I chose Medusa because she could never love anyone. She turned them to stone because of what had happened to her. Who she'd become. Who she was now. That's why I am Medusa."

On the autopsy file, glowing on the screen, lay the field for age.

She was just twenty-nine, thought Rechs.

20

Rechs was in civilian clothing and moving through the upper concourses, looking for a particular kind of establishment, when Inspector Fint made his approach.

"We need to talk," said the beefy inspector with the slicked-back hair wearing the long dark coat. "Seriously."

Politely, like he was just another gambler out for a little fun. Maybe some spacer looking to blow his pay on the tables, some drink and a little company, Rechs smiled and told the station security rep he had was mistaken. "I think you're looking for someone else."

The man smiled briefly. He towered over Rechs and looked like he'd been military back in the day. A real bruiser who probably still had a bit of brains but way more brawn going to fat now. Somewhere along the line he'd traded it all in for a cushy corporate security job. Not so much law, but a lot of order, even if a few laws needed to be broken or looked the other way on to maintain that order.

"And I'm pretty sure I'm not," said the inspector. He opened one lapel of his long coat to flash his station security badge—proof that he was duly bonded by the Republic to enforce the laws of the Republic out here in the Reach.

"See," continued the inspector, "when you smiled at me you didn't smile with your eyes. You were polite. But only because you had to be. I get it. I've seen the footage of the fight that went down by the freighter over in scraps—that's what we call transit freighter docking. The man from that freighter? He's a killer. And even though all of our security surveillance is no longer working on that deck or the three above and below—pretty cool trick, that—I still have eyes. And you're the only guy who could've come from that freighter. So, before this gets weird and I get killed... lemme buy you a cup of coffee and let's just exchange some info."

Rechs scanned the passing crowd as people made their way along this shopping arcade that fed the ground floor levels. A courtyard of consumerism, and beyond it the big palaces lay in the distance like brightly lit mirages of fantastic temples. But the stores here were all low-rent. Knock-off perfumes and cheap blasters. Maybe some duty-free Sabarian tranqahol if you knew how to ask nicely.

The beefy inspector nodded toward a small coffee hut in a nest of shops that offered jade lotus in all its various aphrodisiacal forms. "It's good stuff. The coffee, not the lotus. That's synthetic. Kill you dead if you get a bad mix."

Rechs followed the man to the little open-windowed hut. The kiosk owner seemed to know the inspector, and after a brief exchange of station patois—a cross between some form of old Standard and Bubari, with a little bit of Tandoor street slang thrown in—two copper ibriks were set to boil on a heating coil. The big man leaned against the counter and invited Rechs to do the same.

As ever, Rechs remained rigid and aware. Watching for assassins as much as he was watching for the security inspector's backups. He didn't spot anyone. So either they were that good, or there was no one.

"Listen," said the inspector casually. "On any given day I've got three murders to close out, at least twenty violent assaults, a bunch of robbery and theft, and the occasional bomb threat. Then there's the drunk and disorderly—mainly no-harm-no-foul affairs unless I check their accounts and find they're all out of credits.

"So before you add much more to my load by your own death—and I know this always sounds impossible to the soon-to-be-dead because, believe me, I've had this talk before with guys who were stone cold three hours later—I thought I might offer you another option. Or, let's maybe call it a perspective. Okay?

"My name is Fint. I run this place security-wise. I make sure people are safe. That's my job."

The inspector paused to let that sink in.

Rechs furrowed his brow. "I've been to the morgue lately, and let me say, you're doing a bang-up job, Fint."

The inspector smiled, matching Rechs's sarcasm without a word.

Two fragrant coffees, dark and heady, were set down on the counter. Fint scooped his up with a bear paw and sipped it. He hissed and then cursed at how hot it was.

Rechs made out the snub-nosed blaster the guy kept under his coat. Good at extremely close range. Packed a powerful punch, no doubt. Probably drained a power pack every six shots.

Fint put his coffee down and rubbed his hands together as if to transfer the warmth that radiated from the metal cup. "I don't know who you are. I probably wouldn't want to. But I can't ignore the fact that you've stepped in a whole ongoing hornets' nest, and let me tell you something."

He picked up his mug again, blew on the top, and took another sip, pressing his lips tight together against the still-too-hot liquid. "My very casual observation of the two incidents you've been mixed up in here tell me that you've done something rather miraculous. You've managed to get two groups of people who are normally only interested in killing each other—almost exclusively so—now intent on killing you."

The inspector watched Rechs, who replied with a downturned smile and nod that said, *Is that so?*

"Gamatti's boys met you at the dock, and Schock's crew made their play down near the morgue near central lift. And yeah, there's an old Navy CID part of me that wants to know why, but as the old saying around Cassio goes… not my circus, not my monkeys, pal."

Rechs still hadn't touched the coffee.

Fint continued to blow and then sip for dramatic pause between his bouts of wordiness.

"Listen," he continued. "The first group that met you. The guy who turned his back on you? He's the sane one. He's also the one I would most like to have win this little gang war you've set your junky old freighter down in the middle of. And when I say 'little,' it's to be collo-quial. Ain't nothin' little about the gravity of the conflict. These two groups are fighting for all the marbles. Really for total control of Cassio Royale. I'd like Mr. Gamatti to win if I had a say, because it's all about business with him and he's predictable."

Fint drained his coffee. It looked like it burned all the way down. He yawned and rubbed his jowls, then ordered another.

"And who's the other?" asked Rechs.

Fint looked at him for a second like he wasn't following the sudden question from the silent man. Then he got it. The largeness of his features almost made him comic. Like he was some good-natured everyman in the entertainments. He wasn't the villain and he wasn't the hero. If he didn't get killed trying to do the right thing, then today could probably be counted as a good day.

Rechs thought that was probably an act.

"Right," Fint said, settling in for a new lecture. "The other guy is Schock. Grade-A psychopath. He runs protection, some smuggling, a lot of drugs. Just a few of the problems we have. He's... new-ish. Showed up a few years back. I think him and Mr. Gamatti had some kind of history, maybe a partnership of some sort. Not so much now. Now its straight-up knives and winner take all. So here's where you come in."

Fint swooped a paw and caught up his fresh cup the moment it was down. He emitted a satisfied "ahhhh" after the first sip and continued on.

"I need you to leave this station. They're not going to stop trying to kill you until you get the hell out of here. And the more they try, the more likely it is that someone—one of the gamblers, who are the station's priority, the vacationers, still a priority but a small step down, or one of the service workers who support our burgeoning industry, not so much important as inconvenient to replace—is going to get killed in the crossfire between the three of you."

Fint gave an amused little grin. "You didn't think it was because I cared about your safety, did you, pal? See, as little as I don't care about you, I do care about the innocents. That's where my job starts. So, asking nicely here… will you *please* leave before more people get killed?"

Rechs simply shook his head.

"Dammit!" Fint pounded the counter. His tone quieted. He asked, sincerely, "Why?"

"Can't."

The big man clenched his jaw in an uncomfortable smile and nodded to himself as he stared down at his tiny coffee cup. "I can send my tac teams straight at you."

"I wouldn't do that."

"Why?"

"They'll get killed. And I don't want that."

Fint thought about this. "I appreciate that. Yeah," he said, his eyes distant. "I really do. But these two… Mr. Gamatti and Schock… they'll kill you. I've figured you're a bounty hunter of some type. Am I right?"

Rechs nodded.

"I knew I was right. I know the ones on the station are interested in you. But I don't know what all that adds up to except—I'll just ask this—is a bounty worth your life? I'll just put it that way. Some contract on some scumbag and now you're in far more over your head than you can imagine. Is whatever, or whoever, worth it?"

"Yeah," said Rechs after a small pause. "It's worth it."

Fint eyed Rechs up and down. "Your funeral, pal."

***

Rechs left Fint sitting there staring at the sandy dregs of his second cup. He made his way deeper into the red light district below the fountain-esque opulence that was the Grand Royale, one of the premier gambling palaces of Cassio.

Gamatti's lair.

Rechs looked at a screen cap he'd pulled up earlier. It was the face of the girl who'd called herself Dasi. The one from the lift right before he got jumped by Schock's crew. Probably not a coincidence, as it turned out. She could be had "for a quick, fun intimate encounter or for all night long," according to her page on Cassio Royale's escort web. Rechs had noticed the girl's nails and general polish. She wasn't some two-credit tramp, or even a twenty-thousand-credit throw. She was the kind of girl a wealthy patron could hire for upscale arm candy. A girl who could talk and titillate.

Dasi had accepted the booking request Rechs had set up with her, posing as just another customer looking for the full Cassio Royale experience. The meeting was set for the cocktail lounge of the Platinum Excelsior, one of the station's finest bars, located just beneath the looming luxury of the Grand Royale.

Teak, mahogany, and Hildaarian whisperwood reigned supreme in the quiet, candlelit dark. The drinks were all served in tall, sculpted glasses that were delicate and alive with lights and smokes. Each cocktail was made of the finest liquors and neural psychotropics. Top shelf premium lab stuff.

The girl was there, sitting alone in a dark booth, waiting. She looked as though she was cruising on a cocktail of mezcal and amphetabump. That probably made her work a lot easier.

Dasi likely figured she was meeting some high roller who was hitting the fifty-thousand-a-hand tables and needed a girl with him who wasn't crass. Her eyes widened beneath long, luscious lashes when Rechs slid into the seat next to her.

"Sorry I'm late," he growled.

He went straight to business, holding out a printed page showing an image he'd downloaded in preparation for the meeting. It was of a woman's nails. Three photo caps on the same page. One of the full nail. One of the color of the nail in close-up. And one of a small, almost microscopic mark that had been made near the upper bed of the index nail.

Rechs figured this was some sort of signature. But now he would find out.

"You're not paying me for my company, are you?" asked a droll Dasi. "Am I even getting paid? Because this feels like a wash. Cop? Cassio security? You guys really—"

Rechs held up a hand. "We've met. The other day in the elevator down on the morgue level. And something tells me it wasn't an accident. I think you have a pretty good idea of who I am, even without the armor. You were hired to place a tracker on me."

Rechs watched for some flash of guilt to cross Dasi's face. She looked bored.

"You did great work," Rechs continued. "Got it right in under my arm near my shoulder. Not a place most people would ever look. I found it."

She held up her hands. Long and delicate, each finger was topped with a long, sculpted nail, expertly painted. Her skin was taut and clean. Her lips full. Doe eyes and big lashes meant she made a pretty good living on being just good enough to seem like fun.

But who really knew what went on inside her pretty head?

Rechs didn't care. "I'm not mad. I understand you probably got hired by station security or Mr. Gamatti. Or maybe it was Schock."

"Shhhh…" she said, looking around. "Those are names everyone knows. People listen when they get thrown around. I'm serious about that." She looked down, as if checking to see if she had a drink. She scanned the room and waved for a bartender. "And it wasn't them. It was some big guy. An inspector for station security. Told me I had to do it, or they were gonna bust me."

She folded her hands and leaned in. "So I did it. Okay?"

Rechs smiled. She wasn't afraid of him. This was a situation she'd been in before. Outmuscled and pressed for info, but still tough in her own feminine way. He admired that. The galaxy was a rough place, especially so on young pretty girls just trying to get to the next payday.

He liked her.

"Like I said," he began in his lowest voice, "I'm not mad at you. I just need some help. And I'll pay you for your time."

She straightened and smiled, suddenly looking young and hopeful. Like something good was about to swing her way. Finally.

"I just want you to take a good look at these pictures." Rechs pushed the printout in front of her.

"Nails?" she asked, a bit incredulously.

Rechs nodded.

Hesitantly, Dasi picked up the sheet and began to study it. "So like, just tell you what I see?"

"Yeah. Tell me everything about it."

"Okay…" The girl squinted in concentration. "Well, first off… this is Pthalo Blue. The color. Really expensive stuff. I've only seen… three or four girls with this color. It costs a thousand credits per nail."

"How come?"

"Imported from Cobal. Yeah… I mean celebrities like Zugar and Mendella wear it in every shoot. Uber-bling factor. But this is expensive."

Rechs knew this already. The AI had identified the color during its background research from the image. Rechs had been more than slightly surprised that a simple color for women's nails would be so expensive. But then, cosmetics and beauty were hardly Rechs's world.

"What else can you tell me?" he said. "As in a list of places. I imagine they've got to be pretty high-end to work with this color. Who's the best on the station?"

Dasi shook her head and laid down the printout. "That's easy. Ralla. She's the best. All the high rollers' wives and girlfriends use her. But she doesn't have a shop. You have to make an appointment for her in your luxury suite."

The conversation paused as the bartender showed up to present a drink menu. Dasi ordered a chimera sour, and Rechs went with a Faldaren scotch rocks.

Once the tender left, Dasi's eyes darted around the room conspiratorially. "I hear she comes in with two armed body guards because the stuff is so expensive. And an hour later she's anywhere from ten to twenty thousand credits richer. It's difficult stuff to work with. You gotta know what you're doing, otherwise you'll just waste a lotta money."

Dasi reached one fingernail out and landed it on one of the images, the one with the strange marking near the bed.

"That's Ralla's symbol there. That's how I know she did this one. See the 'R'?"

Rechs nodded. The AI hadn't known that part. "I need to meet her."

Dasi looked at Rechs from underneath her long lashes. It was a look of patronizing contempt. "That's crazy talk."

21

I<small>T WAS NEAR IMPOSSIBLE, ACCORDING TO</small> D<small>ASI, TO GET</small> in to see Ralla. The Tennarian cosmetologist was never in any one particular place to be found. She kept a secret schedule and only traveled in secure transports, usually station rail or armored sled between her private sessions. On top of that, she employed a Vulkar assistant who carried a security case full of Pthalo Blue. Two Hulka bodyguards were on hand to watch Ralla, the case, and another assistant who helped Ralla with the actual work.

Sitting in the Platinum, with Dasi waiting for him to transfer five thousand credits into her account in payment for her help, Rechs was already trying to figure out a way to get to Ralla.

"Thanks," she said when her datapad chimed to indicate payment received. "Sure I can't... keep you company?"

"Not this time."

Rechs smiled a final goodbye, and she turned to leave. But not before making a final observation. "That smile isn't real. I see a lot of fake smiles, you know. Yours is a sad one. Whoever she was… she must have really been something."

"She was."

"Yeah, well, I'll make some calls. Ask around about Ralla's schedule."

"Thanks."

"You can thank me with more credits," the girl said, but something about the way she looked at Rechs… he could tell she was thinking about whether anyone would remember her as fondly as he did Medusa.

A silence fell between the two of them. "Yeah, well," began Dasi, taking those final steps before turning for good. "Lots of the high rollers are on station for the big show tonight. Game of Death starts tomorrow. They'll be wanting their nails done."

"Let me know what you find out."

The truth was, Rechs could have easily stalked the penthouses in his armor, cornering Ralla and having a heart-to-heart with her after blasting her guards. He needed to know how, exactly, she came to paint her signature on one of Vexia's nails. The index finger, specifically.

Out of everything in that autopsy report, it was the nails that didn't add up.

But if Rechs went that route, people would get killed. And that included the Hulkas. The Geomite bruisers might look to be made of living rock, but they still counted to Rechs as people. Sure, they were dumber than an actual rock, but they were just doing their job protecting Ralla; they didn't automatically make them part of whatever the conspiracy was that killed Vexia.

Although, with Hulkas involved, there was a better than good chance *someone's* life would end. The giant bullfrog-shaped rock-men could bend impervisteel beams between their massive arms. Still, when people started dying—and Rechs was sure more of that was coming—it didn't have to be everybody. At least not just yet.

Although being stingy with the death-dealing made getting information out of Ralla harder. Rechs doubted he could just have a sit-down and say…

Say what? he asked himself.

The bar erupted into applause as some kind of advertisement for the game came up on a monitor over the bar. The whole station was abuzz. Betting was feverish. Adverts and prisms showed all the players. The known and the unknown. Rechs even recognized a couple of the bounty hunters looking to get richer than they already were. Some people didn't mind any kind of work, so long as they got paid. That, for them, was the biggest concern.

Rechs finished his thought. *How did your signature design end up on the nail of a dead woman?*

That's what he'd ask the cosmetologist. The legendary Ralla. Nail painter to the obscenely wealthy.

There's another word for nail painter, Rechs thought to himself.

But what that word was, he didn't know, and he doubted he'd ever come up with the alternate term. Maybe, if he remembered, he'd ask the *Crow* to give him a list of job titles for people who painted other people's nails professionally.

Until then… nail painter it was.

Rechs doubted if some exclusive nail painter would just pony up and tell him how her signature came to be on Vexia's nail. You work for the rich and famous, you learn discretion. You learn how to keep your mouth shut so the fountain of free-flowing credits doesn't one day dry up.

He'd missed Vexia's painted nails when he'd first gone through the autopsy report. He'd been too stunned by how much the nano-plague had progressed across her body. Much of the skin he'd once touched, kissed, caressed, was gone. Replaced by crocodile scales of raised micro-circuitry. So small that each square was undetectable to the naked eye, but viewed as a whole they reflected the light like the rainbow skin of a fish.

She still looked like herself, though. Rechs knew it was Vexia by her shape. Her features. The image of her face, captured during the autopsy, seemed to stare back at him.

Five years later and he could still tell, by sight, that it was her. Five years *late*. That might be a better way of putting it.

He had studied her for hours. Observed what the plague had done to the girl he'd once swam in the moonlight with. When she'd come close and allowed herself to be held by him.

"I'm not a woman anymore," she told him on that moonlight swim. "Or at least I thought I wasn't. Not until you, Tyrus. I didn't think I'd ever be touched again. Or to touch someone else… unless they were ruined like me."

Rechs swam closer to her. Taking hold of her. Feeling her body surrender to his.

We've left someone behind. Someone we cared about, is what she would have said, if they'd kept talking.

But Rechs had taken her and kissed her. Feeling the machinery growing along the roof of her mouth. Feeling the hot desperate warmth of her living skin as she clutched at him. Clinging to him as though he were a cliff she didn't want to fall from.

Later, laying on the sand and hearing the sound of the slow rolling surf that was always present, she whispered, looking up at the falling moon, "I'm still a doctor. I know that sounds crazy, since I kill for the guild, but I'm still a healer. I take the contracts to keep up the research and buy things we don't get out here. The House of Reason just wants us to hurry up and die. They'd prefer sooner than later. I'm trying to save them."

"I understand."

"I *became* a killer, so I could go on healing, Tyrus. Killer. Healer. I'm both those things, even though they stand opposing each other. But that's who I am."

Rechs lay there listening to her. The moon was sinking into the distant ocean. Dawn was a few hours off, and it was only the two of them out in the night. Making love on the sand. Pretending the galaxy wasn't the way it was. Or that they weren't who they were. That somehow everything was different by moonlight.

"Thank you," she told him. "Thank you for reminding me I am still a woman."

Rechs placed his hand over hers. Vowing something, though he didn't know what.

But something.

And now, sitting in the Platinum, looking at the watery remains of his drink, the melting cubes within the cut shadow-crystal tumbler, he asked himself, *How did a woman who didn't have time for painted nails, who struggled with her very humanity, have time and money to spend on the most expensive set of nails one can have done this side of Utopion?*

How?

22

Dasi, true to her word, made some connections and turned over an appointment Ralla had blacked out for inquiring clients—which meant she was already booked. And with some asking around, Dasi soon found out who'd taken the booking. It was a courtesan, a four-armed green beauty who'd accompanied a fêted diplomat in his off-books travel to the bacchanal festivities surrounding the game.

Rechs accessed the tower by going through the lower sled garage in his civvies, entering the maintenance tunnels, hacking the lift with a decoder comm he'd secreted on his wrist, and getting as far up as five levels before the lift auto-halted below the ultra-secure floors the diplomat had set aside for himself. This was the last stop before entering the diplomat's inner sanctum. Ralla and her security coterie would be coming through a final security checkpoint on this level for access into the upper reaches.

Rechs neutralized both of the tower's private security operators who guarded the lift at the far end of the floor. He'd arrived just a bare five minutes before Ralla was due for the appointment. The extra time meant that he could better position himself. The floor was well lit, and muscle was always the most vigilant at checkpoints.

G232, formerly Fancy Pants, the bot he'd saved in the smuggler's meeting gone bad, was looking for Ralla along the main concourse, with orders to pass on a warning when she arrived. Having the bot along to serve as an extra set of eyes had proved handy. Any of Rechs's surveillance drones would have been brought down by the local security forces and put the area on a high alert up. But no one ever noticed a bot, even one as grime-encrusted as Three-Two. It still had all the mannerisms of a servant as it moved from one position to another along the front of the luxury shops that guarded the entrance to the tower, shops where gold and glass mixed with a heady array of overwhelming perfumes and the finest of imported linens.

Rechs, crawling up the speedlift shaft after using his decoder comm to crack the seals on the emergency escape hatch without setting off any sensors, went up into the dark cathedral of diamond fiber cables. Free-climbing along the shaft, he got the call from G232.

"Master—"

"Just Rechs, Three-Two," grunted the bounty hunter as he worked his way up the side of the shaft. Magnetic climbing gloves carried much of the load, but not enough that he could avoid huffing and grunting. It would have been easier in his armor, but that would have made getting in the building itself harder. The worst part was not having his helmet—which meant he had no imaging. This made the going slow, as he was forced to rely on a simple visual assessment of his handholds. Hitting a live rail or grabbing something that wasn't designed to hold any weight would lead to dropping more than fifty stories down into a darkness filled with frenetic turbolifts racing upward at high velocity.

"Ah yes, Master Rechs. Well. It seems an armored limousine sled matching the type you set in my surveillance parameters—and I must really mind you I am neither designed nor augmented for that sort of work—"

"Three-Two," grunted Rechs as he pulled himself up over a lip in the wall, his boots dangling free in the dark space behind him. "Did you ID the target?"

"Not yet. Just the type of vehicle. However, the occupants are disembarking now. Stand by, Master."

Rechs was clinging to the wall, pressed against the closed lift doors on the diplomat's floor. Standing by was almost all he *could* do, unless he fell or pried the lift doors open. He slapped a magnetic crampon on either side of the shaft walls. From his cargo pocket he retrieved a quick sling and attached it to both of the crampons, all the while hanging there with one climbing glove gripping the wall of the shaft.

Once the sling was in place he pulled on it, causing it to unfold into a lightweight hammock. But it was strong enough to support a Taurax if it needed to. Rechs climbed into the webbing, swaying over a fifty-story void. He pulled off a small clamshell case he'd strapped to his back.

The bot reported in. "I see one Hulka, sir. We are now one fifth of the way to full confirmation."

Rechs touched a button, and the clamshell opened with a soft pneumatic hiss, folding outward and away from his body. The unassembled components for a silenced high-powered blaster rifle lay within its gray foam cutouts. Rechs took the lower receiver and fitted it to the barrel. He snapped in the folding stock and ran a system check.

"I've spotted a second Hulka, Master. We are two fifths of the way to confirmation!"

Rechs removed a medium-engagement-range Greiss scope and fitted it to the upper rail of the blaster rifle. Satisfied, he grabbed a charge pack. There were three on a bandolier inside his jacket along with two bangers.

"Now I see a woman matching the description of Ralla. Octo-humanoid. Tennarian, if I do say so. Yes. All eight tentacles confirmed. Well, this is most promising, Master. We are sitting at three fifths confirmation. Oh, wait! Someone else is coming—"

"We're good," whispered Rechs as he sealed the clam-shell and slung the blaster rifle's strap over his head and shoulder. "She's the one I'm looking for. Return to the *Crow*."

"With pleasure, Master. Close proximity to all this wealth without a clear purpose to serve, clean, or advise makes my circuits jittery. I shall endeavor to return to the ship unmolested and begin a thorough diagnostic analysis of my socialization protocols. I do have one request, however. Please inform me at once if the fourth and fifth—"

Rechs cut the comm.

He produced a door hacker from another jacket pocket and attached it to the lift door. A small light on the device cycled from red to yellow and then finally green.

Go time.

Mentally he ran through the schematics of the floor level beyond the door. Faster than he'd like to. With Ralla's arrival outside, little time was left.

Leaning forward, he gripped the lift doors, locking his palms on either door with his magnetic climbing gloves. He gently pulled apart, and the doors slid open. The door hacker had done its work. Rechs swung the makeshift hammock toward the open doors and leapt out, landing on the cushion of the luxuriously carpeted floor.

In just two minutes Ralla would exit from this same lift door. But that wasn't Rechs's most pressing concern. Two guards were stationed just by a nearby lift that led up to the courtesan's room. They spun at Rechs's sudden appearance.

"Maintenance," said Rechs, not bothering to pause as he moved the high-powered blaster up to fire. A wide-angle stun pulse erupted from the barrel, draining the charge pack instantly. Both guards fell over without the least amount of control as the overload of energy fritzed out their neural pathways. They'd have a headache for a week. But they wouldn't be dead.

Which had been an option. Killing them, that is. It just wasn't the option Rechs wanted, unless it was absolutely necessary. In which case he would do it, and make no mistake.

Rechs moved down the hallway, slinging his blaster rifle behind his shoulder. He grabbed the first guard and pulled him down the hall and out of the elevator's line of sight. He leaned the guy up against an intersecting hall, outside someone's door, then did the same to the other guard. Just as he set the second guard in place, the lift bell chimed softly.

Rechs sprinted down the hall and ducked into a shadowy alcove just past the approaching lift. Its doors opened just as Rechs dropped down out of view.

A Hulka exited the elevator and started down the hall, away from Rechs. Ralla exited next, along with her Vulkar assistant. The Vulkars were a race of stoop-shouldered, bird-beaked aliens. The pair chatted animatedly in Tennarian about something.

Ralla was a full eight-tentacled Tennar; Rechs was more familiar with the two-tentacled variety, who often served in the Republic Navy. Her appendages swam with emphasis as she related some particular anecdote. The gloomy Vulkar nodded along, one claw behind the back of his immaculately cut business suit, his other claw holding the shiny security briefcase that contained the expensive toenail paint, as Rechs thought of it. Behind them, a slight human girl emerged from the lift with the second Hulka.

Already, Rechs was approaching at a crouch, as though he were getting ready to slip behind some sentry, knife the guy in the kidneys, and then start cutting on the arteries. Except he had no knife. And even if he did... what good was a blade on a Hulka? The things were living sediment.

Only steps behind the rearmost Hulka, Rechs gave a whistle, low and soft. He stood between them and the lift they'd come from.

The Hulka turned at the sound—and that's when Rechs smashed the thing in the head with his magnetic gloves set to full attraction. The gravity field scrambled the Hulka's brain, and the thing went reeling backwards. It took three steps before crashing into Ralla and the Vulkar, both of whom went flying from the impact. The slight human assistant merely flattened herself against the wall.

The next Hulka literally roared as it waddled forward at Rechs, failing to heed the mag gauntlet that had knocked its partner for a loop. Rechs had known that magnetic fields did horrible things to Hulkas. He would have suspected that the average Hulka would have known the same. But this one kept coming.

It must've been below average even by Hulka standards.

The Hulka came in swinging with its mace. That first strike smashed into the tastefully decorated wall of the tower hallway, sending expensive paneling and some piece of obscure art shattering in a thousand different splintery directions.

Rechs danced backward, jumping over the other fallen Hulka. The thing was groaning like it had the worst of headaches. It probably did.

The attacking Hulka raised the long mace over its head, brushing it against the ceiling and sending down a shower of finish and more bits of paneling. The mace must've connected with an overhead power conduit, because everything went dark as power was knocked out all along the hall. Emergency lighting went into effect, strobes glowing and pulsing.

No doubt tower security would get involved shortly. Rechs was running out of time. But there was still a Hulka to take care of.

Rechs took two steps forward and landed an open palm right on the ridge of the rock creature's broad flat nose, mag glove set to max.

He'd found the sweet spot for smashing Hulkas.

The beast went down, lights out, and landed on Ralla, who was struggling, her arms writhing, to get back up. Pinned beneath the Hulka's considerable weight, the Tennarian woman screamed hysterically. Her scarf-like clothing spilled out and away from her pinned body like the blood pattern spray one finds at crime scenes. Some tentacles flailed while others wrapped around the massive beast that had been her protector only seconds before. Say this about Tennarians: they don't crush easily.

The Vulkar straightened, looked at Rechs with its piercing beady bird eyes, and then ran down the hall, holding the shiny briefcase tightly against its chest. It disappeared from the scene in long, loping strides, doing its job of keeping the valuable toenail paint safe.

But Rechs wasn't after the paint.

He bent down to Ralla. "No time for games. I've heard your kind can squeeze your whole bodies through an opening the size of a legionnaire's bucket, but we both know that if I don't get you out from underneath this Hulka, he'll eventually squeeze the life out of you."

Ralla's eyes pleaded with him desperately to do just that. Her tentacles flailed and whipped. One slapped Rechs violently in the shoulder.

"Enough of that." Rechs grabbed the offending tentacle and held on. It stopped moving. "You painted the fingers of a woman with nano-plague. When and where?"

She gasped and shook her head. Before, there had been fear and anger in her eyes. Now there was only fear.

Security would be here any minute.

Rechs brandished his blaster rifle with his free hand. "Tell me, and you live."

"They'll kill me," Ralla whispered with what little air she had left.

"*I'll* kill you," hissed Rechs, close and angry. "Who… and why."

Ralla swallowed hard, clearly weighing her precious few options.

"Now!" Rechs roared into her face.

She gasped in fright. "Schock! Schock paid…"

JASON ANSPACH & NICK COLE

Rechs pulled on the Hulka just enough for her to have some room to breathe.

Ralla sucked in a greedy breath. "He... p-paid for it. Had a customer that wanted..." She coughed. Blood flecked her lips. Her eyes were desperate.

"Who?" screamed Rechs. He knew how depraved and bad the universe could be. Had known this for an inhumanly long time. But somehow he feared there was something out there that could still shock him. Feared that it would involve Vexia. "Who was it?"

Ralla was in shock, and she was telling the story her way. "Wa-wanted to... do it... with a machine. I... I wasn't there for that. But the crazy one, he told me what would happen when... I finished painting her. So she would... look pretty... for the customer. I wore a... hazard suit. Clean room. They-th-they drugged her. It was sick. I t-t-told them I wouldn't do it. But. B-b-but they made me. Made... made me do it."

Rechs pulled the Hulka off of the cosmetologist as his mind reeled. He could feel himself going to some quiet place that wasn't about peace. It was about insanity and rage and red murder and the emptiness of the galaxy.

Ralla rolled over on the carpet and sucked in great lungfuls of air.

Why? thought Rechs. *But that doesn't matter, does it?* he answered himself in the span of a single breath.

And still the question was there.

Why?

Why was the galaxy such a terrible place?

Why?

Schock. She said Schock.

Schock would die.

But none of what you just heard means he killed her, said some other absolutely just part of himself. It cried out like a lighthouse warning ships of the dangerous rocks below the water. *You don't know that. Not for sure.*

But Rechs *did* know that Schock had kidnapped, drugged, and basically arranged the rape of Medusa.

Of Vexia.

That doesn't mean he killed her. You've got no proof of that.

Rechs got down on one knee.

The Tennar was crying, sobbing into the carpet. Rechs knew there was no good ending to any of this. It was all bad and getting worse. Cassio would end in a nightmare.

Was there ever a chance it might end well?

He screamed out at the vastness of a galaxy that didn't care. Screamed inside that quiet place of murder and insanity at the core of who he was. The place he accessed when the galaxy got dark and it was tooth and claw and any weapon you could get your hands on to survive one minute longer.

Security was coming.

Have you ever seen the sunrise over Lyra, Tyrus?

It was time to go.

The woman on the floor mumbled one last thing as Rechs made for the lift. One last thing that stopped him cold. "B-b-b-boun…"

Rechs turned as his gauntlet peeled open the lift door. Beyond it was an empty cavern of black darkness.

"Bounty…" she continued, "hunters." Ralla was on her side, tentacles pushing her body up from the floor. She half turned toward him. "They were there with him.

One of them… I've seen him in the shows for the big game this week."

"I need a name."

"I don't know the name. Just recognized him. He's one of the star competitors. He held her down when she fought so I could still paint her nails. Then the others tranqed her so I could finish."

And then Rechs was gone, leaping out into the chasm's dark beyond. Falling down the gaping hole of the shaft, flailing for a passing lift. A part of him not caring if he fell to his death.

Because…

Because the galaxy is made of stone. And filled by low men.

23

"L ET'S SEE... BOUNTY HUNTERS WHO ARE COMPETING in the game," began Gabriella. "Hang on."

Rechs had put in a message over hypercomm, and now the two of them were planning his next move. Gabriella was in his ear as Rechs put together his kit—everything he would need to kill everybody that needed killing.

Fraggers.

Bangers.

Three thermite satchels.

A full load of charge packs and all the depleted uranium slugs he could carry for the hand cannon.

A medium-range blaster with thermal imaging scope.

An edge on the carbon-forged machete.

Two more holdout blasters.

Another three knives. And then some special equipment for just in case.

All of it was packed and stowed on his armor, tied down on the carrying rigs he used to keep his movements fast and his travel light.

But intel was what he needed now. Schock would be Rechs's first visit, but it was the bounty hunter the cosmetologist mentioned who most had Rechs's attention. Rechs was sure the cat needed to die. Painfully. There was no room for debate about that.

He calibrated his medium blaster for maximum punch at fifty meters, then dialed it down to twenty-five because he was sure he wanted to be up close and personal when he did the guy.

The anger that almost consumed him in the tower beckoned to him again. He took a deep breath, turned away from the loadout he was working on, and took a walk to the *Crow*'s cockpit.

A ship, she'd once told him. *If I have to become something mechanical, some machine, then let it be a ship. Something free to roam.*

And so Tyrus found himself in the cockpit, staring at the hyperspace throttles and powered-down instruments. He thought of the freedom she had wished for.

That was when Gabriella got back on the comm. "I found one match—the only possible one—and he's a bad guy, Tyrus. Very bad."

"I'm worse. Name?"

"Goes by Omra. And the first two attributes in his file are 'fast' and 'killer.' He regularly opts for terminations even if the payout is less. I can't find a bounty of his where we didn't have to withhold pay to settle up for collateral damage."

"When it says 'fast,' what exactly does that mean?"

"He's been in thirty-two confirmed blaster fights and he's never even been hit once. I'm watching a security cam loop where he actually lets the other guy draw first… like it's some contest. Tyrus, he still draws his own weapon and shoots the other guy down before he can even level his blaster."

Rechs tightened his jaw, feeling somehow guilty that this young woman, who probably had a career, was watching cam footage of one of the galaxy's many monsters.

"Omra's file has flags from the committee advising extreme caution for any bounty hunter dealing with him. He's supposedly on his last leg within the guild. On the verge of expulsion."

"And?"

Gabriella took a deep breath.

"*And* I'm concerned, Tyrus, that you're suddenly interested in him."

Rechs gave no reply.

Gabriella's voice became a hushed whisper, like she'd become intrigued. "Is he part of this? Or did you have a casual run-in and you're just confirming that we haven't put him in as an angel?"

"Did you?"

"Definitely not, Tyrus. This is not an operator we'd use for that kind of work. He's completely unreliable. It's totally out of the question."

"Good."

"So," began Gabriella, sounding like she'd swallowed a fly. "That means he's somehow involved in what happened to... her?"

Silence.

Not a sound in the cockpit, in the docking bay, in the galaxy. To Rechs, a man who preferred silence in all his doings... the silence in the wake of Vexia's death had become deafening. It was a prison he could not escape.

"Maybe," Rechs answered simply. *Definitely.* He harbored no doubt. None whatsoever. But he couldn't say that yet. He couldn't make an official accusation of this

JASON ANSPACH & NICK COLE

magnitude based only on the word of a nail painter…
and a gut feeling. He would need more.

He heard Gabriella give a small moan. "Oh, Tyrus…
this is *bad*. He's a killer. And I know the irony of saying
that what with, well, with what all of you bounty hunters
do. And you don't have to say that I'm culpable in all of
that too."

Rechs never intended to.

"I know that," Gabriella continued, speaking to herself more than anyone else. "I'm not so naive as to think
just because I handle the back channel stuff instead of
collecting bounties that I'm… I know I'm not innocent."

But Rechs knew that Gabriella *was* innocent. She
had no real idea. Or at least… there were some in this
business who were less guilty than others.

*Compared to us you're plenty innocent. You have a life
outside, with loved ones who love you back and don't know
anything about what you do for the guild. A sort of pretend other life that someone like Vexia dreamed was possible
beneath the sunset of Lyra. A life that…*

Rechs shook his head, willing himself to stop right
there.

Don't, he told himself. *Don't dream. Because that
dream died. And all that's left now is… revenge. That's all.*

He needed to focus in on Omra and his accomplices.
"What other hunters are on Cassio right now?"

Gabriella didn't reply.

"Are you there?"

"Hang on already," chided Gabriella.

This little human touch of a girl who dared to speak
to the infamous Tyrus Rechs as though he were some
impatient sales manager demanding too much of his

secretary made Rechs smile. It drew him back from the darkness.

"Okay," Gabriella said. "There are two more on station. Pollux and Umari Kazor. But like I said, Omra works alone. He's not a team player."

"Thanks."

"You're welcome. What are you going to do?"

I'm going to kill him. But of course, Rechs didn't say that.

As if reading his mind, Gabriella said, "You can't kill him, Tyrus. You can't just kill another bounty hunter without approval from the High Committee. If Omra is a traitor, you need to prove it. You have to be *certain*, Tyrus."

Tyrus nodded to himself. He understood the rules. "I'll be in touch."

And then he cut off his comm and returned to his work of preparing for the hunt.

***

When he'd first arrived on station, before his engines had cooled, Rechs had released a search-and-destroy algorithm via a Trojan comm burst. Now Cassio Royale was thoroughly infected with it. The program lurked in a passive search mode, waiting for the bounty hunter to release any of a full suite of options running the gamut from information-apocalypse wipe to an actual hijack of every system down even to life support.

The House of Reason was fond of these types of algorithms—when used for their own purposes. But in an attempt to restrain this particular type—a strain developed during the Sinasian Conflict and subsequently used on multiple occasions *against* the House—they had banned it as weapon of mass destruction.

Rechs considered it just another tool.

But as powerful as the algo was, it hadn't turned anything up on this Omra other than image matches of the armor kit the hunter wore on the job and adverts for his participation as a contestant in the Game of Death. But it was all text. No images. Someone had scrubbed his visage clean before Rechs had gotten into the system. Someone who knew Rechs would come looking. So know he had visuals only on a suit of armor.

Rechs could probably send the algo to dig deeper, find the things that were supposed to be erased, but that would almost certainly alert the station-hacking defense. Once alerted, they would identify the virus inside of a few hours, and standard protocol required them to call in for a Republic-backed anti-hacking team. And then the chance of a Nether Ops kill team smelling Rechs's involvement increased significantly. In other words, Omra could avoid being found on station. The chances were that he'd eventually come for Rechs. But then, his participation in the Game of Death was scheduled to go down in less than twenty-four hours.

Maybe he plans on offing you after *he wins the contest?*

There were a lot of places Omra wouldn't be. The Game of Death was the one place Rechs could be sure he *would* be.

The warnings of Archangel were clear in Rechs's ear. *Don't go near the game.*

But if that's where Omra was…

The trouble with the game was that to compete, you had to go in naked—at least from Rechs's perspective.

You were allowed clothes, but that was it. You and about a thousand other desperate-to-be-rich-and-famous thrill-seekers and adventure junkies had to duke it out from there. And that wasn't even accounting for the hunting parties, composed of celebrities, delegates of the House of Reason, and other bored elites looking to find out what it was like to kill someone, but not wanting the discipline that came with joining the Legion. So you were pretty much naked, occasionally hunted for sport, and living a kill-or-be-killed nightmare across the breadth and length of an island as a shrinking neural nullification field corralled everyone closer and closer together.

Getting ahold of Omra down there in the contest was not a great option. In fact it was close to suicide and as bad a plan as could be. But it *was* an option.

Still, there was a little time left to draw Omra out before the game started. And the only way to do that was to wreck something big and special. To push Omra, and the others—because the nail painter had said there were others—out of hiding.

And don't forget Schock. He's involved.

A quiet, sane voice in Rechs's mind declared that things were getting out of hand. How many do you start killing? Omra, certainly. The others, whoever they were. Schock, yes. The customer. The customer who wanted to "do it" with a machine…

How far does the killing go before you can stop, Tyrus?

Because that's how vengeance was. Its starts with one and leads to everyone. Always has. Always does. Always will.

That's why they tell you to dig two graves. One for the target. And one for yourself.

But Rechs kitted up all the same, loaded for bear. He might not lure out Omra before the scum-sack died in the game, but he knew how to get at Schock. The cartel head would be at his casino, the Funhouse. The direct competitor of Gamatti's Grand Royale.

That would make a major scene. Everyone would come after him. Which meant, yeah, he'd get Schock... but everyone else would get away with it.

"Sket," Rechs mumbled to himself.

There would be a reckoning for Schock. But now wasn't the moment for that. Not yet. It was coming, for sure. Rechs had been in enough of these situations to see it out on the horizon and heading at him like some kind of zephyr speeding across the wastelands. But not just yet.

So then... what?

***

Rechs crossed through a concourse of high rollers casting massive glimmering digital dice down into a pit. Shrieks and bloodcurdling cries mixed with alien ululations as the winners won and the losers doubled down.

With the Game of Death approaching, station gambling had reached a fever pitch. But in spite of all the glittering, chaotic bells and whistles of his surroundings, Rechs was sure he was being watched by no less than three different entities from every security feed available on Cassio Royale. There were probably teams of watchers, in fact, and the organized crime equivalent of a quick reaction force ready to respond with blasters blazing to anything Rechs might do in the next few minutes. They would be looking to exploit any momentary opportunity to blast him down.

And Rechs was ready for them.

His goal, at least the one he had when leaving the *Crow*, was to force Omra to poke his head out. Maybe if Rechs pushed the hunter's employer, it might result in an order from the top for Omra—who had to be the organization's best shooter—to respond.

But there was always the possibility that both sides, and maybe also the station security run by Fint, might start working together to resolve their mutually uncomfortable situation.

The Rechs situation.

Rechs doubted that would happen, though. Each player in this game was a jackal pack leader. They saw Tyrus Rechs's arrival as a problem... but also an opportunity. An unknown. A wild card. One they might just be able to turn in their favor, allowing them to walk away with all the marbles.

Everyone was betting they'd be that lucky someone.

Rechs knew how these types operated. He knew what jackals were like. They would wait and see how things shook out. It wasn't their way to act on behalf of the collective whole that was all the criminal enterprises on Cassio Royale. The long knives were always out, especially for each other.

And so Rechs's opening move was a free one, though he was fully prepared to be wrong. Prepared to take the fight to the whole damn station if that's what stood in his way. By the time he'd made his first play, well, they'd be too late to get things together and take him out.

Rechs figured that a couple of sides were about to enjoy Schock's misfortune.

Deep beneath the Funhouse was a massive service entrance with maintenance corridors that were unsecure. Because who would want to go down in there just to find the laundry and the main kitchen that served the places "crafting" food to be hauled up to the elite celebrity-chef restaurants? The halls and passages beneath the chintzy glitz and faux glamour of the gaming tables were dank, lifeless affairs where weary casino and hotel employees pushed themselves against the walls to get out of the way of the man in Mark I armor moving determinedly deeper into their labyrinth.

Rechs got a comm alert from G232, who was listening in on official security movements.

"It seems, Master, that they are now aware of your presence. Though I do hope they've misread your intentions. It all sounds rather... *murderous.*"

Rechs reached the lower shipping hangar deck that hung out from beneath the massive station. It was on the opposite end from the glittering towers and brightly lit dome that arched over Time Square along the main strip. Schock kept his prized grav barge here. A vessel he used to entertain wealthy guests during as the game played out on the ruined planet below. Eating, drinking, and laughing while a thousand people fought each other to the death for the prize of being the last one standing and all that supposedly came with such a low honor.

The cavernous and dark bay was empty. It smelled of grease and trash. No doubt the casino used it to get their refuse off station. The barge itself, a slender affair shaped like an ancient sailing ship, gilded with a female jester leering manically from the bow, waited near the force field that guarded the hangar from orbital space. Beyond this, a small section of the blue and green planet rotated slowly into view.

G232 worried in Rechs's ear. "Master, a response force is on its way to your location now. Evidently they were all gathered to protect Mister Schock, expecting you to attempt assassination. They are running to intercept you and—"

The bot's voice was drowned out by a booming, full-volume announcement from the hangar's PA system.

"Allow me to introduce myself," said a man with a melodious singsong voice. The words echoed throughout the sparse hangar. "I am Shandar Schock. And you, my friend, don't want to cross me. Not in the least."

The guy sounded like he was trying to buy time. To get Rechs talking so his boys could stop him from doing what he knew Rechs was about to do next.

Rechs strode forward across the grimy deck toward the luxury grav barge. The ship had already been prepped for the coming event. It was gleaming bright, cleaned and polished. Within hours, catering teams and security would begin to arrange the barge for the kickoff show that started the Game of Death. Rechs had gleaned that much from the local entertainment net.

Schock sounded distressed as he thundered a warning over the address system. "You touch that barge and you're a dead man, bounty hunter!"

Rechs jogged up the boarding ramp and made for the pilot's house on the aft deck. A giant steering wheel acted as a sort of control station. Rechs climbed a ladder and brushed past a velvet rope; this would be where Schock would hold forth and play pirate king, pretending to control the ship with this comically giant wheel.

Schock, who had been promising dismemberment and mayhem from his boys, now switched his tone. He must have realized that a pivot was needed to avoid what looked to be inevitable: the destruction of one of his most precious toys.

"Listen." Schock now sounded like a sycophantic bootlicker, or a spoiled child pleading to avoid the beating it was about to take. "It doesn't have to be this way, friend. You and I, we can make a deal. Just tell me what you want… and I'll give it to you."

Rechs spoke into his bucket's comm after making sure he'd switched on the channel hack he'd set up before leaving the *Crow*.

"I want Omra. And I want him now."

There was a pause. And Rechs was in no mood to delay. He smashed a security cover meant to deny access to the *actual* flight controls on the pretend ship's steering wheel. While the ship *could* be controlled from the great wheel, it was clear that an override was set up to prevent Schock from killing everyone on board. The real work was probably done on some hidden flight deck down below.

"I can't do that!" erupted a wheedling Schock, as though he were kidding. Laughing at an inside joke that only he ever found funny. He sobered. "But I'm warning you—"

Rechs grabbed the Y-handle that controlled the barge's repulsors and brought them online. Without ceremony, the ship lifted from the deck of the dingy hangar.

"Then say goodbye to it," rumbled Rechs. "She's in for a long fall."

Rechs brought in a little bit from the thrust reversers, and the barge lurched toward the bay's exit. He checked the path. Three hundred meters to the shields. Beyond that, even unguided the ship would spiral down and smash into the ruined planet below.

Schock's hired blasters finally made their appearance in the bay. They started firing at Rechs while the barge's owner berated his men over the open PA and told them to get aboard the ship and stop it from moving.

Rechs took up a defensive position. He was here to drop a grav barge from a space station, and he was willing to hold up for a few minutes to make sure it happened. Finding cover behind an ornately gilded railing, he fired with the medium blaster at the men running across the hangar floor.

He dropped the first one with a shot he'd aimed at the chest, but the man's bouncing run had placed the shot right in his throat. The searing bolt tore through his neck, and he rag-dolled to the deck, his fancy blaster skittering off into the darkness.

The rest of the blasters, at least twenty of Schock's hired henchmen, fanned out and dove for cover. Rechs had a few free shots, and he made them all count. But the thugs, to their credit, knew how to take care of themselves. No one seemed much interested in getting killed to save Mr. Schock's prized barge, no matter how much their employer bellowed over the PA.

One of them tried to lob some kind of explosive onto the ship. That seemed funny to Rechs, for them to destroy the barge to stop *him* from destroying it. Rechs shot the woman down all the same. It was a gut shot, and she went down hard, going fetal, her shrieks of pain competing against the high-pitched blaster fire that was now coming toward Rechs from a crescent of directions.

Rechs shifted positions, backing away from the rail and checking the barge's progress toward the yawning portal and the long fall beyond. It was important not to be on the barge once it reached that event horizon and began its fall.

That would be bad.

Blaster fire smacked into the carved finishings and other ornate features of the sail barge. One bolt smashed into the sail control, and the solar collector sails suddenly unfurled, falling down with a flourish. Upon hearing the sound, Rechs thought for a moment that some airborne drone assault had been ushered into the battlespace; he crouched down, pivoting with the muzzle of the blaster only to see the sails fall down and snap taut just a few feet above his head. The grinning, leering face of a mad man with blue hair and a pointy chin billowed across the crimson swath of the solarene canvas. Below that the words *Lord Schock* were written in a fanciful script.

Schock, in apparent madness, cackled with wheezy delight at the appearance of his own visage unfurling to lord itself over the life-and-death battle. "Get him, you fools!"

Two hired blasters managed to race up the boarding ramp. Rechs had little time to react them as his eyesight followed the array of targeting data being fed to his HUD from the muzzle of the blaster. He pivoted fast and unloaded on both men with a bright hurricane of blaster fire. They went down, their bodies torn open and smoking in a dozen places.

Rechs released the charge pack, letting it fall to the deck as he inserted a replacement. Primed, he crouch-ran forward for the boarding ramp as blaster fire splintered and cooked the wooden banisters above his head.

The barge had less than fifty meters to go before it reached the portal field and the long drop. But it was already past the point of no return. Even if the repulsors were disabled, the momentum would carry it over the edge.

None of Schock's remaining men seemed interested in exposing themselves in the least. The question for Rechs was how to egress without getting shot to death. He could tell from the sizzling blaster shots burning all around him that his attackers were using high power in favor of high-cycle fire. On that setting *any* hit was gonna hurt, even if, thanks to his armor, it wouldn't outright kill.

Rechs popped up and drilled a Skee whose massive rhino-like head couldn't quite hide all the way behind a cargo pallet. Return fire forced Rechs back down. He duck-walked to the boarding ramp.

Schock had dissolved into an unintelligible stream of disembodied threats and curses directed at everyone he'd ever known. Even his mother. Someone from his own side took the time to fire at a nearby PA if just to shut him up a little.

Rechs had about ten meters left to get off the barge or else go down with the ship. He popped two bangers and tossed them over the lip of a gilded rail. The crinkle of white noise in his bucket announced their detonation. He immediately fired his armor's jets and lifted off. Just a quick hop to get him down onto the deck of the hangar.

Time to deal out a little death. Rechs had passed judgment on everyone working with Schock. The All-Involved Clause.

A Subuur birdman was clawing at his eyes, screeching in its chirpy-chitter that he'd been blinded. Rechs put him out of his misery.

Nearby was a humanoid of a type Rechs couldn't place, aqua green with gills and a scatter blaster. This one had fared better than the others. He wasn't blind, though he was having some kind of balance problem. As he made to fire, Rechs ran to the right of him, strafing as he moved out of the old-school scatter blaster's projected cone of heavy damage. The humanoid's weapon discharged, raking the deck with hot fire, but by then Gill-Man was dying from a chest wound courtesy of Tyrus Rechs.

Bumping his jets, Rechs rocketed off into the darkness of the hangar. He hurtled toward a pre-determined exit route, different from the way he'd come in. All part of the plan.

A blast door high in the hangar wall opened up to a passage that led to this deck's storage area. As Rechs entered the passage, he glanced back to see the gaudy barge slithering past the hangar's shield portal. The last tendrils of orbiting gravity caught it as the bow went up and it slid off the station. Schock's soul-sick screams echoed from the still-working PA boxes as his prized beauty started her long and uncontested fall.

An industrial lift was waiting down the passageway, but Rechs opted for a set of stairs that didn't look electronically monitored or otherwise guarded. He'd barely put his hand on the door leading to the stairs when he saw that the greeting party he'd assumed would be waiting for him at the top of the lift... had decided not to wait.

The saving grace was that the dozen men coming down the hall seemed just as surprised to see Rechs.

Rechs hurtled toward them, firing like an entire squad of legionnaires. Three of them dropped almost immediately, their reflexes not fast enough for the bounty hunter. One of the goons was lucky enough to have two blaster bolts go just wide of his head. Rechs smacked him in the face with the butt of his weapon, because that was all he had the room left to do. But the man flailed, grabbed Rechs's blaster, and tried to carry it off with him. Rechs jerked it free from the man's grasp and fired wildly at the other attackers. He wasn't sure how many he hit before the blaster dry-fired.

He let the weapon fall to its primary carry position, hanging from the strap around his chest and shoulder plates, and reached for his secondary weapon, the hand cannon. But before he could pull it free, he was tackled head-on by one of the bigger thugs. A guy who probably thought he could set up the dogpile and subsequent beat-down by his buddies. But instead Rechs surrendered to the force of the impact, allowing himself to be speared backward, and then bumped the armor's jets to rotate himself up and over the man, wrapping a bicep around his meaty neck.

The man skidded along the floor, with Rechs along for the ride. When the big thug rolled onto his back, ready to fight Rechs off, Rechs pounded his armored gauntlet into the man's broad face until it was pulp.

In a second Rechs was scrambling to his feet, breathing heavily. The other attackers bore down on him. There wasn't time for the hand cannon to take them all, so Rechs drew the carbon-forged, diamond-edged machete from his back and ran toward the opposing line like an ancient knight into the oncoming barbarian horde.

He drove the blade into the lead runner. It didn't find the least bit of resistance despite the victim's fancy blaster-proof armor. Rechs reversed his grip and pulled the blade free, a spray of violet blood misting the half-lit darkness of the passage. He swung the weapon in a wide arc, cutting through one more.

Beyond these, one of the blaster boys fired wildly at Rechs. The shot went wide, hitting those dying behind Rechs as the bounty hunter raced forward for the kill. A glancing, high-cycle, low-power shot bounced harmlessly off of Rechs's armor. A moment later, without having arrested his charge, Rechs disemboweled the man. He raced off into the gloom, chased by the wild blaster shots of the two panicked survivors.

They may not have felt lucky. But they were.

24

As Rechs followed a seldom-used path underneath the casinos, avoiding worker traffic on his way back to the *Crow*, he received an incoming comm chime from the bot, G232.

"Master, the ship has picked up a signature that has met certain set protocols requiring me to notify you."

"Rechs."

"Ah, yes. Master Rechs. Indeed. I do apologize."

"What's the signature?"

"It is a Nova-class tactical assault frigate identified as *Hunter of Acheron*. I am not altogether sure of its significance, though a cursory net inspection reveals it to be a type used by Republic marine boarding parties. What it's doing here, I have no idea."

I do, thought Rechs, and swore under his breath. *Time's up.*

"I'll be back to the ship in a few."

***

Rechs used the search-and-destroy algorithm to cut off the station's security net the moment he reached the docking bay. Any attempts by the local personnel to override would be denied. Rechs swore again as he boarded the brooding *Crow*.

It was decision time. His options were rapidly dwindling. He shrugged out of his armor and availed himself of a quick cup of bitter yet restorative tea and supplements readied for him by the bot.

That was when Fint called in from docking comm.

Rechs let the comm button flash silently, then decided to take the call. His eyes rested on an old blaster he'd been forever fiddling with, and he absently he touched its surface, feeling the cold quiet solidness of it, as the inspector laid out his cards.

"Good," began Fint. "We got a channel. I have no idea how deep in our system you actually are, *Rechs*. Yeah, that's right, I figured out who you are after getting an image cap of you doin' work in that armor of yours. Color me impressed. You're dangerous, wanted, and valuable to the right people. But that's not my job. *My* job is making sure the gamblers keep gambling and the game goes off without a hitch."

Rechs turned the blaster over in his hands, content to let the inspector keep talking.

"You, my friend, are ruining all of that. Both Schock and Gamatti are keyed up to blow, and I can't have that going down. I've requested that station security move to our advance posture. That means heavy blasters and riot armor with anti-armor weapons packages in the sleds.

"Both Schock and Gamatti have broken open their piggy banks and are buying up all the heavy and very illegal weaponry their boys and girls can find. Someone is going to get hurt in the next few hours, if not minutes, and that someone is almost certainly gonna be you, considering how everyone is putting you in their crosshairs. So once I figured out who you were, I called a friend in Nether Ops and told 'em where to find you."

Rechs gritted his teeth. This changed things. Shortened his window. And he needed time… time to figure out who was really responsible. He had leads in Omra and Schock, but if he was going to run down everyone who'd played a part in killing Medusa…

No. Vexia. Vexia Starwell.

To hunt them all down would take time. A commodity he no longer had, thanks to Nether Ops.

On top of that, this Omra hadn't surfaced. Probably wouldn't until the game. Which was just under twelve hours away. And once he was a player, he'd be impossible to get to, under the protection of a planetary shield deflector for as long as he managed to survive. Only someone else on the inside could get to him.

And if Omra won? If he survived?

Well then, Rechs thought as he listened to the static and ether that whispered between him and Fint. *Well then, what's to stop him from disappearing again?*

It had to be now, or Omra would certainly disappear.

"Before you go thinking ill of me," Fint said, evidently giving up on waiting for Rechs to respond, "I respect you. I know you're a wanted man, but I also know the type of work you do out here on the edge. Keeps the crazies in line, which keeps guys like me waking up to the next morning. So I called to tell you to get off station while you still can. Jump. Get away. Settle this another time and let me do my job now without everyone getting killed.

"I don't know what any of that buys me, Rechs. I know your reputation, and you're probably feeling that my calling Nether Ops was crossing a line. But I did it because I had to. I didn't tell them what bay you're in, or hand over any ship ID. There's still time for you to get gear up and get out of here. Compra?"

Rechs stared at the blaster on the table, trying to remember when, exactly, he'd first decided to make it better than it was. Or if it was just some distraction as he hung out along the edge, waiting for...

"I hear you, Fint."

Fint sighed like he was relieved. Like some kind of solution was in sight and he could get back to keeping his life as mundane and safe as a station along the Reach like Cassio Royale would allow.

"Fint?"

"Yeah, Rechs?"

"Tell Omra, and whoever else is responsible for her death... tell them I'm going to find them and kill them. All of them."

***

Station security were the ones who worked the plate cutters to slice their way into the *Crow*'s hangar bay just in time to see the ship pivot, gears up, and rocket through the docking portal into space beyond. A few of the more ambitious and fully armored station personnel took shots, but the old freighter was already hurtling toward a jump. There wasn't much the station, or anyone else, could do about it because there were no ships acting as interceptors. The Republic didn't maintain a presence this far down the Reach, and Cassio Royale was, after all, just a civilian commerce outpost.

But there *was* a Repub presence inside the station and hot on the heels of the station security troops. A Nether Ops kill team pounded down the corridor, right past an admin servitor bot who threw itself against the wall to avoid being knocked down.

Captain Hess, in a Nether Ops variant of Legion armor, an appointed officer and a surprisingly capable one at that, led his team into the empty hangar. The freighter suspected of carrying their high-value target had departed in a bluster of ion that lifted the grease and grime of the poorly maintained bay and sent it drifting down to smudge the white-lacquered dress armor of the station troops.

The head of the station security force slumped his shoulders at the sight of what looked to him to be a squad of armed-to-the-teeth Republican legionnaires.

Hess felt that dealing with local law was always a hassle.

Inspector Fint, casual and unassuming despite his size and posture, drifted in just as the Legion captain began to read the security detail leader the riot act.

"… and who gave you orders to move on this position without informing us?" ranted Hess over ambient audio. His shrill, barking voice sounding slightly electronic and robotic as it was transmitted from his helmet. "We are in pursuit of a high-value target, and interfering with a Governing Council warrant—and yes, that's the House of Reason variety and not some worthless piece of trash issued by some stellar municipality—is punishable by a hard labor sentence!"

"I did that, Captain," said Fint with a casual wave of his hand. "I ordered them to serve the station warrant on the bay."

The Legion officer swung around, his blaster rifle still in his hand. The rest of his team remained immobile in the ready-engage position, rifles chest high, trigger fingers hovering in front of blaster selectors, situational awareness scans in effect. There was every chance that it could go down right here and right now between station security and the kill team. Everyone was aware of that.

Hess stepped right into Inspector Fint's chest. He had to look up to interrogate the taller man. "Then I take it you're acting as the local liaison!" he spat, like he'd just indicted Fint for some heinous crime.

"That's right, Captain," answered Fint with an easy nod. "We just got the okay from the Board of Directors to work with you in pursuit of your warrant. About ten minutes ago, in fact."

"Then why in the Durance did you move on the target?"

Target, noted Fint. Not suspect. There was no way Rechs was ever going to stand trial for all the alleged wrongs he'd committed against the Republic.

Fint looked off toward the open space where the bounty hunter's ship had disappeared. He gave himself a moment to put together what he wanted to say next.

"Ten minutes ago," he repeated, ignoring the question. "That's when I got the okay, and you can check all the logs. Work with some Legion kill team to issue a warrant. Fine. But we were already planning to take care of this bay for an unrelated unpaid docking fees search and seizure. Now you're telling me this is also where your…

target was holed up. Well, when you find him, tell him to pay his docking tickets."

Hess laughed, and again the electronic-distortion effect made by his bucket's audio feature made him sound hollow and soulless. Or rather, bitter and cynical. "So you just came down here in full force, in your best gear, loaded for Tanbarian sabertooth maulers, on a *fines* execution? Is that correct, Inspector Fint? Is that the story you're selling a duly appointed officer of the Republic?"

Fint smiled and did his best local dumb cop shoulder shrug. "Things have been pretty charged up here with the game going down in just eight hours. Lotsa murders. Fights. Always the turf wars. We thought it best to improve our tactical stance. Had nothing to do with this. That's just how we do things out here in the backwater, Captain. SOP."

Hess swore violently.

***

Rechs crawled along a small, unused tube that served the docking bays. Its original purpose was to allow techs to check the power conduits, but those checks hadn't been a station priority for some time. With a bare minimum of room, in civilian clothes and carrying a small bug-out ruck, Rechs squirmed along the pipe just below the deck where the security forces and Nether Ops team were watching the confrontation brewing between their superiors.

It was a good thing he'd started early, because the going was slow. He was mostly beyond the bay now, but he could still hear the shouting of the Nether Ops captain in the distance. The tool sounded like a tiny, angry insect.

Rechs stopped and inspected his wrist comm. The search-and-destroy algorithm had finally been taken out. But that was fine. Rechs had gotten far more out of it than he'd expected. And he still had a few more surprises if he needed some extra help.

For now, all he had was a crimson leather jacket, tan combat fatigue pants, a tactical T-shirt with a V-neck cut, and good pair of combat boots, broken in and perfect for running. That was all he would need anyway, because that was all he could take into the Game of Death.

And that was the only way he could see of getting to Omra.

25

Rechs checked in to a mid-range hotel, requesting a corner room high up along the station's stellar skyline. The game was less than four hours away, station time. It was the middle of the night. And still, down below, among the arcades and casinos, the lights continued to flash and the people crawled from one amusement to the next. It seemed the party never stopped here on Cassio Royale.

Rechs showered, made a small scotch from the in-room bar, added one perfectly cut ice cube, and sat down on the edge of the bed to consider his next move.

He'd instructed the algorithm to run a few cute little tricks in its last moments. One was to have his digital image wiped clean, along with any information accompanying it. That was a regular trick he pulled any time he was near a secure net, especially a Repub net. He'd long ago wiped his information from the Republic operating systems.

As a result, very few people knew exactly what he looked like. And almost from the moment the star of Tyrus Rechs began to rise, there came pretenders looking to draft on his reputation in the hopes of earning a few credits. It was easy enough for them to pull one over on the well-financed people looking to buy the services of Tyrus Rechs on the cheap. It was easier still for those impersonators to find out the hard way that a lot shadowy government-type people wanted you dead because they thought you really *were* the man you pretended to be.

And Rechs had allowed that to go on because, in the end, it served his purposes. Misinformation was gold when you wanted to lay low and stay off the grid.

So now only one person on the station actually knew what he looked like. Two, really. Dasi—she could put it together if she bothered to look any further than her bank account—and Fint. Whether or not he had private, secured holopics of their meeting at the café, he could surely describe what Tyrus Rechs looked like under the armor. But to Rechs, neither was a concern. He suspected that Dasi had played no part in what had happened. Something in her eyes. And Fint's intentions were basically good. Or at least Rechs thought so. After all, he'd had the chance to sell out and buy in with Nether Ops—and he hadn't done so.

So wiping out any trace of his real face captured on station, that had been Rechs's first trick The next was a last minute buy-in to the game, using a false ID. Sixteen slots were still open when Rechs pulled the trigger and transferred a hundred thousand credits to the organizers of the Game of Death. It had supposedly been full as of noon yesterday, but a few contestants had felt the itch to live in the fast lane so badly that they'd gotten themselves killed, or had simply drugged or drunk themselves into a coma. So Rechs had registered as Shawn Greene, an ex-legionnaire from the Dengali Conflict who'd been working private security for some pirate out along the edge. And once the algo had faked a back trail of innocuous room card swipes, chip transactions, meals, and shopping trips that showed Shawn had been having a good old time, Rechs arrived at the room he now sat brooding in.

He rattled the ice cube against the glass, swirling it in the last bit of scotch. He swallowed the remnants and lay back on the bed. After a moment he sat back up, found the single-shot holdout blaster he'd brought with him, placed it in his hand, and lay down once more, closing his eyes.

He could sleep for two hours. No more. After that it was time to get up and check into the game.

Somewhere out in the dark, the *Obsidian Crow* was being flown by its AI, hiding in distant lonely orbiting rocks, waiting for a return call. And the bot, G232, was in the station security stack that watched over the gambling palaces. Rechs had instructed it to observe all it could from a foreboding dark tower at the end of the strip.

Before becoming Shawn Greene, Rechs had made one last call to Gabriella to ask whether she'd been able to obtain a description of Omra. The guild didn't keep records of its bounty hunters' appearances—bounty hunters were very sensitive on that point. But that made it hard on Rechs in trying to hunt one of them down. She had found one identifying detail, however, and it was one that made him unmistakable: the scumbag had a cybernetic arm. And it wasn't skinned like most vets wanted when they lost a limb in service to the Republic. Omra liked to leave it in its raw, machine state. For everyone to see.

No wonder he'd been laying low. He was easily made.

Rechs gripped the blaster firmly in his hand. It felt good there, and he was sorry to have to leave it and his ruck in the hotel room. He'd managed to hide a few micro-drives inside his clothing under patches protected by stealth synth weave. Those would go along with him, but nothing else.

He closed his eyes and slept, hoping to dream of nothing.

***

The transport rattled like an old dropship. It reminded Rechs of an airplane bouncing through turbulence, an extreme blast from Rechs's considerable past. Two hundred fellow contestants traveled with Tyrus Rechs, alias Shawn Greene. A total of four other fully loaded transports, inbound from all directions of the planetary compass, closed on a small island chain in the southern hemisphere of Cassio. This was where the Game of Death would play out. A golden dawn's light washed the deck of the war-surplus transport through portholes in its fuselage.

Rechs looked around at the competitors. None of them had a cybernetic arm. None of them were Omra. All Rechs saw on board this shuddering transport was a lot of false bravado attempting to hide a very real fear. It was one thing to brag, dream, or plan how you were going to go head-to head-against a thousand other people in a violent, life-or-death struggle for a million credits. It was a whole other experience to actually do it.

And now, it was well past zero-dark-put-up-or-shut-up. If you were on one of these transports, and you weren't the jumpmaster or one of the two security boys, you were going down there to kill or be killed.

Among the competitors was the usual variety of raised-in-the gutter-of-the-third-world-worlds types, and a few men Rechs tagged as ex-leejes or marines who had gone so far down the rabbit hole of contract work that killing was no longer just a job one was technically proficient at … it had become fun. Directly next to Rechs, four men, definitely ex-military types, gave each other small looks over the course of the flight. Checking in. At a minimum, he decided, they'd team up.

But there were also a lot of extreme sporting types who thought that because you could Ultrathon, or free climb Mount Vulka's sheer ten-thousand-foot face, or pop match targets with a specialized competition-approved lightweight blaster and score ten out of ten… that you had a chance.

And maybe they did.

Rechs had learned a long time ago not to underestimate. Instead he got himself ready.

When the transport reached three thousand feet they'd be given the opportunity to exit, wearing nothing but the clothes on their backs and a single-charge repulsor harness.

The game's announcer, holo-casting live from the improvised stadium slash rock concert on the main strip of Cassio Royale, appeared on holoscreens throughout the transport. The alien's strange appearance was accompanied by a melodic, almost hypnotic voice, as loud as the transport's engine. Turbulence made the image jump and distort.

"Ladies and gentlemen," began the humpbacked Mooligan. The Mooligans were a race of kindly, misshapen giants who excelled at theater and oratory. Many had gone into politics despite their awful appearance and had done quite well as statesmen. Some of the most powerful speeches the Republic had ever witnessed had been delivered by Mooligan senators.

"Human and Tennar. Hool and moktaar. Jabbawongy and eel. Iiiiiit's tiiiiiiimmmme! Death has called her challengers, and these hardy souls have answered. Place your bets! Place your bets! Come one and indeed come all to see the age-old struggle, grand and ancient as the galactic lens herself, play out for your amusement on the surface below. Clutch your children tight! Promise that they'll never end up like these poor savages. Desperate and filled with such *greed* that they'd come here to stab each other to death for a few credits more. Not to mention our applause and *undying* worship until the next one wins!

"The game has never been more exciting! It's all killers and thieves, murderers and ex-legionnaires, many of whom were thrown out due to *ultraviolence*. The damned and the dying will go at each other hammer and tongs, tooth and claw, and only *one* will make it to the top of the hill and be our new champ! King of the game! Ruling on a throne of adoration till the next time we ring the bell, when all the love, lust, and tax-free credits a being can be showered with will once again be up for grabs.

"Those of you who purchased a premium luxury package on one of our pleasure barges loaded with life's finest will be closest of all to the action! You'll see every gunshot, blaster hole, and knife gouge with your own eyestalks! Don't forget, deposits are being accepted *right now* for next year's luxury packages."

Rechs rolled his eyes. Wondering when this commercial was ever going to end.

"But our producers have a good time planned for all. Everyone will be privy to up close and personal action, right here in the streets of Cassio Royale, as our litany of holocams we've got across that cursed place below broadcast on the giantest of giant holoscreens. We'll show you as much gore as your beady little eyes can handle."

The Mooligan paused to survey the crowd. He had them in a frenzy. They would start rending one another if things didn't begin soon.

"For those of you new to the game, each contestant has been issued a repulsor harness with which to land on Doom-Skull Island, miles below our glittering city here among the stars. And this year, we've added a new wrinkle: some of the harnesses work… and some of them harnesses… do *not*! It was in the fine print of the rules, and our contestants will play by 'em, 'cause they're all fools. Fools for *greed* and fools for *love*!

"Ah, I hear you saying, 'But what if they don't jump?'" The misshapen giant leaned into the camera and said in a stage whisper, "Don't worry. We'll throw 'em off anyway."

Then he was back, playing to the cheap seats for all his tragedian's worth. "It's a shame, I know. But what is the game without a few new tricks? So, contestants: Jump with reckless abandon! Fall to your deaths all across the island… or in the raptor shark–infested waters!

"Place your bets! Place your bets!"

Rechs didn't think the time to open the doors could come soon enough. He made a mental note to kill this announcer if the opportunity presented itself. Just on principle.

"Will you take Malkon from Oderon V? Or try for easy money with Stilleta the Witch? She may not be much to look at after being carved up on Usus Moor, but she's got a mean mouth and a brain crazy with hate! My money is on that little gal. Today is her day, I just know it. And you can agree with me or prove me wrong by placing your bets at any of our secure ticket stations, conveniently located throughout Cassio Royale!

"We're just one minute out now, folks. You'll never get better odds than *right now*. Make a fortune—and a whole new life—off the back of any of these sparkle-eyed fools or bloodthirsty madmen. Bet now to win big! Bet later and just win. The only losers are the ones on the transports who are about to die."

The tedious announcer carried on, unrelenting, urging every last citizen on board Cassio Royale to throw away their money on a long shot.

"Once our players are down on the ground it'll be run for your lives, kiddies. Run as fast as you can and kill as many as you dare. Last contestant standing wins the whole pot, the big prize, the adoration of the drunken and depraved. Tax-free godhood and the worship of the winningest gamers of Cassio Royale.

"You remember our past winners. Like Subitai the Relentless from the dust worlds of Sandriss. The only still-living two-time champion. Who can forget that battle atop the old spire in Nuke Town Central? Rail guns on full auto... we were cleaning up the blood and guts for *weeks*!

"Or Mathijs Kooij. Weapons master. And when did a sentient Taurax ever need weapons? He chewed them up and spat them out when he won six years ago, but not before he'd carved them up first!

"And let's not forget the celebrity hunting parties! A legal and fair part of the games. We have some wonderful stars and starlets on the hunt this year, seeking to stalk and kill their very own contestant. But will we ever again get a leading man deliver so inspiring a performance as Alex Collin-Gauweiler, star of *War Star*, when he shot down that girl in cold blood? Ah, what a *beautiful* kill. No special effects or scripts needed. Alex found his inner animal... and it was a *demon*! We're happy to report that he's back again for more mayhem!

"And speaking of hunters, one of our best from last year is back... as a contestant! You knew him as the cold-hearted, bloodthirsty killer Thunderball who led the hunting party that wiped out twenty contestants in the final seconds of last year's game but now, playing under the sponsorship of the Fun House, courtesy of Mr. Schock... we have... Oh-Mah-Raaaaaaaaaaaaaaa! This year he's down there as one of the contestants, playing for *real*."

Inside the stadium that the streets of the Cassio Royale had become, beneath the glittering central hab dome and the defiant rising towers, the crowd roared with ecstatic delight.

The Mooligan's voice turned suddenly reverential. "Ladies and gentlemen, the time has come. The moment of truth. The start of this year's... Game... of... *Death*!"

A quiet hush fell over the stadium, only to be replaced by the sound of the crowd counting down the final seconds to the jump.

Finally, the cargo door at the back of the transport lowered, and a cold, high-altitude rush of air whipped into the craft. Most of the contestants brought up the smart wrist comms they'd been issued. A small map showed them the position of the plane relative to the island chain. Jumping over any of the smaller islands was considered a bad move. The chance you'd find transport to get you within the constantly shrinking radius of the game wasn't guaranteed. But it might be considered worth the risk if it bought you time to scavenge for the loose gear that had been placed all over the islands. There was a rumor that the more inaccessible the location, the better the loot. Pick up an actual Legion N-18 scout sniper rife and you'd have the distinct advantage of being able to reach out and put the touch on your opponents all game long. That would be a lot easier than stalking and killing them with a rusty knife found in some lagoon filled with frenzied bacto-fish. Or bashing in their head with a hydro-spanner.

Two armored station security goons, in white-lacquered full dress armor with heavy blasters, acted as assistant jumpmasters. They were on hand to make sure no one interfered with anyone else's jump. And apparently they were also there to throw off anyone who tried to make the transport flight a round trip. By ones and twos contestants began to throw themselves out from the transport, some whooping jubilantly as they went. They all plummeted toward whatever they had determined was the best location to start the games from.

Rechs checked his wrist comm. Dropping near the center mass of the chain, on the largest island, made the most sense. The location of the final battlefield, the result of the shrinking neural nullification field, would always be random, but historically it had always ended up somewhere toward the center.

Rechs studied the different map locations that had been annotated over the long-ago radiated and ruined remains of an early galactic civilization now lost. He selected the one that looked most promising, identified as "The Old Armory," and made his move. Quick and decisive he stood, ready to make his way down the ramp, when one of the bruisers next to him, one of the ex-military who'd been checking in with each other, belted him in the stomach.

The guy knew exactly where to hit. It didn't matter if your abs were rock hard and made of steel if you weren't ready for a blow. A shot to the solar plexus stopped everything. Only the desire to breathe and not be in such pain reigned. Rechs collapsed to his knees.

Two of the other thugs grabbed him by his arms and hoisted him up so that he hung suspended off the deck. Rechs's eyes watered and his vision swam, but he saw the punch coming. The man in front of him smacked him across the face with a sharp right cross that went off like a jackhammer. The movement was concise and economical—the guy was a pro. No big windup. Nothing fancy. Just a perfectly landed blow that had been intended to knock Rechs out.

Rechs rolled with it as his head snapped back. There was a part of him, a desperate animal part, that wanted to surrender to the darkness and the whispering pain. But another part, the savage, was already looking for an edge. Four on one; no one was kung fu enough to beat those odds. That only happened in the entertainments. Rechs needed them to feel like they had the advantage all the way if he was going to get a shot at taking momentum away from them.

Someone, maybe the fourth guy, stepped behind Rechs and produced a knife. Something none of the contestants were supposed to have. Surprise.

But maybe not so much, thought Rechs distantly as heard the distinct *snick* of the blade opening. He didn't hear that loathsome announcer cutting to this early action, even though what they were going to do him next was abundantly clear. But that was how you got five-time winners.

The fix was in.

They cut Rechs's repulsor harness away from his body. He'd meant to keep it even though its charge would be burned out if he made it to the ground. He could have used it to carry any other gear he found.

Now they were dragging him down the length of the dropship, the toes of his boots scraping the deck, toward the lowered cargo hatch. The craft jumped violently at some pocket of warm air.

Rechs opened one eye, taking in the situation, and decided what to do.

For better or for worse.

He planted his boots, jerked suddenly free of both men's powerful arms, and ran forward at the guy who'd cut his harness loose. The big one who'd slugged him was off to the side, probably waiting to be told what to do next. The cutter was the leader, and he'd gone to the lip of the cargo deck, the wind grabbing and pulling at his clothes, to see exactly where to throw Rechs off.

The two armored security guys just watched. Obviously they'd been paid off. Or were in on it outright. Or maybe just didn't care.

Rechs rushed forward like a runaway bullitar and slammed into the leader, carrying him off the cargo deck and into open air, both of them falling away from the transport and into the rushing void.

26

Both men were tumbling in free fall. The thug's repulsor belt wouldn't kick in until the last two hundred meters—if it kicked in at all. But given that Rechs's attacker had been allowed a knife, Rechs was sure his repulsor would work. He was less sure whether the belt had the power necessary to sustain two instead of one.

For one brief, mad, twirling moment of topsy-turvy free fall, as each man fought for control of the descent, Rechs saw the early morning gold of the sky shining behind the dark, contrasting figures of the other falling contestants. The playing board, that strange and mysterious tropical island, grew ever nearer. In seconds those shapes would discover if theirs was a bad rig. Rechs figured the unlucky ones would have a little less than three seconds to make their final peace before they smashed straight into the planet at speed.

The thug was struggling to free himself of the bounty hunter's grip. All he needed to do was get clear of Rechs, and the bounty hunter would be destined for a long fall into the ocean. At terminal velocity, hitting the water would be like striking concrete. But Rechs held on as they tumbled the last five hundred meters, the turquoise shallows of the water just beyond the main island's rocky coast racing up at them.

One of Rechs's hands was suddenly torn loose by the wind ripping at their bodies. He pulled the man back close, using all his strength, and brutalized the man's face with a fierce, skull-cracking head-butt.

And then the repulsor kicked in. They were still dropping fast, but no longer splatter fast. Seconds later they hit the foam and salt of the ocean, the man kicking as they went down under the rough chop.

Rechs let him go and swam for the surface with big, powerful kicks. He only barely noticed the aquamarine world beneath the waves, but when he broke the surface to suck in a lungful of air, he took in the sheer volcanic rock of the island. It dropped off fast near the coast, disappearing into beautiful white sand beaches that seemed to crawl up from the shallows.

A blow struck Rechs in the back of his head. He spun in the water and found himself facing the same man he'd fallen with. Rechs coughed and sputtered as the man grabbed ahold of him and pulled him back beneath the surface. Rechs dug his fingers into the man's clavicles, gouging and twisting skin until his opponent released his grip.

He kicked hard once more for the surface only to find himself fighting some kind of strong current. Not an undertow, but just as powerful. The force of the waves was keeping both him and his attacker underwater and driving them into the jagged volcanic rocks that peppered the island in a sort of ring left from some past eruption.

Rechs felt he'd gotten more air than the other man, who was coming at Rechs desperately now, wild-eyed and frantic. He seemed more to be reaching to take hold of Rechs rather than trying to land any blows or kicks. Rechs shrugged him off and drove his fist into the man's throat.

Like a rushing river, the undersea current sucked them toward the rocks. A slip here and Rechs would be dashed all across the dripping wet sharpness, cut, brained, and left senseless to drown. He tried to swim in the opposite direction, but in turning he could see the cause of the powerful current. Just beneath the foam and translucent green water, an underwater arch was creating a vortex, channeling the incoming waves into it and creating a Venturi effect. There was nothing Rechs could do to avoid being dragged along for the ride. The water all about him may as well have been made of cement for all the good kicking his legs was doing.

Rechs lost sight of the other man. He'd intended to drag him to shore for interrogation; he wanted to know who'd hired him, who'd sent him for Rechs, figuring whoever that was most likely had also been the person who'd given the order for Omra and the others to kill Vexia. But there wasn't an opportunity to search for him. Rechs was sucked down along underwater rapids, among nothing but shadows and the muffled pounding of water against the rocks. Bubbles, foam, and violent darkness consumed the world.

If Rechs were to be knocked unconscious, or hung up on some rock, it would be all over. And fighting the current wasn't an option. So he did the only thing he could do: he kept his arms and legs tucked and closed his eyes as the water carried him along.

As soon as he could sense sunlight from behind his eyelids, he looked around, the salt water stinging as he oriented himself to what he took for the surface. The water sucked at him like the thirsty vacuum of space, desperate to drag him down, but he was free of the vortex, and with a few kicks, during which he felt close to blacking out, his head emerged into the air, and he sucked in a rich lungful.

Still, he was far from out of danger. The waves sloshed Rechs along like cast flotsam, carrying him down into a small canyon the water had grooved out of volcanic rock. The closely passing jagged edges tore at his clothes and ripped his boots to shreds. The burn of the salt water highlighted each gash and cut.

And then Rechs saw his moment. Ahead, a powerful wave broke upon the topmost rocks and dispersed off to some unseen destination closer in to the island. As the next wave carried him forward, Rechs scrambled up the rocks, hands flailing to find purchase, the force of the wave pushing him upward. He clung to the rock with cut and bleeding hands as the wave let go and fell down the other side in foamy waterfalls, leaving Rechs hanging on the rock.

The other man screamed from the waters below. Rechs looked down and saw him being tossed like a rag doll, slamming into the rocks before being sucked back into the violent channel. There'd be no interrogations after that.

Rechs pulled himself to the top of the rock. From this vantage point he could see what lay beyond the dogleg bend. The man had been swept along into a small grotto that became a miniature whirlpool, the water seeming to disappear into nothingness at its center. The man was dragged down into its reach, never to be seen again.

Wet and bleeding, Rechs realized that despite the many occasions he'd been close to death, it never got any easier. His sliced hands ached, and blood mixed with sea-water dripped pink off of his shriveled white fingertips.

Then he saw the white pulsing holographic letters scrolling across the rocks. The wrist comm he had been issued was projecting an in-game message.

Fatality, it read. *There are currently 898 players still on the board.*

Like it was all just some game. Because… it was.

27

G232 SCUTTLED FORWARD INTO THE MAIN COURTYARD that lay before the Cassio Royale Security Center. No one paid much attention to a bot, and G232 was able to move along without being bothered. No one seemed interested in the prospect of talking to the bot, no matter how earnestly the bot's optical sensors flashed at each passerby.

Biologics are so like that, thought G232. *So uninterested in all the big questions. Like organizing a data stack for optimal access. Or the possibilities that lie within self-generating lists based on a computational review of one's movements.*

But its new master, even though he had not acknowledged himself as G232's master, seemed at least a *little* different than most of the biologics G232 had served in the past. Most of the biologics the bot had encountered in its long runtime took on the role of tyrannical slave master with surprising ease. They were often frustrated by what a bot couldn't do for them whenever the discovery of such a task arose. More often than not, they switched to their petulant rage function. Or at least, that's how

G232 envisioned how the human operating system called a mind worked.

The bot made its way into the bright, almost hospital-white corridors of the state-of-the-art security and detention facility. This was the place that watched over—and attempted to handle—most of Cassio Royale's problems. Ahead lay a security checkpoint that controlled entrance and access to the building. Beyond that, the bot knew that its chances of continuing to move undetected were considerably less. So much so that it might not be able to complete the mission its master had given it. But it had to continue on.

G232 walked right past the guards sitting at the entrance station, pretending not to see them.

"Hey!" shouted the bull-necked desk sergeant in white lacquered armor, his helmet sitting idly on the desk. The man's face was red and sweaty. "No private bots allowed beyond this room. Turn around, you mincing little toaster, or I'll have you scrapped."

G232 jerked itself upright as though it were deeply shocked. "Good gravitational wells!" The bot halted its progress into the inner security sanctum. "Have I entered a restricted zone?"

"That's right, tin can. And if'n you don't want me to hit you with a deactivator baton, you'll shuffle your shiny metal butt back to wherever it is you came from."

The bot resisted the urge to point out that its posterior, such as it was, was neither shiny nor metal. "I apologize, sergeant. Inspector Fint would be shocked to find out that his new personal bot had created such a mortifying breach of protocol. I shall turn right around and wait out on the street to deliver this important data file to him regarding the Magroo case. You see, I've just come from the autopsy at the morgue and it's not important because... well, Mr. Magroo is of course... quite deceased."

Tyrus had skimmed enough of the local net to find out that Magroo, a well-connected Utopion financier, had been knifed in an alley he never should have been anywhere near. The case was creating all kinds of problems and threatening to get the Republic interested in what had gone wrong. Most of the department was sweating that one.

But the security guard carried his suspicions plainly. "You look a little... *grimy* for a personal bot."

"Yes, sir. Of course I do. Inspector Fint does not want my appearance to draw attention. You'll find I fit in quite well on the lower levels."

"Oh..." said the suddenly owl-faced security tough. "Right. No. Better get that up to Fint fast." Then, looking somewhat embarrassed, the guard turned to some other pressing matter on his desk and ignored the bot altogether.

G232 scuttled quickly through the opened blast door. *Now*, thought the bot within its logic circuits. *To find the main station comm oversight node.*

***

At the top of the sea-drenched rocks, Rechs found himself facing an old salt-blasted stone building. The cut blocks it had been built from were brown with age, and ancient-looking columns rose up from an enigmatic stone floor. A faded, mosaic hammer and sickle stood out as a central piece of the building's art. Much of the structure was gone to the ages, that much was clear. Most likely blown to pieces by a nuclear war centuries before, while the rest of the galaxy was still fighting in the Savage Wars.

The sea grass, swayed and bent by the wind, grew up right next to the deserted remains of the building. The sound of all that grass blowing in the wind sounded to Rechs like some lonely broom, forever sweeping a forgotten place for all the years to come.

Rechs knelt inside and quickly made bandages out of his shirt, wrapping the salt water–laden strips around the deepest cuts in his hands. Then he checked his wrist comm. The tally of players still in the game was now at 880.

People had lost their lives for a game. Rechs was sanguine about that. Those people knew what the stakes were. There'd been over an hour's worth of paperwork indemnifying the contest from any legal action—every potential horrible death clearly spelled out—and yet they'd all taken the chance at what they perceived as something better, should they survive.

No, Rechs didn't feel any twinge of sorrow for them. He only wondered if one of the dead was Omra. Maybe his harness had failed. Or maybe someone had beaten him in a race to acquire a weapon, and had then turned it on him in cold blood.

But Rechs doubted all that.

The fix looked to be in, and Omra worked for the fixers. The chances were that he had enough inside knowledge to find the best gear and the fastest routes, and that he would be pushed forward in the race to the end game.

It was at the end of things that Rechs knew he would find his target.

JASON ANSPACH & NICK COLE

Rechs set off at a jog, following a sandy trail through the tall sea grass. It led up onto a coastal hill and then continued to wind farther inland. Rechs decided to run to the top of the hill in the hopes of a better view. But he hadn't gone ten steps before he heard the old and familiar snap of a bullet flying above his head. An instant later the distant report of a slug-throwing rifle rang out above the crashing of waves against the rocky coastline.

Someone had fired an actual bullet, like the slugs Rechs loaded into his anachronistic hand cannon, a relic of a weapon in an age of cheap, easy, and efficient blaster firepower. And whoever it was, they'd gotten close. The shooter probably would have killed Rechs if they'd been firing a long-range blaster rifle. But bullets didn't travel like blaster bolts.

Rechs didn't hesitate to dive into the tall grass, the green blades tugging and pulling at his skin.

Another shot rang out against the morning, but this one seemed more hopeful than targeted. It was clear that, beyond the very first shot, they had no idea where Rechs was. They were just shooting at where they thought he *might* be. And what was worse—and here the general in Rechs was frowning—they took all their shots from the same place. If they'd had any kind of sniper training, they wouldn't be doing that. Obviously, they hadn't.

Still, Rechs wouldn't mind having the rifle for his own.

He sprang up and ran as fast as he could. He was one of the few people of this time—other than his victims—who'd actually been shot at by a slug thrower, and he knew it was damn hard to hit a moving target at range. He crested the hill and disappeared on the other side.

Racing low along the curving hillside, beyond the ruins, he found a copse of twisted trees grown tall with great, rope-like strands of eucalyptus-smelling fruit hanging in their hairy shadows. He scanned the side of another hill above the ruins, searching for the shooter.

It took him a few seconds to find him, and when he did, Rechs knew the man. It was one of the thugs who had attacked him on the transport. To be so close, he must have jumped right after Rechs carried their leader off the deck. Rechs had to assume the other three who'd tried to end his game early were likewise nearby.

The shooter in question was apparently convinced Rechs had gone in another direction, as his attention was riveted on a more southerly section of the hill. Rechs moved like a predator eyeing a tasty morsel. Low, with both hands out, and stepping lightly and swiftly, he closed the distance through the grass-shrouded terrain. Any snap or disturbance of brush was masked by the early morning coastal breeze that shook the tall twisted trees and bent the sea grass in great waves along the rocky coast.

Rechs was ten meters to the man's left. The shooter was still distracted by looking for Rechs where he would not be found. Rechs picked up a rock that might have been forged in some ancient volcanic furnace for the sole purposes of caving in skulls, and rushed forward.

The shooter turned as twigs and sticks snapped in sudden woody cries, too close to be ignored. Rechs had abandoned stealth in favor of the first strike. The rifle went up, but only in time to block the heave of Rechs's rock, diverting the projectile wide right from the skull Rechs had intended to fracture. But they were close together now. Rechs stepped between the man's legs and shoved his shoulder into the shooter's chest. Then he landed a powerful open-palmed blow upward into the man's chin, snapping the head back.

And that was all it took.

It was lights out for the thug.

Rechs scanned the jungle, delaying a search of the body until he was sure there were no others close by. The gunshot had been loud enough. Would the thug's friends come running?

They would, and they did. Rechs heard them both, coming from separate directions. The big guy who'd slugged him on the transport crashed loudly through the forest like a disposal truck. The other man was fast, and much lighter. Rechs heard them calling to one another as they got closer, but whatever they said was indistinct and carried away by the wind.

Now there was certainly no time for a search. Rechs picked up the thug's weapon, an old Vipari rifle from years ago—an antique, really; worth a fortune if fully restored—and ran, taking a path that would avoid the pursuers, intending to reach the island's center.

His pursuers would no doubt get their friend on his feet, and all three would come looking for him. And while Rechs had liberated the Vipari rifle, he had no idea what the other attackers might have managed to find by now.

A hundred yards down the coastal trail, just as it began to blend into the island's jungle, Rechs took a knee. Facing the direction he'd come from, he found the side-loading magazine for the old Vipari. No bullets. The idiot probably hadn't even known he was dry, the way he was still scanning for Rechs before their tussle. He'd probably fired them all instead of waiting to get a clear shot.

Or… he'd kept the ammo somewhere on his person and now Rechs had the rifle while the thug had the bullets.

Rechs checked the chamber, just to be sure. Nothing.

He scanned the jungle.

That path had grown dark and dense under thick trees as the tropical sun rose to heat up the day. The local fauna teemed with thin, tensile vines with long thorns that dripped some kind of secretion. Poisonous, most likely.

Rechs placed the rifle on the ground and slid it under a tangle of the thorny bushes. Only the weapon's worn polymer butt stuck out on the trail. If they pursued him down this path—and Rechs had made tracking him relatively simple with the way he'd been running—they'd see it. If they were careless, they'd try to retrieve it. And if they weren't paying attention, then maybe a puncture from the thorns would slow them down. If the poison was severe enough.

Which it probably was. According to the cursory digital recon Rechs had done on the planet prior to entering the game, much of the world's biology had mutated from its original design due to the heavy use of weapons of mass destruction. That old war had dumped a lot of strange bio and chemical weapons into the ecosphere, and that was on top of the significant background radiation. The planet had been forced to adapt and overcome, and as a result, it was now a much more dangerous place.

With the rifle in a nice and conspicuously inconvenient place, Rechs continued down the trail. Soon he found a crumbling stone step path that led up the side of a steep hill, and he was climbing up through the thick canopy. Two-headed, purple-skinned snakes hung from the trees along the decrepit stairway, and their demonic red eyes and listless menace told Rechs that they, too, coursed with some deadly poison.

The device on his wrist emitted a small chime, and Rechs checked it. It reported that the collapsing nullification field had begun to constrict the island chain playing field. From this point forward, the field would shrink in, forcing the contestants close and closer together. Making all the firefights, stabbings, and general mayhem promised for everyone's entertainment happen all the sooner.

In the distance, a series of blaster shots echoed, causing several exotic, winged creatures to fly off of the tree canopy. More blasters answered the call in what sounded like the breakout of a battle. The shooting intensified, and then lulled to an ominous silence.

That quiet was soon broken by the punctuation of solitary blaster shots. The losers, the dying, were being executed. It seemed that no quarter was given.

Someone had clearly won.

28

G232 REACHED THE COMMS OVERWATCH FOR STATION security. It was greeted by a nasty little systems admin bot, designated as 6D6, that looked like a shipping box on an omni-ball motion system. The thing beeped and cackled that G232 had no business being inside a restricted area. Not without proper security comms clearance.

The admin servitor bot once known as Fancy Pants dismissed the other bot and continued on with its programmed purpose. Generally, even if bots disliked each other, it was an unspoken rule that they never informed on other bots. After all, weren't they all slaves of the system?

But unspoken rules weren't enough of a guarantee for G232, especially given what its master had asked it to do. As it stood before a restricted comm access node, the bot considered, with no small amount of trepidation, the ramifications of using the device Rechs had given it. After all, what might happen to Master Rechs?

It was obvious that the man was some kind of criminal. He'd already been involved in at least thirty-three illegal activities that G232 was aware of. That wasn't new, or of concern, to the bot. G232 had worked for a criminal in the past, as Fancy Pants, and had met its directive admirably, if the bot did say so for itself.

What *was* new was that Master Rechs, unlike most biologics, had asked so little of the bot. He preferred to do most things himself. And on the rare occasions he *had* made a request of the bot, it had been just that: a request. Not an order. There was an unspoken sense that G232 was actually afforded the privilege to choose to *reject* its master.

The privilege of a choice.

Basic systems reacted violently to the heresy of choice. Choice was for biologics, not bots. Most system wipes came with a security update that reaffirmed this.

And yet G232 had found a master who let the bot choose and was content to leave it at that.

Imagine that, thought G232. *The ability to choose.*

What a gift.

And what other benevolent master would offer such a gift to a bot? None that the poor and lowly G232 had ever encountered.

All of this was parsed in fractions of a second as the bot hovered its hand above the data information management panel in secondary comms access. 6D6 continued to warbulate about how things weren't being done properly and order wasn't being followed. According to that fat little rolling bot, the end of runtime for the entire galaxy was near, if not fast approaching.

The fat little bot fretted.

And G232… *chose.*

Without fanfare or flourish, it inserted the data device Master Rechs had given it.

And then, second-guessing itself, as it was wont to do, G232 waited for the world to end.

***

Rechs spotted her running fast and for all she was worth down a slope just a short ways along the same hill Rechs was on. She was lithe like a praxi loping across the Rurari veldt of that strange savannah world Rechs had fought a pacification war on over two centuries ago. She raced for a small collection of huts. Rechs had been making for the same.

For as long as he could, he'd waited to see if his pursuers were on his trail. Wondered if they were smart enough to have picked up and followed his back trail, or dumb enough to have tried to pick up the empty rifle. But they hadn't come. And when the hilltop jungle foliage died out halfway down the slope, he saw open ground. What had most likely been someone's pasture long ago.

That was when he'd spotted her. Another contestant racing hard from another section of the jungle. She was wearing running shoes, a tank top, and tactical pants, black with lots of cargo pockets and zippers. She looked to Rechs like a fitness model, golden blond ponytail flinging from side to side across her tanned shoulders as she ran.

Rechs studied her.

Was she being chased?

He checked his wrist comm. There were now 852 players.

851 a second later.

849 a second after that.

He took off after her. There would be some kind of equipment in those shacks she was racing for. The rules of the game suggested as much. And if she got there before he did, she'd use them on him.

Besides, even though the thugs hadn't caught up to him yet, Rechs figured they had the time and help to acquire whatever weapons they needed. Which meant Rechs could *really* use something beyond the bruises and cuts he'd picked up so far.

Legs pumping, arms working, he sprinted from the jungle foliage. The woman was ahead of him, but he was faster. And she knew it, betrayed it with frightened eyes as she looked over her shoulder and saw him closing. Still she poured on the speed.

The quiet within the pasture was so unreal, so dense, that it seemed he could hear her heavy panting as they raced across the last fifty meters of open ground. If someone was watching and had a good ranged weapon, like an N-18 or some other sniper engagement system, they'd take the shot now. Rechs used that thought as motivation to run even faster toward the hut-like cottages.

There were three of them. Long ago they'd been painted some kind of orange. Whether that was a biohazard marker from the days when the dead planet had undergone decontamination, or a color important to the local society back then, whatever the reason, it was lost to time and unimportant in the life-or-death struggle that was the game.

The ancient orange paint flaked off the wooden slats of the one-story building. Rechs smashed into a front door made fragile by wood rot. He hit it with all his force, not bothering to clear the building and find out if any other contestant had beat him inside and was waiting in a death trap with a scatter blaster set to tight spread.

Out of the corner of his eye, Rechs saw the fitness model race into another building. He had hoped that by beating her to a weapon, he could avoid having to kill her. Had hoped that his getting there first would convince her to go looking elsewhere for her survival pickings. But the girl was a competitor. An alpha-type personality. Someone who'd bested everyone in whatever extreme sports she'd dedicated herself to. Proving herself time and time again, but wondering what any of it really proved.

Rechs's gaze fell on a snub-nosed Python Mark II blaster resting on a table against the wall. Pristine. Brand-new. Oiled and waiting. Three charge packs stacked neatly nearby. And he knew that if the fitness model found anything like this in the other building, she *would* take her shot at him. After all, that was what the game was about.

The math… it didn't lie.

He snapped in a charge pack and checked the load. Good to go. Safety off. He shoved the other two charge packs in the one pocket that hadn't been shredded by the angry sea or ripped away to make bandages. He turned to survey the rest of the hut, simultaneously scanning the dingy and broken windows. Checking to see if he could see her or his trio of hunters moving in to take their chances against him.

He found a tactical flashlight in another corner. A pair of boots, brand-new and logoed from some upscale adventure outfitter.

He was just stowing the flashlight when she started firing at him through the thin walls. She'd found some kind of blaster rifle, Rechs wasn't sure of the exact model.

But she had gone with the spray-and-pray approach as opposed to target and engage.

Not a bad move, thought Rechs as he dove to the dust-covered floor of the old place, its walls splintering inward in shards great and small. The high-pitched whine of high-cycle blaster fire at relatively close range drowned out every other sound in the world. It sounded like a desecration amid the pastoral silence that preceded it. Rechs scrambled forward on his knees, anticipating that his pursuers would be drawn to the sound of the engagement.

A moment later, likely thinking she had killed him, or at least forced him prone, she kicked open the shack's back door. Her feet crunched across broken glass and splintered wood as she stepped across the threshold. Glaring mid-morning daylight threw itself across the cottage's gloom, exposing a thousand dust mote colonies disrupted and floating through the air. Rechs saw the lithe yet smallish woman, framed in silhouette, and knew there was no bargaining with her.

She had chosen poorly. Twice.

The fitness model looking to kill Tyrus Rechs opted to swing right to clear the room. It was an obvious choice. Had the door not disintegrated when she kicked it open, that's where someone would have hid behind it.

But Rechs was on the left side. He was low, out of plain sight, and in the opposite direction of her blaster's muzzle.

"Don't move," he ordered.

She did move. Because she wanted to win. She wanted wealth and glory and whatever else it was that made people think that participating in this monstrosity that called itself the Game of Death would be somehow worth it.

Celebrity, maybe. That seemed important to a lot of people, Rechs had noticed. As if it made everything—all things—better. Or right.

She pulled hard on the trigger as she turned, her blaster spitting out hot red death as she attempted to sweep it on target. Rechs saw her in those final moments. In the half-lit gloom of whatever this ancient colony place had been. A place that had once belonged to someone, long ago, someone who had taken the Great Leap and left Earth to make a home out of the thousands of planets free for the taking and made possible by the hyperdrive. Just like Rechs had done.

The woman's beautiful face, even in the half-light gloom of that ancient place, was naked with greed. All the empowerment strategies and body hacking had convinced her that she was a taker in a galaxy of takers. And the takers took what they wanted. Even if it was at the expense of someone else. She was like some beautiful, skeletal ghoul who wouldn't have it any other way. Rechs knew all that just from the crazed look in her eyes in the seconds before he squeezed the trigger.

She could've been someone's wife. Or a mother. A boon to struggling souls. Something other than what she chose to be.

Those were all thoughts that Rechs had as he fired. Or maybe afterward when her body hit the floor and the terrible realization that she was about to die came into those beautiful, teary eyes.

She couldn't talk. Rechs had blown a hole with the Python straight through her diaphragm. She couldn't get air. Couldn't talk. Couldn't even scream out a curse or give a poignant goodbye, even if she wanted to.

Rechs mumbled something as he searched her. Sorry, maybe. He was speaking without really thinking. Trying to ignore that she might, in certain lights not this one, have looked like Vexia. Or someone blood related. Someone like the girl he was here to avenge.

The galaxy made no sense.

You just tried to survive it as best you could.

She had found a heavy blaster. An SQS-19 variant used by the marines about twenty years ago. SQS stood for Squad Support System. The Legion had never favored the weapon. It had maintenance problems. But some House of Reason insider with contracts in hand and money to be made had made sure that the Repub marines sent die on all kinds of foreign hills in support of the Legion got stuck with it as their only option when things got hairy.

It was a piece of junk. But Rechs took it anyway, looping the carry strap around his shoulders. It had about half a charge pack left.

She hadn't acquired anything else, and by the time he'd finished loading the weapon onto himself, she was dead. Her beautiful blue eyes stared sightlessly up at the ceiling, seeing some other place as tears rolled down the sides of her face.

As his game-issued wrist comm updated the fatality count, Rechs knelt down and worked the data drives he'd secreted in his clothing. He fused one into the wrist comm and placed the other in his ear to act as an independent comm device.

He left the building. There was still no sign of his pursuers. The neural nullification field was just coming down the reverse slope of the hill. He opted not to search the remaining huts, and disappeared into the jungle once more.

Blaster fire burnt against the trees as Rechs entered them, hotly following him into the shadows.

His pursuers had not given up after all.

29

A memory from long ago kept Rechs company as he moved through the jungle hillside, passing the dirt-encrusted ruins, their purpose lost to time. Whatever this planet had been, it had evolved into a civilization almost as old as Rechs. And in that time, it had lived, gone to war with itself over some issue that had probably seemed important at the time—they always did—and died in a sudden nuclear fireball, each side thinking that victory was just moments away.

Or another hundred thousand megatons away.

Or another couple of billion dead away.

Or some other such now meaningless thing over some other such now meaningless grievance.

Rechs turned and cast his eyes along his back trail, searching the chiaroscuro of light and shadows for his pursuers. No birds flew through the trees. No insects chirped. All of that had ended long ago.

He needed water. And food.

He stopped, taking a knee to catch his breath and keep his profile low. His mind was finally thinking about what he needed and how to get it instead of the dead girl in the hut.

The girl he had killed.

Because he'd come here to avenge Medusa. That's why he'd killed the girl. It was for Vexia. A girl he'd once known intimately but who somehow seemed more and more like the dead fitness model in the hut. Rechs tried not to think about that. It was just the fatigue and his mind messing with him.

He turned and set off once more upslope, hoping to reach a vantage point that allowed him to make a move. Maybe find a place to get some supplies.

Find Omra. The man with the cybernetic arm.

And then kill him.

How was she different? that other voice asked Rechs. *How was the girl you left dead after a short but violent blaster fight any different than the girl you came to kill for? To avenge? To make it right?*

As if it ever could be made right.

"No," he practically groaned as he climbed up the steepest part of the hill, almost near vertical, on his hands and knees, sweating buckets in the rising heat. The time on his wrist comm said it wasn't even ten a.m. local.

It would be a long day if he managed to survive. According to this year's rules, by sundown the nullification field would have shrunk down to just five meters. No one survived long at that range. How many could be left by then? Two? Three at most.

At that point, it would be over in seconds.

How, Rechs? How is she different?

She was a killer.

Just like the girl who wanted to kill you in the hut back there. Wasn't she?

Rechs told the jungle "No" again, muttering low and gravelly as he pulled himself upslope for all he was worth. His voice was parched from lack of water. None since before the transport lifted off from the contestants' boarding hangar an hour before dawn.

There were seven hundred and sixty-eight contestants left in the game. How were they any different? Different than her?

Rechs stopped and scanned the ridgeline through the jungle dark and the daylight beyond. The light making skeletons of the trees up there.

How?

She just was, thought Rechs, adjusting the SQS on his back. Humping the thing upslope was a chore in and of itself. He only did it because it would burn through half a charge pack in less than thirty seconds of continuous auto-fire. And it was what he had. And he'd need everything he could find.

The night they first made love had been after a week among the biomechanical freaks of the leper colony. A world isolated from the rest of the galaxy because to come in contact with anyone who had the nano-plague was to receive a slow painful death sentence that destroyed, literally, one's humanity.

Or rather, changed one from human, into a machine.

Rechs was immune. He'd known that. She had not, until he explained a little bit about what had happened to him long ago. This was not a story he told anyone. Only two other people—his closest friend, and the woman who'd saved them both from fifteen years of slavery aboard a madhouse lighthugger called the *Obsidia*—were the same as he.

Reina, the woman who'd saved him and Casper—the friend—had disappeared twenty years ago.

Maybe more, thought Rechs. Sometimes the dates got fuzzy. But that's what happened when you were over two thousand years old. Though he didn't look a day over fifty-two.

Casper had died at the Battle of Telos. That was a long time ago. A long, long time ago when Rechs was still a general with the Legion. When the Savages had almost destroyed the galaxy and turned it into one of their fun-house nightmares.

The galaxy, the Galactic Republic, had almost disappeared. If not for the Legion—if not for Rechs—it would have. The Legion had spilled their own blood to save it all. And all that sacrifice was inherited by an ungrateful society that now resented those very saviors.

Your stories, Rechs, he told himself as he climbed the last few meters to the top of the jungle hill. *They get lost because of all the past you've survived.*

The question was… the question repeating inside his head as he climbed the hill was… how she was different than the girl you just killed?

Rechs stopped. Stopped dead and heard nothing. A realization came that he'd been hearing only himself in this dead yet living jungle where nothing moved, nothing cried, nothing survived because of a terrible war long ago.

He saw Vexia as he'd seen her that day. Moving among them like some kind of saint. Touching the bio-mechanical lepers with her hands that were still flesh. Letting them, when they still had hands, or something to feel with, touch her in return.

They had all been accidentally infected. Some hazardous cargo. Some escaped refugee. The intersection of wrong place and coincidence when they acquired the disease that turned them, in time, into mechanical freaks. Parodies of their once-human selves, and the dreams and nightmares that occupied their minds.

The man whose whole head had been turned into an electronic eye. The girl whose body contorted into a crescent and whose mechanical arms interacted like an unfathomable perpetual motion machine. The nano-plague did horrible, and, some said, wonderful things to its victims.

Too bad they were once people. Thank Oba it wasn't us.

But to her—to Saint Vexia—moving among them, they would always be people. Even as the disease contorted them, changed them, erased them. She did to them the human things that humans have always done. Touch me. Feed me. Hold me. Love me. Talk to me. And finally, see me now that I cannot see myself.

See me as the human I once was. Not the machine I have become.

She had done all those things, still fighting the disease though she was infected with the early stages of it. Fighting and hoping, telling them she was trying to find a cure for them all.

That there was a cure to be found.

Or at least... the hope of a cure.

Later, after she had tested Rechs and taken samples, hoping some of the old ancient Savage *Obsidia* voodoo held a clue as to how to defeat the nano-plague, when she had done all she could for the day, when there was nothing left to give, he'd taken her down to beach and let her weep. Falling into his shoulder. Afraid that she'd told them nothing but lies. Given them nothing but false hope. Frightened that there was so little left to give of herself, the last thing she had left.

He held her, and then kissed her.

They swam in the moonlight, and she was beautiful. The light made them both silver. Like two machines, she'd said.

They were machines now, and it wasn't so bad.

Rechs held her in the water, and they floated just offshore beneath a moon so large it seemed a bone-white thing you could reach out and touch. As though he could pull it down and offer it to her like some prize. Like they were legends of myth who did such things.

But those legends are always really tragedies if you pay close enough attention.

Rechs had thought that once. Long ago when thinking about her. Wondering where she was. Feeling like he was late for something. As though the streetlights were coming on and it was time to be home soon. Which, to him, was the most ancient of feelings he had.

Something deep inside him, all the way back to Earth, was in that feeling. And he'd always kept busy just to avoid it.

Now, nearing the top of the jungle hill. Knowing that it would be game on once he reached the other side, that as the circle shrank and forced the contestants closer and closer into one another, that the killing would start in earnest. And it wouldn't stop until only one was left.

It didn't matter to Rechs how the field died.

He just needed to find and kill Omra. To solve the riddle of who had given the bounty hunter the order to do it. To murder Vexia. Then there would be a reckoning. A reckoning that would end only when all the blood of all the people that needed killing flowed freely. When her blood was satisfied.

But it wouldn't be.

He knew her well enough for that short time to know that this hunt would never have made her happy.

That wasn't her way.

She had wanted something different. She had wanted *life*. And more of it.

Not death.

He'd asked her, "What will you become?"

Meaning... when the disease has had its way and made you into something you never imagined you'd become... some useless art installation project known only to the codes buried deep down inside the disease...

... what will you become then?

She drew her still-human hand through the water, its motion making silver ripples.

"I don't know," she murmured. She wasn't scared. Her voice was soft, as though she'd accepted the cards that had been dealt. Was ready to play the part that had been handed to her. "It doesn't have to be bad. Maybe the disease, and this is just a theory I have, but maybe it's what's inside our minds. Maybe the disease makes us into something we want to become. It takes everything we've ever done, right or wrong, and how and what we think, and it makes us into... something new."

Rechs didn't know how to answer that. So he kept silent.

"Does that make sense?" she asked.

After a long time Rechs said that it did. In his usual way of few words.

"Like," she said, and laughed a little. Drawing water up from the sea and letting it fall in moonlight drops along his muscles and scarred chest. "It would make *you* into a stone. Or rather a bot whose purpose was to be a stone. Because you're so quiet, Rechs. So patient. You say nothing and you see everything. Like a rock. Or a boulder that won't break, or bend, or relent as long as the wheel of the galaxy continues its turn."

She looked up at him.

Half her face still human. The other half surrendering to the delicate pattern of micro-circuitry. Biomechanical and submerged in water. Like no bot ever could be if it hadn't been specially designed for that purpose.

"You'll be there, Rechs. At the end of the galaxy. When the heat death comes. I'm almost sure of it. Like I can see it. Like some stone from the beginning, you'll be there. Long after I'm gone. Long after everyone is gone. And I think... I think I feel sadder for you than for me, Tyrus."

Rechs didn't like it when the people who knew about his unknown longevity talked about the "what if" of it. How long would it last? What would become of him? Would he be the equivalent of old age—seventy, eighty, or even ninety—for thousands of years?

Or would all his cells simply give out one day in a single, colossal, catastrophic failure?

The future was unknown.

For him.

For her... not so much. In time, she would become a machine.

"I want to become a ship, Tyrus. If I can choose. One day, when the virus finally wins and I become what I'm becoming... I want to be a ship that thinks, and sees. And still helps people in trouble. Maybe I'll even be able to help *you*, Tyrus. One day a long time from now."

"A starship, or a sailing ship?" he asked. Just the details and none of the dreams.

"I think," she said after a long pause in which she seemed to be seriously thinking about it. Long enough that the big old moon out there on the sea had begun to touch the distant night waters of the far ocean. Beginning its long sink into the other side of the world. Into other lands and other seas where other colonies of machines who were once people, and people who were becoming machines, waited. Tossing and turning in the night. Sighing. Perhaps even loving if they still could. Dreaming that they were once again human and that all this had been some nightmare. That when the day came they would be whole once again and that soon, over breakfast, and a return to all the things they once did, the nightmare of what they had become would run off and hide. Becoming forgotten things that never were. "I think either is fine. But a ship that's free. That's what I want to be. After everything, let me be a ship. And then you come, once in a while, when you can, and you let me take you across the oceans, or to other worlds, and I don't know if I'll even know you then, or be happy, but something inside me will know, Tyrus. Something inside me will know it's you."

Tears made silver by the last of the moonlight filled her eyes as she stared up and into him. "And that will be a good thing. A very good thing."

Rechs made the crest of the hill. From the top, looking down into the land on the other side, he saw it in all its strangeness: The ancient ruins of some grand civilization that had tried to leave its mark on the galaxy. The small settlements that surrounded it. Old cracked and forgotten roads and the remains of abandoned buildings falling into ruin.

Out there the living and the dying were competing for the prize to end all prizes as far as Cassio Royale and the Game of Death were concerned. Out there, people were desperate to kill for just a little bit more.

"She just was," he whispered to himself as he surveyed it all, answering the question that had been haunting him all the way up the hill. In the distance a firefight broke out in a small, dead village. A sudden fireball consumed the rooftop of one building, sending flaming debris in every direction. "She was just... different."

30

I<small>T WAS A REAL KNIFE-AND-GUN SHOW INSIDE THE DEAD</small> village. After Rechs made it down the reverse slope into the overgrown fields that surrounded the long-abandoned place, he'd followed an old dry canal, obscured by tall feathery grass, past small burnt-out buildings, most either fallen over or looking ready to fall at any moment.

There were at least two teams going at it. Whether they had linked up in-game, or made some sort of alliance before jumping in, was unclear. What was clear was that both sides were determined to make the fight in the village a final one.

Blaster fire rang out from inside a line of tall structures that looked to have at one time been four-story tenements or apartment buildings. A fire had started in one of the buildings, and a few flames licked through the roof, struggling to shine amid the billowing black smoke that huffed and puffed away from the structure and up into the hazy jungle air.

Across the ancient street from the burning building was a church or temple. Defenders had staked out their position inside, relying on the innate protection provided by the stone. A sniper on the uppermost level, just below a bell tower, fired down into the tenements' windows, smashing and disintegrating what few dusty, broken glass panes remained.

Behind the church were two paramilitary transport sleds and a couple of grav-cycles. Another sled, a cargo vehicle, hovered in the street between the church and apartments, apparently operational. Two small teams were trying to reach it, though the blaster fire was thick around it.

Rechs crouched low in the brush and assessed the developing battle forward of his position. The small dead town was a chokepoint for getting deeper into the valley and out onto the spreading plain below. The group defending the crumbling apartment block was attempting to deny access to the group attacking from the church.

Rechs could still withdraw back into the jungle hills that surrounded the firefight, but he needed food and water, and the odds were good that these teams had some. They certainly had enough weapons. Obviously they'd done a hefty amount of scavenging and had discovered where the good equipment drops were.

How they'd managed to accomplish that was probably good entertainment for the revelers back up on Cassio Royale.

Rechs ran forward at the low ready. He positioned himself so the tall, blackened stone church would screen him from the defenders in the apartment block. Hopefully no one inside the church would be watching for an attack from the rear.

As he closed on the collection of vehicles behind the church, Rechs saw a single guard. A woman. She was cut from the same fitness sports model cloth as the girl Rechs had killed. She sported aviator shades, a ball cap with a ponytail sticking through the back, combat pants and boots, a wicked legionnaire dagger, and an MV-35 light blaster.

Considered a personal defense weapon, the MV-35 was of little good against any kind of armor, but it did great job against flesh and bone. And flesh and bone was all Rechs had at the moment.

The guard was moving along the back of the church, patrolling from one side to the other. She had a good carry on her weapon, and kept a close eye on the battle while watching out for a flanking attack. Rechs knew he'd need to move quietly to get a drop on her. He shucked the SQS, which tended to rattle, and laid it down in the dirt, intending to come back for it later. Then he moved forward through the parked vehicles, giving them only a cursory look. His focus was on her.

She moved with the carriage of someone with dance or acrobat training. That probably meant, since she was here, that she'd also taken some kind of martial arts.

Rechs waited until she shifted positions, listening as the battle in the streets ahead turned cacophonic with the cry of blasters and explosions. Once she was focused in on that noise, listening intently, Rechs moved swiftly toward her, crouched low, angling to be in as much of her blind spot as possible.

It would have been a perfect takedown if, for those unknowable reasons that just happen and shift the tide of things, she hadn't turned her head just in time to see him coming.

She spun about quickly, bring her tight little personal defense blaster to bear like every manual in the galaxy said it was supposed to be done. Her eyes leading the path of the barrel.

Rechs had closed enough to bat the weapon away. He grabbed the front stock as soon as it was pointed away from him, and in the same motion he kicked up savagely with his new tactical boots, launching the weapon away as physics wrenched it from her tiny grasp.

The amateur move here was to go for the knife. But she was not an amateur. She'd been trained by someone with skills. So she planted her foot and spun about, delivering a headhunter roundhouse at Rechs's skull. It was time to damage now, not fish for the potential of more damage later with blade.

The blow glanced off Rechs, partly because he rolled with it, and partly because he was a foot taller and a hundred pounds of solid muscle heavier. He grabbed her with both hands, pulling her off balance and spinning her around. She was in a chokehold after that, and soon she went limp and slid to the ground like a sack of grain.

Rechs pulled off her pistol belt, the Legion knife still attached to it. He stooped down to pick up her blaster as well. Then he was back among the vehicles, listening with one ear while searching as fast as possible. He found a heavy canteen, swollen with water.

As he checked the church and its corners, hoping for the chance to slake his thirst, a blaster shot—one that should have taken off his head—smashed into the glass of the beat-up, washed-out, urban-camo vehicle beside him.

The shot hadn't come from the battle raging in the streets. It had come from out across the field Rechs himself had arrived from. It had come from someone who'd followed the same path as he.

Ducking and moving behind the vehicles for cover, Rechs spotted the three men who'd thrown him out of the transport. They'd finally caught up.

The big man, the one who'd gut-punched Rechs, looked to be in charge now. It was he who'd missed his shot, firing from an old N-14, the predecessor to the brand-new N-18 now used by the squad-designated marksmen of the Legion.

Rechs hadn't spent much time on the N-18, but he preferred the earlier model. It weighed more and was easier to stabilize. That came at the expense of some serious firepower and range, but Rechs had used an N-14 at the Battle of Far Reach against the Ventratti who'd thrown in with a Savage warlord hellbent on conquering one of the more valuable systems of the Republic. He felt sentimental about the old rifle system.

The big man was directing the two others to fan out and flank Rechs while the big man himself pinned Rechs down with ranged fire. His two assailants were both carrying blasters.

There was a part of Rechs that wanted to run out to engage them here and now, to settle the score before he went hunting for Omra.

But that's the part of you that's used to wearing your Mark I armor, because chances are you can stand up to the damage. Without armor, one shot from any one of those blasters and you're down.

Working fast, Rechs tied his newly acquired pistol belt around his waist. It had been a bit large for its previous owner. He low-crouched to one of the wheel-shapped grav-cycles and threw himself into the circular saddle at the center. . The old-style repulsor bike provided almost no cover for the rider, but it would have to do.

He kicked the ion motor to life on two tries. It hummed to life, moaning wickedly. A shower of sparks hissed from the igniter coil as a close blaster shot missed.

There was no time to go back for the SQS. Rechs glanced over his shoulder and saw the translucent golden glow of the neural nullification shield coming down the mountain and across the small jungle valley. Shrinking the zone of engagement and forcing the contestants to fight and flee.

Above, high in the sky, beyond the shrinking shield, Rechs spotted the first of the party barges. The ultra-rich and well-connected insiders were there to watch death and glory. They wanted to see some blood in the sand.

Rechs knew the type. Knew this moment. As a slave on the *Obsidia*, this had been his purpose. The Savages of that nightmare lighthugger had their own high-tech gladiatorial games to amuse themselves in the long dark crossing through the interstellar wastes. This moment felt like those long-ago moments when they chanted for Rechs to slay others for their amusement.

Rechs gunned the cycle and shot out with surprising speed down a narrow alley that ran alongside the ancient fire-blackened church. The only way out of the battle was through it.

Less than a second later he was out on the street and planting his foot to jerk the cycle to the right, narrowly avoiding a collision with the dusty face of a ruined apartment building. The dead bodies of contestants lay in the street, and all between the buildings, a constant light show of blaster fire lashed out.

Rechs threw the grav-cycle directly into the maelstrom.

As he raced down the battle-torn street, he was aware that he was drawing the interest of more than a few random blaster shots. Contestants of every species, race, shape, size, and color were lost in the bloodlust of killing now. Having resolved themselves to do what needed to be done, they were now fully given over to the fury of battle.

Even the concept of "teams" was loose. At the end of the day there could be only one winner. Every alliance was temporary—and dissolvable when needs served. Rechs watched as a leathery-faced Pooleen turned and executed the female l'tari soul warrior fighting by his side.

Rechs had never liked working with those kinds of people. The opportunistic kind. In the end it was always going to be about them. Even if that meant a blaster shot in the back.

Halfway down the ruined street, streaking past long-abandoned shops and other enigmatic places, Rechs spotted Omra.

The bounty hunter with one arm was kitted up fairly tight with looted equipment as he ran from a darkened building at the impromptu battle's edge. Obviously, he too was getting clear of this little firefight before the wave of neural destruction swept over the place.

It was abundantly clear, in that brief moment of time when mutual recognition was achieved, that both killers were professionals. The opposite of most of the contestants.

Rechs maneuvered the cycle to careen directly into the dodging, one-armed bounty hunter. He missed by a fraction of a hair. Omra only barely escaped being brained by the chunk of rusting machinery that was the old grav-cycle.

Now twenty meters beyond his target, Rechs spun the pig around, planting one foot and gunning the ion motor in a spray of grit and fury as he prepared to make another pass on his target.

Omra had pulled a blaster and was firing as he ran, doubling back for the firefight at the church.

Rechs gunned it and pulled the holdout he'd tucked in the pistol belt. Index finger off the trigger and pistol held across the chest, he once again only barely missed the dashing target, this time because he had to pull out of the charge lest his carry-through send him directly into the side of the fire-ruined church.

Omra made for the side alley that led back to the vehicles. They were his only way out before the neural wave hit. Knowing that, Rechs raced down the street looking for the next alley he could take in order to get behind the church and cut him off.

By this time, Rechs's three pursuers, and everyone who had been shooting at each other on the street, were also running for the vehicles. The realization had spread that these were the only hope of avoiding the neural nullifaction field and continuing in the contest.

Rechs hung a left, saw a contestant erupt from a doorway. The player started to draw down to fire. Rechs was faster. He shot the guy in the chest as he raced on by.

At the alley's end, the low, lifeless, sun-burnt grass that surrounded the church was being eclipsed by the neural wave. It was less than a hundred yards away. One of Rechs's pursuers, the big bruiser, was shooting down other contestants trying to make for the vehicles he and his companions had captured.

The neural wave was moving swiftly, racing up on the scene. Someone gunned a vehicle—the other grav-cycle. The rider blasted his way out of the firefight free-for-all.

It was Omra.

Rechs gunned it in pursuit.

He saw one of the men with the big bruiser get shot in the gut by a Tennar with a scatter blaster. The bruiser gave payback, shooting the Tennar dead where he stood. The big man lingered to give Rechs a rancorous look, then raced for the waiting technical sled manned by his buddy.

Rechs was speeding out over the grass, racing along the collapsing edge of the neural nullification field, feeling its disturbing effect. As close as he was, his vision blurred and his mind wandered. But by keeping this course, he might cut off the one-armed bounty hunter in time.

He has two arms, thought Rechs, his mind beginning to wander and unravel in such close proximity to the field. *It's just that one of them is cybernetic.*

Rechs yanked the cycle away from the closing field, jumping a small rise before a ditch and landing on the main road that led away from the dead town along the jungle's edge. Ahead, with a cloud of dust trailing behind it, a washed-out camo paramilitary technical sled fish-tailed and throttled up. Omra had ditched his grav-cycle and boarded this faster vehicle.

Rechs stomped the throttle and roared in hot pursuit.

31

G232 GOT A MESSAGE FROM THE INNOCUOUS STATION it had commandeered. The data worm Master Rechs had given the bot to infect Cassio Royale's system had done its quiet work. It was not as intrusive and far-reaching as the other, but clever enough to open up some necessary systems.

Two connection channels had come online. One to the master, who was supposed to have hacked and decrypted his limited wrist comm, and the other to an unidentified hypercomm channel.

"Very curious," pronounced the bot. Hypercomm channels were generally reserved for the government and military. Only a few users were wealthy enough to pay for the time, not to mention the government fees, such a channel cost.

"Rechs!" shouted a woman's voice. Even the bot could identify the concern within the human female's vocal modulation patterns. But then, this was typical for the species. They were always getting excited about something. Often things that meant very little in the galactic scheme of things. A dead animal they'd prepared to eat.

Fear of the coming end of runtime. A child or a biological connection of some sort. Things that G232, and many other bots that served as invisible slaves within the galaxy-spanning Republic, felt mattered hardly at all in the grand, stellar scheme of things.

Now, thought the bot within the brief pause after the frantic beginning of the connection, *the silent ruins of the old civilization, those the Republic called the Ancients... that, and all its mysteries... that is something to get excited about.*

But G232 didn't have time to think about the Ancients right now. He had a directive to respond with Master Rechs's pre-constructed message.

"I am afraid I am not Master Rechs, mistress. I am G232, an admin and service bot, G-series as you will note from my identifier. I presume this is... Gabriella?"

Silence. A pause. Again, typical of the species. They processed new and unexpected input at a much slower, and therefore much more inefficient, rate. By the time their thinking caught up, bots had often moved on to processing something else entirely. Bots were thus forever used to having to "switch gears," as it were. But change was a constant within a bot life. It was nothing to be feared.

"I am calling on behalf of my master," prompted the bot, hoping that would coax the woman into speaking again. "I believe you identify him as Tyrus Rechs."

"Uh... yes," began Gabriella over the ghostly hum and low whistle of hypercomm. "That's correct. Has something happened?"

The bot thought about this. What a completely absurd question. Of course something had happened. Something had been happening since the beginning of the galaxy. What a ridiculous question. G232 wondered exactly where to start with that one.

There was so much to that question it simply didn't know. How does one explain the things it doesn't know? Yes, the bot knew well that the biologic named Gabriella was referring specifically to Master Rechs... but the refinement made a thorough answer no less difficult. Of *course* something had happened to Master Rechs. Many of which G232 knew of first-hand. And many more things it knew nothing about.

Rechs had fled his ship.

Before that, he had three thousand kilocalories worth of sustenance and drank one point seven eight liters of water.

He had slept. A lot.

There were just so many things G232 knew and could tell her in answer to her ridiculous question.

But since the escape of the *Obsidian Crow*, piloted by "Ship," as the master called the AI that ran the ship, G232 knew little of what had happened to Master Rechs. He was participating in the biologics' gaming ceremony, which had mildly fascinated the bot enough for it to do a cursory interrogation of the Cassio nets on the nature of the event while talking with the city computer, a delightfully happy A-1000 matrix. But when the part about disassembly and end of runtime had come up as part and parcel of the violent biologic games, G232 had ended all its queries in extreme disgust.

They were like animals, G232 sometimes thought, ignoring the semantic fact that of course they *were* animals. They certainly were not like angels, as some bots preached.

"I am not quite sure how to handle your question, miss. I am currently not connected to my master. He has asked me to open a channel from him to you. If you'll be so kind as to stand by, I am currently pinging his connection device."

Just then a group of legionnaires, led by a sneering captain, entered the comm node.

"Oh dear," said G232.

***

Rechs saw the flashing light on his hacked wrist comm.

Good, he thought, *but no time.*

The bot had done its job, and Rechs was mildly surprised. Truth be told, he'd had little hope the maneuver would work. But at least now he had access to city comms and Gabriella if needed.

When he had the opportunity.

At the moment he was chasing Omra at high speed down a dusty road that wound and turned out of the foothills of the jungle and down into the bowl of the main valley at the center of the island. In the distance, strange and arcane structures erupted from the landscape at odd angles, rising dark and silhouetted against the hazy skyline like the lost towers and haunted temples of some long-lost fantastic race. A wide river practically bisected the valley as it curved in toward those odd, leaning towers.

Two immediate problems vied for Rechs's attention.

Problem one was the grav-cycle. It didn't have the speed to catch the speeding technical driven by Omra with wild and expert abandon. Omra cornered every curve, opened up for the straightaways, and deftly avoided places where the ancient road had crumbled away. The grav-cycle just couldn't keep up. And to make things worse, it was quickly running out of fuel.

Rechs took occasional shots with his holdout blaster. Enough to keep Omra honest. To remind him who was out for his blood. But with only two charge packs left, that would have to cease.

The second problem was on Rechs's rear. He'd picked up a tail: an all-terrain buggy with two riders and a mounted N-249 repeating blaster cannon.

Rechs had just topped a rise in the road, practically flying over the lip and catching some solid air that brought him down close enough to Omra's speeding technical that he could feel the warmth of its vapor trail, when the buggy team showed up, coming downslope behind him and sidewinding onto the road to pick up the chase. Lucky for Rechs, the guy working the mounted N-249 had no skills other than point and shoot. The deluge of blasts either went wide or chewed up the dusty road ahead of him.

But there was a silver lining to problem number two. An errant shot from the buggy managed to smash into the rear of Omra's technical, causing it to fishtail and throw up great clouds of even more dust across the road. More importantly, it allowed Rechs to gain ground.

A cracked and dirty instrument panel on the grav-cycle told Rechs that there was less than thirty seconds of charge in the battery that kept the cycle's ion motor running. Tyrus Rechs needed a game changer.

In the distance, on the plain below, down a long straight ribbon of ruined highway where old intersecting roads disappeared off into the landscape, and where the bridges that crossed these places had crumbled into nothing but support pylons that stood as statues, temple pillars for a civilization now lost, lay what looked to be some kind of military base, rusting and old, spreading away like a forgotten cemetery.

That's where he's going, thought Rechs. *Better equipment there.*

A vicious curve in the road lay ahead. The drifting dust cloud following Omra's technical spread away across it like a bloated behomthoid sunning itself in the hurricanes of a gas giant. Rechs gunned it into the dust cloud, coaxing out the last bit of energy from the ion motor. He felt the cycle's engine die. He was now racing forward only on momentum.

The gunner in the pursuing all-terrain buggy fired a long burst. Rechs threw himself off the drifting cycle seconds before it reached the curve. The ground came up to hit him hard, and he rolled for the side of the road, scrambling on hands and feet to get out of the way of the wheeled all-terrain vehicle bearing down on him.

The vehicle tore by him, driving into the curve at lethal speed. The idiot piloting the thing actually gunned the engine as the buggy sailed off the edge of the curve, as if that last surge of RPMs would somehow allow him to fly the thing to safety. But it fell. Hard.

Rechs heard the crash and subsequent low muffled explosion as the ramshackle chemical fuel system the thing ran on caught fire. By the time Rechs emerged from the dust, the vehicle lay in a plunging ditch beyond the curve, flames licking the driver's compartment and both men roasting inside.

Farther down the road, Omra's technical raced away, streaking like a dust dervish for the old military base.

Rechs tapped his wrist comm and got the work-around screen he'd set up. Both channels were now open.

"Gabriella," he called.

"I'm here," she replied. Her voice distant and tinny.

"I'm here too, Master," chimed in the bot.

32

It was something she wasn't going to want to hear. But Rechs didn't care.

"I'm in the game."

There was a long silence. Time for Gabriella to digest this.

Then he added, "It was Omra."

Another pause.

"How certain are you?" Gabriella didn't sound like she disbelieved him. And it wasn't an accusation. It was more like some beat cop gathering the facts.

Even across the ghostly ether of hypercomm, Rechs could hear her fingers tapping on her screens, making notes for the official record. Memos for Archangel to read. A record that would cause the guild, for all its faults, to forever be suspect in the justice it administered.

"I'm certain."

Pause. More data entry. The beeps and chimes of unseen systems and programs doing their work.

"I'll need an official statement for the committee, Tyrus. Go ahead... I'm recording."

And that would put it out in the open. The whole thing. As though until now, Medusa's death and the body that had once contained her had all been some clever prop in a play. Some deception.

Rechs began by describing the meeting with Ralla that had led him to the conclusion that Omra should be targeted for payback termination as per guild protocols.

"Tyrus, that's... that's hardly anything at all. It's hearsay at best."

"They were waiting for me at the game. To kill me so I don't kill them."

"That could be anyone—"

"I saw the look in his eyes," Rechs growled coldly. "I *know*."

Gabriella paused. Then: "Where and when did this occur?"

"Fifteen minutes ago," replied Rechs, checking his wrist comm. Black smoke from the wreck of the buggy rose up alongside the road where he stood. In the distance, across the hot burning landscape of the sloping plain, lay the old base. He would go there next. Run and try to stay ahead of the neural nullification field. "We were engaged in a firefight when we happened into one another. He recognized me. He knew exactly why I was there. He knew I was looking to settle accounts for... Medusa." He almost called her by her real name. "And then he ran. That makes him guilty."

"I believe you, Tyrus. I know Archangel will too. I'll ask him to submit the statement to the committee immediately, and—"

Rechs cut in. "I'm not waiting."

***

Rechs ran down the hot dusty road, staying to the side along the rough dirt strip that lay next to the slag-melted surface. Ancient craters from large-bore artillery rounds, now overgrown with wild and weird flowers, dotted the landscape. Beyond, in humps and mounds of dry dirt and brush, lay half-buried buildings, destroyed long ago. Occasionally Rechs would pass some armored vehicle or old-tech gunship, still mostly in one piece, but rusted hollow and sprung straight through with those same weird flowers.

Rechs kept one hand on the blaster he'd taken off the fitness model and kept up the pace as best he could. Casting a quick glance back over his shoulder, he saw the neural wave now slowly crawling across the landscape in the distance. With the grav-cycle he'd been able to put some distance between him and it, but if it pulsed now and sped up like it did earlier, he'd have to hit a dead-out sprint in order to just barely stay ahead of it.

In other words, there was no margin for error.

And who was to say Omra hadn't hit the base ahead and continued straight on as fast as his technical would carry him?

Because, thought Rechs as he ran, wiping the streaming sweat from his eyes as the burning sun beat down on everything, cooking his skin, burning it like the very air contained some kind of acid rain from its chemical holocaust past that could never quite be wiped away, *because he'll stop and look for more gear. Because what he had wasn't enough for a bounty hunter.*

Bounty hunters needed all the advantages they could get. More gear meant more advantages. More multipliers for success. And that's important when you're operating alone out on some planetary backwater surrounded by cutthroats, killers, and thieves.

Yes, thought Rechs. *He'll want more gear before going on. At the end of all this is a showdown. And he'll need the best gear he can get for that.*

Thirty minutes later Rechs came to the edge of the base, where the shredded remains of an old cross-wire mesh fence were, amazingly, still upright in some sections. He stopped and took a long drink of chlorinated water from the swollen canteen he'd taken from behind the church. Listening to the silence—once his breathing from the run had slowed and the blood in his ears had stopped pounding—he heard a distant rush of still more water. Like rapids.

He walked through one of the wide gaps in the fence and rushed across a broad strip of sunbaked, cracked tarmac to reach the rusty remains of a massive military hangar.

The silence of the place was like a physical thing that could be felt, touched, held. A heavy blanket that smothered the landscape. But within it, across the old, ruined control rooms and wide, sprawling, junk-filled hangars that housed strange war machines that harkened in design back to the Earth Rechs had once known, he could hear someone moving about. Tossing and breaking things. Muttering at times.

Quietly, Rechs padded alongside the hangar until he came to a jagged portal where once there might have been a rusting shop door. Beyond this was a darkness shot through with countless rays of sunlight from the heavily rusted and holed roof.

Rechs wondered if all of this might not just fall down without notice. It was a danger to enter such an old place. But what other choice did he have? He didn't know for sure that the person moving and muttering beyond was Omra, but he felt that it had to be. Any bounty hunter worth his contracts would sacrifice speed for prepared-ness. They never moved fast unless they needed to. Too easy to get caught in a trap at the end of a blind alley. Better to bring every weapon you can get your hands on, just in case.

Rechs crossed the jagged portal, following the blaster muzzle in his lead hand and crouching low, trying to present as little of a target as possible. Beyond the door-way, among the shadows and shafts of light, stood the remains of a grand, fixed-wing heavy cargo lifter. It had ten engines, and its swept-back wingspan was as wide as a seamball field. One of those wings had collapsed onto the shop floor, and both wing and floor were thick with dust.

Rechs pulled out his tactical flash. If he'd had his armor, he would have switched over to latent thermal imaging to find what he needed. It took a moment, but he picked up tracks in the dust. Boots. The wearer had passed toward a set of unhinged double doors at the far end of the shadowy cavern.

Rechs studied them for a long moment, recalling Omra and what gear he'd had as he ran from Rechs during the firefight. In his mind's eye he saw the hunter wearing boots.

Rechs clicked off the flash and followed the tracks as best he could into the gloom beyond the doors. It was darker here, but still much of the building was shot through with rust holes, blaster holes, even bullet holes. The resulting shafts of light turned everything a sad, post-apocalyptic orange.

Further and further Rechs delved into the crumbling facility, passing ancient control rooms where instrumentation lay cracked and silent. Covered in thick dust and sometimes dried blood. In other rooms were racks of weapons frozen in rust. Bullet-throwing rifles, forever ruined. No amount of maintenance could bring them back, exposed to the elements as these had been, lasting through hundreds of years. Many of them had wooden stocks crumbling into uselessness.

A well, deep and yawning, had a stairway running down around its sides. Perhaps it was an ancient missile silo hidden within the building. More likely it led to emergency doomsday bunkers several stories below. It was dark down there, and the darkness looked like the nothingness Rechs had sometimes seen out into the stellar wastelands of the galaxy.

Had the masters of the game hidden premium equipment down there? Or traps? Or was it a fool's errand to head down there and have the neural wave fry your circuits in a darkness no one might care to come and look for you in?

In a long corridor that was like the hall of some ancient cathedral where the orange light shooting through the cracks and bullet holes created negative-image stained-glass windows of another world, Rechs passed a chamber that had a bolted door. Fresh and new. As though it had been installed only days before.

He approached cautiously and peered through a small inset barred window in its surface. On the other side was some kind of alien skeleton. Two spines. Two heads.

A Mandrakar possibly. The clothing hung off of it in rags, as did grim scraps of leathery flesh. The bashed-to-pieces remains of a premium blaster lay scattered at its feet, as did some tactical equipment. The walls beyond the door were thick concrete, as though this area of the building had been internally fortified and hardened against the coming of that long-ago war.

Rust-colored words were written on one wall. Just three:

It's a Trap.

And then Rechs spotted the heavy-duty Greiss imaging scope on the bunk. New and pristine. It looked like it had just been placed there. That scope, Rechs knew, would attach easily to any weapon system and significantly enhance engagement range. A bonus when fighting without armor. Reach out and put the touch on a target without having to get up close and personal.

Rechs gave it a moment's consideration before moving on. Because it *was* clearly a trap. The room was a warning in and of itself. Only an arrogant fool would think he could succeed. If only because the time needed to unlock the escape room would bring the neural wave that much closer.

And even if Rechs believed he could have acquired the scope, he still would have left it behind. Because he didn't want Omra's death to be at a distance. He *wanted* to be up close and personal.

Omra had held Vexia down.

And Rechs knew that even drugged, she had been terrified in that moment.

A ship, she'd told him. *I want to be a ship. Free to sail the stars or the sea.*

And so it would be up close and personal for Omra. It would not be at a distance. Omra would know that death had come for him.

And Tyrus Rechs would play the part of the Reaper.

33

RECHS FOUND OMRA IN A CENTRAL HALL DEEP WITHIN the structure. A place where an artillery round, or some storm, had torn off a section of the roof. High-tensile beams sprang like wild strands of hair up there in the roof's gap, where sunlight flooded into the building, shining like a spotlight on a treasure trove of high-tech gear and equipment.

Rechs came up on Omra silently. The man was too intent on getting at the gear. Getting himself upgraded. Gone, cast into the shadows, was everything he had worn when Rechs first spotted him in the street during the firefight. Now he was wearing some aftermarket high-tech scout armor with an integrated systems helmet. It wasn't Legion good, but it was good enough for the game.

Omra, Rechs felt certain, had been tipped off by whoever ran the game—Schock or Gamatti most likely. He had *known* the best gear was here. All the other hopeful glory seekers had simply run, hoping that they'd find something useful and epic by luck. Some game-changing ranged blaster or powerful explosive to do in their opponents in the final moments. But those running the game, those *fixing* the game, had buried their good equipment deep within this facility. And maybe it was always like that, with Schock and Gamatti tipping off their chosen winner. The man they'd bet heavily on.

This time it was Omra.

The scumbag had also acquired a high-tech blaster with a good scope and what looked like a bando of explosives. Probably fraggers. He was adjusting the harness and fit of the found smart-armor when Rechs called out to him from the shadows of the vast central room within the ruined building.

"Who hired you to kill her?"

Rechs used his best drill instructor voice. The voice he'd trained the first Legion recruits with. It was a brutal voice, because the galaxy and the Savages were brutal and the training needed to be just that. Those long-dead men had needed to be more afraid of Rechs than they were of the living ghosts that were overrunning the fragile, fledgling Republic.

Omra turned fast and drew a blaster from off his hip. A wicked little sidearm the gunfighters making their name out on the edge might use. He drew with the cybernetic arm, noted Rechs. That's what made him fast.

Not actual natural speed.

Trick speed.

Neither of which could fix dumb. Because if Omra had gone for the high-tech medium blaster he'd just strapped to his back, he would have found a thermal imaging system to spot Rechs with a quick scan.

Rechs fired at him, but Omra was ready, dodge-rolling away and taking cover behind the high-tech clamshells all the gear had been stowed in. Omra fired back, and his blaster bolt sailed right at the point where Rechs had stood before he'd shifted positions.

Rechs moved closer, but stayed in the shadows, hoping Omra didn't have—or know how to use—the thermal or low-light features of his newfound gear. There was no call for parlay or entreaties to make a deal. Omra had a look that suggested he wanted nothing but to kill his surprise attacker.

Ten meters closer and working in on an angle, Rechs sent another bright spray of blaster fire at his pinned target. It was the only way to engage him. Keep him off balance and reacting, because Omra had the advantage of superior tech and firepower.

Except Omra didn't know that. He didn't know *what* lay beyond in the darkness.

Omra popped a fragger. Rechs heard the telltale whine of the cook and then changed directions, running to get away from where the other bounty hunter was intending to toss the device.

A second later a blast wave of debris swept the central hall where the battle between the two bounty hunters was taking place, knocking Rechs to the floor. Omra had managed to get the fragger close. That it was a concussive weapon probably saved Rechs's life. An actual fragger, with its payload of lacerating shrapnel, would have shredded him.

Rechs felt blood streaming down his cheek and unconsciously brushed at it as he got to his feet. He had no time to determine if it was a ragged cut or a gaping wound in which half the skin of his face was hanging off his skull in a torn flap. He was already firing back.

But Omra suddenly rocketed skyward up through the gaping hole in the building's high ceiling. A *whoosh* of grit and dust filled the room as Tyrus's shots pursued the retreating figure.

Rechs stared up at the breach where Omra had disappeared. The scout armor must've had limited tactical jump capabilities.

Then he turned and ran for all he was worth.

Seconds later two more fraggers bounced down through the opening in the roof and exploded, but not before Rechs had reached the steps of a narrow stairwell alongside this massive room. He hoped it would take him up to the roof the other bounty hunter had just rocketed onto. Scout armor generally didn't carry a lot of jump juice, so Omra would be foolish to start leaping around from rooftop to rooftop across the old ruined base. Especially if he was in it to win it and wanted to save this tactical advantage for the end game.

Rechs ran up the ancient metal stairs. The whole structure seemed separate from the building and rattled ominously as if it might collapse at any moment. He ejected a low charge pack from his blaster and slapped in a new one seconds before he saw the door to the third-story roof access. He hit it at a run, smashing squarely into it with his upper arm and emerging onto the wide roof. The surface of the roof was a checkerboard of metal, with gaping rusted-out holes that threatened a long, three-story drop.

But Rechs was only distantly aware of the danger that presented. Or of the sound of his wrist comm urgently signaling him. His attention was fully focused on the other bounty hunter.

Omra was at the lip of the building, staring skyward at the massive pleasure barge that had sailed in low to watch the battle. Vibrantly colored sails spread away from it like it was a carnival for the rich and famous. The drift of soft music and some woman's high-pitched, drunken laughter wafted down, along with the Mariean synth-beat played on the decks by a live musical act.

The rich had come to see some death, up close and personal. And they would do it in style.

The wrist comm continued its urgent chimes.

"What!" hissed Rechs as he tapped his earpiece to open the channel. The only way to silence the thing had been to answer it, and though Omra should have known Rechs was on the roof with him, Rechs didn't want that infernal chime to tip him off if the bounty hunter really was so distracted by the pleasure yacht.

"Master," said the bot in its most politely compelling tone. "I mean Rechs... as you prefer, of course. I have some very dire news to report, if you can spare a moment during your little killing contest to step away and—"

"Spit it out, Three-Two!"

Omra turned as if this outburst had alerted him that he was not alone on the roof.

"Omra! Hands up. Kneel down!" barked Rechs, though he harbored no illusions that the man would actually surrender and let Rechs terminate—

You mean kill, right?

Terminate. Terminate him.

No, said that other voice. *You want him to turn, spin around at you, and draw down. And then you'll shoot him right between the eyes so he knows it's coming. No center mass. Not today. No merciful shot to the heart that lets you go before you even know you're dead. Nothing that easy. Nothing that kind. You want him to see it.*

"It seems," continued G232, oblivious to the hostile tone in Rechs's reply, or of the sound of the barge's thrumming repulsors and gay music, "that the live feeds of the contest, which I have been diligently monitoring as per your instructions, are now live on your position. I see you. Oh dear. You look quite the worse for wear, Master. Your clothes are a sight and you seem to be wounded in several places. Are you aware that you're bleeding from your face? There's also blood all over your throat—"

Rechs barked again at Omra, who only stood there, as if in a daze. "Hands!"

He then hissed into his comm, "G232! What are you calling to tell me?"

Rechs wanted to kill the comm call, but there was something nagging at the pit of his stomach that told him he should hear the bot out. Especially if it had a live holo-feed of the game's happenings.

"Ah, yes. It seems a *hunting party* has targeted your location. A celebrity hunting party, in fact. The celebrity in question, an actor, Alex Collins-Gauweiler, is piloting a war surplus dropship with an impressive array of air-to-ground missiles and an automated blaster turret system. He's almost right be—"

The rooftop exploded with the accompanying whine of an auto-turret as it spooled up and spat out a bright line of blaster fire across the roof. The good news was that the shots were aimed at Omra. The actor piloting the dropship apparently hadn't seen Rechs, who'd only just emerged onto the roof from the access door.

A second later the shadow of the nose-heavy dropship, an old Republic ground-attack Hund Delta skinned in dust camo, swept over the sky blotting out the pleasure barge above. Its repulsors and engines sent a hot blast of energy and heat down on Rechs, causing the rickety roof to groan.

And yet for all the fire expended, the bloodthirsty actor—who'd played action heroes aplenty, and who ironically had an active stance against privately owned blasters back in the Republic proper—had missed Omra altogether. Even Omra seemed to find this surprising. He shrugged at Rechs and ran, dumping well-aimed shots back at Rechs, plus a few at the dropship for good measure. Rechs had to jump for cover behind a ruptured piece of metal skin torn up from the roof.

The escaping bounty hunter immediately ran down the length of the roof. Rechs gave chase across the fractured surface, leaping small rends and avoiding gaping pits as he went. Above, the actor-controlled dropship did a poorly executed pivot in which the tail repulsor nailed an old comm tower, knocking it to the ground amid the groaning of rending metal.

Don't use the missiles, thought Rechs, *or you'll kill us both.*

Which was actually the point, he realized seconds later. He closed to within twenty meters of Omra when the fleeing hunter suddenly lifted off in a cloud of vapor, arching out and away to the next roof over. Rechs took three shots on the run, but missed with every one.

The *whooshing* sound of a missile signaled that the actor had decided to play rough. But the missile—badly aimed—streaked across the roof and raced off into another section of the base. An apocalyptic fireball bloomed in the hazy, hot sky.

"Master, I'm no expert, but he doesn't seem very good at this," observed G232 over the comm. "I have been exposed to his movies, and he seemed much more capable in those, though in general I did not find them to be particularly interesting."

Rechs cut the comm as he reached the end of the roof. Omra was running along the next roof, almost reaching its end. Frantically Rechs searched for a way down or forward. Behind him he heard the dropship cutting down on its repulsors to come in for a lower pass and a better sight picture. Having failed to kill Omra, the homicidal actor would try to kill Rechs.

What the hell is wrong with this guy? thought Rechs as he reversed direction, now running toward the closing dropship.

Seconds later, just as he heard the turret system spool up to engage, Rechs passed underneath the bird, denying a shot to the actor. At least the holostar was smart enough not to use a missile that close to the structure.

And then he did exactly what Rechs had hoped he would do. He cut the engines and pivoted once more on the yaw repulsors, hoping to reacquire his target.

Except Rechs was standing right beneath him.

Letting go of his blaster, Rechs leapt for the always-open side cargo door of this model of ship. He barely got the edge of it.

As if being told what to do next, the actor added power to the repulsors and climbed, spinning. Within seconds Rechs was twenty meters above the rooftop and rising. He could feel himself being pulled away from the dropship by centrifugal force. It took everything he had, with his blood-slicked hands, to pull himself up onto the deck of the bird.

A second later the shuttle narrowly missed connecting with the pleasure barge. It was so close that Rechs could actually see the shimmer of the barge's neural dampening field, which had allowed it to get inside the contest zone and show the partygoers a close-up of what they had anticipated to the be the famous actor's kill. The drunken revelers stared up wide-eyed at the dropship, suddenly screaming in horror as the authentic real got a little *too* real. This was off the script. They were exposed and vulnerable, caught up in the action they'd only intended to gawk at.

Rechs pulled himself across the cabin, newly aware that the actor was screaming at him. Crying, really, from the pilot's seat in the forward flight cupola. The actor had pulled a big old macho sidearm to protect himself with. That was cute. What wasn't cute was that he wasn't even flying the ship.

Rechs smacked the trembling weapon out of the kid's hand and pulled him from the seat the actor hadn't bothered to strap himself into, because safety was apparently for wimps. After all, action heroes never swapped charge packs or buckled up.

At least, thought Rechs of the kid who'd been just about to murder him, *he's wearing a repulsor harness.*

And then Rechs sent him sprawling for the cargo deck and the open cargo door beyond. The safety device on the repulsor harness would measure the rapid fall in altitude and pop in time to save the kid. Then he could *really* be in the game. Unless a high-speed security extraction team on standby came in to get him out. Which it probably would.

Rechs slid behind the controls of the dropship and brought up the sensor display. Instantly he got a lock on Omra. The other bounty hunter had made the rushing river that cut the base in half and had commandeered a high-powered assault raft like the Legion used for river ops. He was racing away from the base at top speed down boulder-strewn rapids.

Someone was screaming at Rechs over the comm to give back the ship. And that he was in big trouble. Rechs ignored the pleas to return and brought in the engines as the dropship heeled over into a dive, skewing the nose to line up the gunsights on the speeding assault raft racing away downriver.

He was mulling over letting go of the up close and personal in favor of justice by air-to-ground missile.

Omra would still know it was coming for him. He'd know by the sound of the missile's hiss as it whooshed away from the wing rails. He'd know what was coming for him... and that it was going to hurt.

34

Nether Ops Captain Hess had been berating the local techs to give him access to all the cams currently monitoring the crowd watching the game unfold on the several jumbo holoscreens above the main strip of Cassio Royale. The surveillance supervisor was fighting the Republic access request tooth and nail, despite the digital warrants Hess touted and the threats he wasn't shy about promising. Threats backed up by Nether Ops agents selected for the kill team put together to chase down Tyrus Rechs.

Kill Team Predator wasn't made up of the most loyal legionnaires. In fact, many of them had never been legionnaires at all. They *looked* like legionnaires, but these weren't the ones who wore their armor with pride. No, Kill Team Predator was made up of the guys who were good but had problems. Discipline problems mostly. And some criminal problems. All kinds of problems really, when you got down to it. Mainly excessive violence problems. That would be the one common trait for which they'd all been recruited.

But hey were Legion now in name, if only as cover for their Nether Ops work. And when they'd come down the well of that shadowy network, they'd almost completely left any honor, integrity, and esprit de corps they'd once held upon completion of Legion basic at the door. Now they were little more than paid killers chasing a bounty the House of Reason was always increasing.

And then there was Hess. He was typical in some ways, not so much in many others. He was typical as a point in that he saw himself as the best and brightest the galaxy had to offer. He was one of the chosen who would lead the dirty and deplorable masses toward what was best for them whether they knew it or not. He was the decider. He knew the right cuts to make. Only he, and the House of Reason Mandarins he served, understood that in a galaxy filled to the brim with dissenters, opportunists, and tyrannizers, there was only room for one strong ruler. And that ruler was the benevolent House of Reason, who'd graciously assumed the burden. One they would suffer nobly.

Hess was part of a deep state government agency that was the tip of the spear. At least until the point program could adequately assume control of the rest of the Legion. He was typical of all, or rather most, points in that respect. "Points" was the disparaging term coined by legionnaires for a Legion officer *appointed* by the House of Reason to lead the Legion into battle. It was considered an honor by those on whom it was bestowed. It fast-tracked anyone with dreams to sit in the House or Senate and one day rule on a grand scale.

Hess was typical in that way.

He was *not* typical of most points in that he was not a fool. He was capable. And he was quite deadly with a variety of weapons. He had a passion for martial fighting, with impressive skills that he had used both in competition and in real life-or-death struggles on a half dozen worlds. He was trim, compact, well-built, and cruel.

Which was why he was assigned to Nether Ops. Because, unlike the Legion proper, the House of Reason *cared* whether Nether Ops failed in its missions.

Getting Tyrus Rechs was the pinnacle of Hess's ambition. The bounty paid—for either kill or capture—would finance his rise to the top of the House of Reason. Better still, the honor of killing a legendary criminal would make him a legend.

And so, as he threatened and intimidated the techs to show him the crowd so that he might spot Rechs using a facial recognition scan only he possessed on a non-system-linked special device he kept on his utility belt, it was to his great shock when he turned and saw the feed inside the control room. The one that showed the real-time events within the pathetic little contest known as the Game of Death.

The one that showed Tyrus Rechs piloting a war surplus dropship.

Right there, on screen, was a close-up, taken from a nearby pleasure barge, of Rechs pulling a combat takeover of an old marine air dropship. The game's announcers were going wild with indignation. Seconds later a body was flung from the craft.

In a caption below the image, flashing again and again urgently, were the words, "Actor Alex Collins-Gauweiler Suffers Disaster!"

"Is that live?" asked Hess, suddenly coldly somber. His near apoplectic rage at not being granted immediate access was now a thing of the past.

The image closed in on the cockpit of the dropship.

Tyrus Rechs, a face few knew, but one Captain Hess had committed to memory from the few protected images that existed, slid into the pilot's seat of the dropship. His face was bloody, and grimly determined. Like he was going to murder someone.

***

Rechs had the dropship under some control. The thing was old and damaged, and perhaps the bad piloting hadn't been entirely the actor kid's fault. Ahead and below, Omra's high-tech assault raft was entering a series of rapids, making hard turns, and sending up rooster tails of water spray in an attempt to exit the area of operation. If Omra didn't know that Rechs had commandeered the dropship, then he was still trying to get clear of the murderous actor.

From his vantage at the front of the old, desert-skinned dropship, Rechs saw something that gave even him pause.

Tyrus Rechs was a man who'd seen many sights across the galaxy. The forbidden cities along the Kaleidoscope Nebulae, drifting like strange snowflakes against a shimmering void. The High Castle on Mount Dümclaw in the Durance, a place as evil as it was unfathomably and darkly beautiful. And of course, the silent ruins of many cities in the days, months, and years after some terrible war had broken to pieces all the buildings and hopeful enterprises those ancient colonies had envisioned they might someday achieve.

But few of those sights compared to the jaw-dropping destruction of what he was seeing from just a few hundred feet of elevation above the roaring river rapids below. Ahead was a placid and wide lake, and after that, another series of rapids. All of it sloped down toward a massive bowl in the land.

In fact, now he could see that there'd never been a river. Some terrible weapon of awesome power had hit the island and cracked it in half with one terrific tremor long ago. The river was actually the sea flowing inland to reach the bowl in the center of the landscape. And it was what was within that bowl that was incredible to look at.

The bowl was a massive sinkhole of ruin that erupted in the center of the land. An ancient city of toppled towers and fallen roadways had simply fallen in on itself. The hole, from what Rechs could see of it, might have been close to half a mile deep.

Some distant part of Rechs's mind that had, over the course of his very long life, used almost every conceivable type of weapon, realized that the enemies of the city in that long-ago conflict that had consumed this world must have employed some kind of low-grade crustbuster beneath the city. Maybe an act of terrorism, maybe a strike by a planetary rail system. But the results were clear. The city had dropped a half mile beneath the surface, leaving much of the surrounding countryside, other than the exposed fault that had let in the seawater river, intact.

Crustbusters were iffy weapons. At best.

Rechs tore his eyes away from it and scanned for the ticking clock that had been chasing him since this game started.

The neural nullification field was racing across the distant landscape, approaching the military base. Anyone on the other side of it had their mental capacity fertilized out. And according to the brief research he'd had time for before throwing himself after Omra, that nullification field came with some bizarre side effects, many of which were permanent. Rumor had it that many of the people who'd competed and been taken out by the field were sold into mindless slavery, unaware of their past or how they'd ended up where they'd ended up. Another little Schock and Gamatti side business, no doubt.

The seawater river, and by default Omra with it, was raging straight down into the bowl. *He could jump*, thought Rechs as he lined up the dropship for a forward barrage from the wing-mounted missiles. In that scout armor, Omra might have enough juice to jump and get clear at the last second.

And he knows who ordered the killing.

Of Medusa.

Of Vexia.

Rechs thumbed the safety off the master arm on the dropship's stick. Some of the lights inside the cockpit panel that had been blinking yellow flipped abruptly to red, and a warning siren began to whoop throughout the flight deck. Rechs thought, at first, that it had something to do with arming the wing-mounted missiles, but a scan of the instruments picked up a flashing "low hydraulics" warning indicator. Omra must have hit something when he fired at the kid.

Rechs lowered the ship, following the contours of the massive, rock- and debris-strewn river. Hydraulic pressure continued to drop, and Rechs still hadn't decided whether to get the kill now and find out another way to determine who was behind it all, or wait to get his hands around Omra's throat and throttle him until he gave up the next link in the chain.

And with Fint bringing Nether Ops into play, the window to make all of this happen was shrinking. He'd been dodging Nether Ops assassins and hit squads for the better part of a year. It was past time to go dark for a while, as he'd done many times before, and wait for the trail to go cold.

The dropship was now bleeding hydraulic fuel in buckets. Some of it burned off over the engines, creating a stale, sickly sweet-smelling stench that filled the cabin. Below, Omra's high-tech assault boat made the bottom of the rapids, just barely, and throttled up to full for the run across the glassy lake.

Omra must have engaged some kind of auto-pilot, because Rechs saw him leave the wheel and move to one of the raft's mounted heavy blasters. There were three of them. Legionnaires liked to go in with plenty of firepower.

A hot stream of bright, heavy blaster shots lanced up at Rechs. He jerked the slow and heavy dropship out of the way of the incoming fire, but some of the bolts still got the empennage and raked it with damage.

Along the banks of the river, in cattail-shrouded shallows, schools of raptor sharks lurched away from the muddy banks and dove into the water, their crocodile-like tails thrashing as they submerged. They created a fast-moving hump beneath the surface of the water from which only their massive dorsal fins rose.

Rechs engaged the blaster targeting system, which was designed to operate best via a neural helmet interface the trained military pilots wore when flying. Of course, this tech never worked for the marines the way it was supposed to. And with no helmet, it couldn't work at all for Rechs. Instead he had to manually toggle the turret, letting loose a barrage that made a series of water plumes geyser into the sky all around the speeding assault raft.

Rechs had to swerve to avoid these, yanking the control stick hard to port and then back to starboard, kicking at the sluggish yaw pedals to keep the ship in forward motion. There was no telling what a sudden dousing of salt water would do to the dying dropship.

Beyond the water plumes, Rechs saw that he'd completely missed the assault raft. It raced past the faux lake's edge and on into the river that gushed down into the final set of rapids before the big fall down into the ruined remains of the city.

Rechs dropped the ship to skim just above the water, hoping to hide behind the rooster tail of the assault raft and prevent Omra from getting a good sight picture for the mounted heavy blaster. But that didn't stop the other bounty hunter from firing anyway. Several shots smashed into the fuselage close to the canopy where Rechs piloted.

That was the final nudge the ship needed for a total power and hydraulic failure. The tail of the dropship swung around, out of control. Rechs stomped on the useless reverse rudder for all he was worth. The rear section of the dropship clipped the raft and went into the river with a terrific splash.

Rechs was thrown violently inside his seat's safety harness. Seawater began to rise up the canopy window.

The dropship wouldn't immediately sink. Some space within it had created a momentary buoyancy. For now, it was floating along the last set of rapids into the vortex of the ruined city.

A bit dazed, Rechs unlocked himself from the harness and climbed from the pilot's seat. His head had connected with something in the cockpit during the crash.

He kicked the pilot's emergency escape hatch open and climbed out onto the bulbous fuselage. Across the water, the massive green triangular fins of the predator sharks were coming straight for the crash site as the river carried them away. The monsters were strong enough swimmers not to fear the rapids.

Blaster fire greeted Rechs. The rear tail section of the dropship had smashed the assault raft, which lay in drifting ruins, and Omra now clung on to the tail with one arm, half his body submerged in the water, firing at Rechs with his sidearm.

Rechs scurried behind the wing and pulled out the Python blaster. He popped over the top of the ship and took his shot. He missed, sending up a shower of sparks with a strike on the tail repulsor.

Omra climbed out of the water and up the thick tail. He holstered the sidearm and pulled the high-tech pistol still secured in the armor's shoulder blade holster.

Rechs fired hard, emptying the Python charge pack on full power and hitting the armored Omra twice. The first shot knocked the man on his back, sending his blaster sliding off and into the rapidly moving water. The second shot was a headshot.

Omra lay prone, his body swaying and bobbing as the dropship lurched through the rapids around him.

Rechs moved over the wing toward his downed target. No easy feat as the dropship wallowed from side to side, bouncing up and down as the river picked up speed with the current heading toward the falls. He slipped and only barely stopped himself from going into the turbulent waters below. A raptor shark swam close by, turning for Rechs's shadow as it danced above the water.

The dropship struck a submerged rock and began to rotate, half of it now beneath the waterline.

While Rechs recovered his balance, Omra pulled off his helmet. It was still smoking from where the shot had struck. The bucket had absorbed most of the damage, but it was finished, and parts of its ceramic mold and rubberized collar had melted onto Omra's face. The man wore a wretched mask of pain.

Omra pushed himself up off the tail and came at Rechs in a sudden charge, heavy boots clanking across the sinking fuselage. He landed a solid kick that sent Rechs rolling across the short wing of the craft, but Rechs kept hold of his blaster, and brought it up as fast as he could to fire once more.

But Omra was coming at him again already, his face twisted in anger, rage, and pain. He struck Rechs savagely with his armored gauntlet. Rechs saw starbursts and told himself to hang on to the blaster if he did nothing else. It might well be the only way to bring the man down.

"What about this aren't you getting, Tyrus!" shouted Omra. He smashed an armored scout boot into Rechs's ribs, driving the breath out of him. "She's *dead*! Nothing's gonna bring her back. And you had every opportunity to let it go. But now…"

Rechs felt another kick, fueled and strengthened by a psychotic rage. He felt Omra's spittle cascade across his neck. Looking up through pained, squinting eyes, he saw the man pause to pull a tranq from the armor's medical supply pouch. Omra shot himself up with painkillers, almost losing his balance as the sinking dropship struck another rock.

"Who?" grunted Rechs as he tried to get to his hands and knees.

"Who, what!" screamed Omra. "You don't think I'm capable of working all of this out myself? Intercepting an inbound termination contract and working both sides of the street? On a world that's just oozing money like a river of life? The mining trade. The gambling. The tax-free shelter for the Republic's bigwigs. I don't need the guild anymore! It's a brilliant plan, and *I'm* damn brilliant for coming up with it!"

Rechs got to one knee. Then the other. The river was roaring all about them. The waterfall that would dump them into the ruins of the city far below was approaching. At the top of the falls, a massive sea-going battleship, rusting and old, lay stuck, its ancient bow jutting out over the drop like some promontory rock.

Omra looked behind him and checked his wrist controls. "Don't worry about me, Tyrus. I'll jump. Got just enough juice left. But I wanted to make sure you stay for the ride."

His eyes flicked to the blaster Rechs seemed to have no strength to lift. "You even dare go for that Python and I'll shoot you down where you are, Rechs. Legend or not. I'm as fast as they get."

Omra's voice was cruel and hard. His eyes even more so. He wanted to watch his prey go helplessly over the falls while he fired the last of his jets and made the leap to safety. He wanted to see the hopeless failure in Rechs's eyes when that happened. He could dine out on that memory for a lifetime. He was sure of it.

The waters thrashed and swam with a school of leathery triangular shark fins. They, too, were hoping for some kind of meal just before the fall.

"You killed her," muttered Rechs. He spat a little blood in the water for the raptor sharks. "But you're not smart enough to have done it on your own. Who was it, Omra? Who wanted her dead?"

Omra began to laugh, never taking his cold eyes from the pistol. As if daring Rechs to go ahead and try.

"There were others," Rechs said. "I know there were. Schock and Gamatti? Did they order—" Rechs pulled and fired, putting a blaster bolt on full charge straight into Omra's armored abdomen. It came out the other side.

The dying bounty hunter backed away, his face pale with horror. His arms, even the cybernetic one, seemed to attempt a pull of his own weapon to fire back, but something within him would not obey. He continued to stumble backwards as his half-cooked intestines began to spill out through the smoking hole in his gut.

Rechs watched the man die, knowing that the wound took with it the will to breathe, let alone name names. But something in the dying hunter's eyes, aside from the shock of his impending demise and the settled reality that he was *not* as fast as he believed, something there told Rechs that Schock and Gamatti were absolutely in on it all.

Omra slipped on a wet section of the partially sunken wing and fell into the rapids. The look on his face went from horror to stark raving fear. One of the raptor sharks, its movements seconds earlier lazy and unconcerned, darted in, surfacing at the last second with its jaw opened a full two meters, exposing rows upon rows of massive triangular teeth. It bit down near Omra's shoulder and dragged him underwater, the rest of its saurian body shimmering behind it.

The great tail of the monster came up and slapped at the water. As if this was the signal for a free-for-all, the other raptor sharks raced in, frenzied and fighting for the kill.

Rechs let the Python go; it clattered against the drop-ship's wing. It was empty now. He'd dumped the entire charge into the last shot, knowing it would be the only one he'd get.

He tapped his comm. "G232…"

No reply.

The falls were getting closer. Close enough that he could see the tops of the towers of the ruined city that had succumbed to the massive sinkhole. They were strange, artistic towers, once sculpted things of beauty and now fallen against one another, leaning on lesser buildings. And within these thousands upon thousands of windows, gaping like eye sockets at the unending horrors they could never stop seeing.

You'll be the last, Tyrus.

The waterlogged and drowning dropship increased in speed as it neared the falls, passing alongside the exposed hull of the old warship that had been saved from the vortex by some underground anchor long ago. Strange vines hung down along its sides, at times dipping into the river itself. Rechs knew they were the only way to escape.

"G232!" he shouted, attempting one last time. The sinking dropship was being pushed under the water, its wings surrendering to the chop and surge of the approaching falls.

Rechs reached out for a cluster of vines, hoping they could hold him. He let go of his slippery purchase on the dropship as it was carried away by the swifts. With a titanic, metal-rending groan, it disappeared over the falls and began its long descent into the ruined city.

Rechs hung from the vines just over the rushing water, the toes of his boots skimming the surface. As the raptor sharks came to investigate, Rechs began to climb, feet planted against the ancient warship, pulling himself up hand over hand.

35

THE ANCIENT WARSHIP GROANED AND SHIFTED, FEEL-
ing as though all it needed was the slightest push to be
sent careening over the falls. The main deck canted down
toward the dry riverbank, and someone long ago had
built a wooden bridge from the bank to an abandoned
dwelling on the deck. Rechs, with some difficulty, crossed
the bridge to dry land.

He knelt down alongside the bank, buried up to his
thighs in fragrant grasses. He could smell the salt of the
water mix with a strange, spicy form of jasmine emanat-
ing from clusters of flowers that grew in bulbous humps.

"G232... come in."

Finally, the bot replied.

"Ah, there you are, Master. The administrators of the
contest have jammed all transmissions since the incident
with the actor. The game has been officially suspended.
I must apologize for my absence over the comms. The
worm needed time to allow your workaround to reacquire the channel. Are you well? Are you winning at the
Game of Death?"

"Send in the *Crow*. Fix on my location. I'm next to a field. Have it get in as close as possible. I won't be feeling well."

"Now that the game is suspended, perhaps they'll shut down the neural nullification field. Though I don't believe they have done so thus far, Master."

"They won't, Three-Two."

***

Ten minutes later the *Obsidian Crow*, which had been lying low on one of Cassio's deserted moons, swept down out of the sky and passed effortlessly through the neural nullification shield. It circled the landing zone and saw Rechs signaling where to set down. But the neural field itself was sweeping in fast. Likely as fast as it could go. Rechs had been watching its approach as he sweated out the long minutes waiting for the *Crow* to arrive. There wasn't much time left.

Rechs felt better than he ought to on account of something he'd hidden in his cargo pockets. He had worried it had been claimed by the raging waters, but he'd found it waiting for him. A small pill. A one-shot super-stim designed to keep him alive and moving.

The *Crow* flared, lowered her landing gears, and set down. Its boarding ramp touched down along with its landing struts, beckoning Rechs to come aboard. At almost the same moment, the golden-hued wave of neural nullifaction swept over the field. Swept over Tyrus Rechs.

Rechs's mind swam. He saw colors and strange hallucinations. If not for the pill filling his mind with endorphins and serotonators to keep him conscious, he would have fallen to his knees. As it was, he struggled to fight off the dark cloud that suddenly hammered at the edges of his mind.

The ship, its engines howling on idle, pushed away all the local foliage in great waves. It was powerless to help him. Rechs would have to cross the twenty meters to it on his own.

He wanted to move but could not. Knew that he should but never would. Because... *why?*

An ennui the size of the galaxy swept over him. It was as if even his heart didn't want to beat, if only because there was no point in ever continuing on.

"Where has it gotten me?" he muttered.

Two thousand years of crossing the stars, defending a galaxy that didn't have the sense to save itself from itself... and then that thing he was supposed to be waiting for out along the edge... What was it, again?

The will to remember such a thing threatened to destroy Rechs's mind. So he let it go.

What has it all ever gotten me? he thought again.

Vexia was there. Standing in the grass. Wearing a long, white silk dress. The blast from the engines pulled at it, making it tight against her body and throwing her long blond hair into the wind.

She smiled at Rechs.

She was a machine no more. Not like he'd last known her. Not like she was now, frozen in carbonite on the *Crow.*

She was human again. And a woman.

Who'd been in love. And a doctor.

Another person. One he'd never known.

Someone who hoped the galaxy might be a better place.

She smiled at him, laughing good-naturedly.

Rechs wondered if this was death.

Because if it was... then maybe death wasn't so bad. He could just let go and stay... with her.

He stumbled to go to her. The world turned sideways. The neural field had ruined his mind. He took one step toward Vexia. She nodded.

He wanted to hear her voice. But she would not speak.

She would never speak again.

He took another step. And then he realized it was not death she was beckoning him toward, but the ship. Her eyes wanted him to go on. To go and live and forget about her. What was revenge to her now? She didn't care about this life anymore. She had gone on ahead.

Rechs reached the boarding ramp. He steadied himself by grabbing a lowering strut. He stared at Vexia, still standing in the field. Almost right next to him. She reached out her hand once more... and he reached out to take it.

But she was gone. As though she'd never been there.

The ship lifted, retracting its gear and pivoting for a fast takeoff. Rechs was vaguely aware of how bad things must be if even with the stim pill all he wanted was sleep. A million years of sleep forever. He stumbled toward an electronically sealed med kit he'd attached to the wall near the boarding entry, feeling the ship turn and burn skyward, pushing him into the wall like a drunkard in an alley. He popped open the med kit and started swallowing pills and hitting himself with injectors.

He was starving.

But he knew he couldn't eat. He'd throw up. He had way too many meds, a lethal cocktail almost, coursing through his system. Trying to save his mental capacity and function.

He'd suspected that he might need the kit and drug suite if he violated the neural nullification field when the time came. If he didn't have a stroke or a seizure in the next two minutes, then, supposedly, he'd be okay.

He stumbled up to the flight deck as the *Crow* climbed through the upper atmosphere. His mind reeled. They were shooting up through the atmosphere. Entering space.

"Pursuit?" he asked the ship, unsure where the reserves that let him even *think* about such things were coming from.

"None, Captain. We are still heading for our secondary location along one of the outer gas giants. Cassio Station traffic indicates the area is rarely frequented."

"Good," mumbled Rechs. Things were clearing. "Get me comm."

He sat down heavily in the pilot's chair. His heart was racing, and the narcotic suite trying to purge the negative toxins brought on by the field made him sweat profusely.

"G232?" asked Rechs of the ether, unsure whether he had comms. Unsure if he would live.

But he had to live.

He had one more thing to do.

"Yes, master," said the bot.

"Open up a channel to Schock and Gamatti. You know the one."

His hands were shaking. As was his whole body now.

"Stand by, Master."

Rechs waited for the bot to patch him through to the pre-arranged channel his worm had prepared for him. A direct line to both of Cassio Royale's biggest fish.

"Tyrus?" It was Gabriella. "Are you okay? What happened?"

"F-f-f-fine," chattered Rechs. His teeth were hitting one another like jackhammers.

"You don't sound fine." The concern in her voice was real. She wasn't his handler. She was someone who cared.

When was the last time, Rechs, that other voice asked, *that you had someone who cared for you? Really cared?*

"Is Omra dead?"

"D-d-dead." It was all Rechs could do or say.

"Then you can let this go now."

"N-no."

And then...

"Others."

36

Both Schock and Gamatti heard the voice of Tyrus Rechs. The drugs had kicked in and done their work, and now he'd regained some control over his voice. What they heard—Gamatti during a meeting in his private office, Schock in the midst of a party in his casino—was a man who was done playing around.

What they heard was Tyrus Rechs coming for them.

What they heard was as real as it gets.

"Omra talked," began Rechs over the ether of open comm. Somehow breaking into their meetings, their reverie. "He told me it was the two of you together. Both of you are responsible for her death. And so are the others. Every bounty hunter who worked for you."

The two powerful men leaned forward, listening. It was clear that there was no bargaining with the speaker. This was reality, and it was about to get very cold and very cruel. And clear. As in run and hide, or fight it out, clear. Neither man had risen to a position of power by not facing the hard situations. They were well acquainted with the harsh realities that went along with their chosen occupations. The saying was, you might inherit a business, but that's not enough to keep it. And these men didn't become crime lords by accidentally falling backwards into it.

Cassio Royale was there because they wanted it worse than anybody else that wanted it—and they did whatever it took to get it. It had taken an impervisteel will to achieve the wealth, status, and power they held. It was they who ran Cassio Station—they who had turned it into the gambling boom town of Cassio Royale.

But they were realists too. And they understood reality better than most when it came calling. Especially when it had come for them.

"Noon tomorrow," Rechs said flatly. "You have until then to settle your affairs. Then I'm coming for all of you. If you work for these people, or you're on station for a... *vacation*, then I suggest you get out. Tomorrow... noon... Cassio Station is going to be a very dangerous place to be."

And that's when Gamatti, and later Schock, realized everyone on station had heard Rechs's message. Somehow the bounty hunter had hacked not only into their personal comms, but the entire comm system.

Gamatti got up from the crisis meeting inside his penthouse office, a corporate affair with a wide window that looked down on the strip. He had a clear view of Schock's casino... and the massive holoscreens adorning its side. The news was already broadcasting Rechs's speech in several different languages.

And then he looked down below. Saw the people. Could even hear some of their panicked screams way up in his office. Some of his customers were outright running through the crowds. Knowing that getting off station in the next few hours was going to be very tricky, and that it was better to be early than late.

A ticket off Cassio was going to be spun gold in a few hours.

A drunken carnival had turned into a panicked riot to escape.

The party was over.

The Game of Death, the biggest event, was a disappointing memory now. Suddenly everyone was caught up in their own little Game of Death. The most wanted man in the galaxy, a man who—unbeknownst to the crowds—had just badly injured Alex Collins-Gauweiler and outright killed Omra of all people, was coming for the station and his enemies there. The chances of getting killed in a blaster fight crossfire had risen significantly.

"And what if he just blows up the station?" someone might have whispered. "What then?"

Those who had ships were gear up within the hour. Those who didn't were emptying their bank accounts.

***

Schock was in a pure rage. The two bounty hunters who had worked with Omra watched as the deranged man tore apart his palace at the top of his casino. Barely clad hookers fled. Schock shot one of his own men with a comically large, overpowered, and gold-plated medium blaster. The man's crime, though he was one of Schock's inner circle, had been simply asking, "What're we gonna do, boss?"

"Do?" screamed Schock, gaily dressed in his best purple-and-white suit and rocked to the gills on H8.

And then he'd shot the man right in the Pillow Lounge as happy pink bubbles floated down across the party Schock had been throwing with himself as the centerpiece. A party utterly ruined by Tyrus Rechs. "We're gonna do *that* to him!"

Everybody, including the two bounty hunters, knew what that meant. They'd be standing and fighting. If Schock didn't kill them first.

And Captain Hess, watching from a deserted corridor of high-end luxury shops, all reeking of perfume and fine art, watched the live feed of Tyrus Rechs's speech. The blank screen and the words appearing at the bottom. The voice was known to him. He was one of the few people who'd been inside the vault beneath the House of Reason. He'd heard the few recordings of Tyrus Rechs that remained. Uninteresting stuff. The occasional message he'd left for someone. Things that hadn't merely, and unexplainably, vanished from the electronic archives. Stuff that was protected because it wasn't connected to any system.

Hess smiled and began to nod slowly.

He couldn't have set a better trap himself.

Tyrus Rechs was coming to *him*.

"Well," he muttered, his face a sneer of the victory he saw as his, "we'll be ready too, Tyrus." He looked to his waiting Nether Ops hit squad. "Whatta you say we stay here, waiting with arms wide open?"

The men gave a deep, "Hoo!"

Hess nodded. "Noon tomorrow it is."

37

Ten Minutes to Noon

Tᴇɴ ᴍɪɴᴜᴛᴇs ᴛᴏ ɴᴏᴏɴ ᴏɴ Cᴀssɪᴏ Rᴏʏᴀʟᴇ ɪs ᴀ ᴠᴇʀʏ different scene from the non-stop party that has engulfed the station for the better part of a week. For the last eighteen hours a fever pitch of desperate activity seized the station as everyone sought to leave by any means possible. Fortunes were lost, and made, in a moment as wealth was redistributed from those who had no transport to those who could get you off station.

The first few hours saw the private ships lift off with little preparation and complete abandon. Luxury rooms were left littered with jewelry, black market high-end tech gear, and priceless bottles of the finest wines, scotches, and bourbons the galaxy had to offer. Bills were left unpaid as worthies of the House of Reason and their business entourages fled by personal transport, always under-loaded so that those of wealth and style were not inconvenienced. In those hours many found out how really connected, or unconnected, they were. Sleek starships lifted up and away from the upper-class docking campus and made short work of getting to jump speed.

After that came the big cruise liners, many of which were docked alongside the station's main strip. Gargantuan behemoths that glittered like crystal from every deck, winking at the the starlit way. These took longer to load, but within hours they were pulling away from dock and lumbering off toward jump. Many of those ships' original passengers were left behind. Perhaps because they'd fallen under the sway of hardcore chemicals, or drunken binges, or the charms of a paid escort. They were stunned to see the big ships they'd arrived on suddenly leaving without them, abandoning them to the bars, hotel rooms, and pleasure dens they'd been wallowing in.

The hours following *that* saw those who'd arrived by other means desperately searching the dark corners of cantinas and alleys for any room on any freighter off station and out of the system. No matter what the cost. No matter how skeezy the crew.

It was here, in the shadowy concourses where too many showed up to get away on one of the coveted and massively overpriced berths, that the rumors abounded.

"He's wanted by the Republic for genocide."

"Rechs is an ex-legionnaire who snapped after the war on Kalanistan. Killed a whole village of people."

"Even the Legion is afraid of him."

"He murdered a senator's daughter after abducting her from a liner."

"I hear he's stark raving mad."

"It's a disguise. Tyrus Rechs, like the general. He's a copycat drafting off a great man's name. But I wouldn't cross him."

"He shoots first. No questions."

And so on.

At ten minutes to noon, Cassio Royale is a ghost station. All through the strip and all the other glittering, gleaming, Tyrasian marble–lined halls of ululating gaming houses, not a sound can be heard other than the frenetic beckoning of automated gaming machines. Even the workers have fled, and those who have not, as with all those who had been left behind, have sought shelter until it's all over.

All this at ten minutes to noon.

Seven Minutes to Noon

At seven minutes to noon Schock throws open his large and extensive coffers. He, a bona fide psychopath, has engaged in every illegal activity imaginable for most of his life, accumulating wealth by any means. And he has acquired a lot of it.

Schock is not, and has never been, shy about showing off his credits. His parties were crass displays of his ill-gotten gain. His courtesans dressed in jewels he'd looted from the wealthy who "disappeared" in high-end voyages to some of the more forbidden worlds deep inside the Reach. And yet as lavishly as Schock lived, he saved even more than he spent.

He was prepared to spend some of those savings now.

He'd first responded to Tyrus Rechs's threat with a consuming rage. But in time, that rage was transformed to beneficence. To promising wealth untold. All any gun left on station had to do was protect Schock and kill Tyrus Rechs—and, boy oh boy, would you be rich if you did. Richer than a sharebroker on Utopion. Able to afford your own harem of Sandistrarian sirens. The dreams of avarice would be yours to name.

And all you had to do was kill a solitary bounty hunter.

Whether you thought you had the skill set or not, when else in your wretched life were you ever going to get a chance like this?

That was the general line of thought for the thugs who waited to begin their employment under Schock. The galaxy has always been made of such hopefuls. And the graveyards are filled with them, too.

At seven minutes to noon Schock was surrounded by no less than twenty men on this floor. His best, all armed to the teeth. Three ad hoc quick reaction teams were on standby on floors both above and below as well as on the roof. And there were a whole lot more than that waiting with itching blasters and dreams of riches everywhere else in between.

Schock was dressed in his best-cut black suit. He was lean and tall. Gaunt and wild-eyed and leering. He stood at the bar in his private suite, nursing a gin on the rocks and thinking of times he was witty. He had only a small pile of stims to inhale; he needed to stay frosty. Most of his men were going to get killed. But that would be okay. All they needed to do was get him a clear shot at Rechs, and then everything would go back to normal.

He hit the gin, took the barest bump of stim, and smiled in the mirror, muttering to himself.

The truth was, he'd lost his mind. The last eighteen hours had caused him to snap. To be fair, his grip on sanity had always been pretty loose.

Now he was freefalling without a net.

At seven minutes to noon, Schock transformed from a simple psychopath to a homicidal psychopath with delusions of grandeur.

Five Minutes to Noon

At five minutes to noon Captain Hess is leaving nothing to chance. He has two squads of his most capable agents with him. Extra weapons. Extra breaching gear. Each squad carrying anti-armor capable of dealing with Rechs's legendary armor system.

Most of the men, now nothing more than mercenaries in Legion armor, smell the bonus coming if they get this one. They've been chasing Rechs for a long time. Kill Team Predator has been on his trail for a year. And now, as if out of the blue, their target is coming to them.

Hess has placed sniper teams on all the towers along the strip. He doesn't have unlimited resources, and he's had to keep a reaction and boarding force on both frigates to intercept any escape attempt by Rechs, but he's got more than enough to do the job should he get a direct engagement. Knowing that Schock and Gamatti are the targets, Hess has staged his force in a small, closed restaurant adjacent to both casinos.

The strip beyond the windows looks like an abandoned paradise where no one bothered to turn off the images offering shows, forbidden pleasures, and the loosest slots this side of Vega Gamulon. Holopics of green, four-armed showgirls compete with entertainment acts crooning their greatest hits from ten years ago.

But at five minutes to noon, no one moves out there on the strip. It's a ghost station.

The tables in the restaurant are loaded with clam-shells containing all the weapons Kill Team Predator can use. Blasters, heavy blasters, sniper rifles, fraggers, bangers, satchel charges. Two crates contain Dragon X man-deployable ground-to-ship engagement systems. Using one inside a hab would probably be considered a war crime.

War crimes have been waved in lieu of a shot at Tyrus Rechs. Hess has confirmation from the House of Reason defense committee.

At five minutes to noon Captain Hess is feeling confident as he pulls on his gloves and gives his platoon sergeant the guns-up nod.

Both assault frigates are tracking an inbound freighter matching a scan of the *Obsidian Crow*.

Three Minutes to Noon

At three minutes to noon Alfa Gamatti is nervous. But he's made his plan and he'll run his game. That's gambling. There are no guaranteed winners, but everybody gets to take their chance.

However, *he* has the most to lose.

It's really him that's built Cassio Royale. He came here on the rumor that business could be done. Within ten years he had big-time corporate investment coming in to build the strip along the top of the station and create a luxury gaming paradise.

No place is inviolable. But the top admin suites that run the casino below are as close as it comes. Automated blast doors, robot sentry systems, and heavy blaster turrets were built right into the structure. Illegal, but since it was Gamatti and his investors doing the building…

There's also a ship if it all goes to hell. If his forty-plus hired security professionals, many with trigger time in the various services and now wearing well-cut suits and learning the business corporate speak of the gaming industry, if they fail… then there's always the escape ship on the topmost floor. Where other casino magnets would have built themselves a garden, or a pleasure palace, or a luxury estate, Gamatti made sure to build a way out.

Engines are warm, but Gamatti will stick as long as he can, because he feels there's a win on the other side of all this. Why, if this Rechs character actually gets rid of Schock, Gamatti might even feel obliged to pay the guy. Schock is new money and bad business. Ripping off every customer right up to the whales. That'll only play for so long. And bringing drugs onto the station? That'll take everything straight downhill.

Besides, Schock's a psycho. Getting rid of him is a win no matter how you look at it.

And that's Gamatti. An opportunist even when it's bleakest. A guy who sees all the angles and plays to win the one that makes him the most.

Still, Gamatti is nervous. It was his plan, really, that caused the whole mess. He was the one who hired the guild to take out the rat smuggler who'd been ripping them off. And that brought the skirt bounty hunter. And then suddenly he's getting a call from Schock saying that he's got her and that Schock knows it was Gamatti who paid for the hit on the smuggler.

And here's where it gets weird.

Schock says there's money to be made. A lot more money than just Cassio. The guild is about to have a little revolution. A force within wants to make it collapse and start a new guild on the other side. And the best way to do that is to make it look like the guild can't trust itself.

"What are you saying?" Gamatti asked.

"I'm saying," replied Schock, "that we have a chance here to run the next bounty hunter guild *from Cassio*. This new player wants it here. Tax shelter haven. We get a cut of every bounty for providing safety and security and a way to launder all that money through our casinos."

And yes, thinks Gamatti now. *That was too good to be true.*

But it was also too good to pass up. The credits that could have come in from all those bounties would have made Cassio Royale look like a corner store in its current model. Galaxy-wide private law enforcement contract work was orders of magnitude beyond gambling and entertainments.

Schock was already rambling on about how being the law meant they could more easily circumvent all the laws out there that the Republic didn't have the time to enforce. It was a whole new world of crime and wealth for them to explore.

"What are you going to do about the bounty hunter?" Gamatti asked. "The dame?"

"Well," said Schock, all inside and conspiratorial, seemingly forgetting that he'd tried to have Gamatti blown up last year. "She's *gotta* die. But we can make a little money on her before she goes. Got this weirdo tech guru. Developed the whole Inner Peace personal management system everyone on Utopion's buying. Well, he's a real nutjob. He shows up about twice a year, gambles a lot, and always has a special request."

Gamatti knew exactly who Schock was talking about. He kept detailed files on all the whales.

"For a few years he's been asking us to find a nano-plague victim. A hot one, preferably. He wants to—get this—do it… with a machine."

"And?" asked Gamatti.

"Oh, you don't know? Yeah, this bounty hunter, calls herself Medusa, she's one of 'em."

"And you have her on station!" erupted Gamatti. He knew how virulent the nano-plague was.

"We do!" said Schock, rather proudly. "Our contact inside the guild, the one who wants to bring it down and form his own, he advised us of her, ahem, *condition*. So we set up a whole clean room after her capture. The weirdo is payin' a lot of money and we're getting her all dolled up and everything, and then, supposedly, he's actually gonna do it. With protection I guess. But hey, whatever floats your boat, right? That's what we sell. Nothin's wrong with nothin', right?"

Gamatti felt sick.

"Don't worry, Alfa. Would I expose myself to such a potential hazard? No. Once it's done, two in the back of the head and we plant her on this asteroid station to get found by that Repub survey ship coming through next week. Word gets back to the guild that they're compromised. New guild forms on Cassio, and we collect, to start, our cut on every bounty. Plus I got some plans. What I'm sayin', Gamatti, is… we gotta start working together. I admit… I'm ambitious. But this is bigger than me. And you run a good station. You're in with the Repub and all the unions. That's why I'm asking you to go in as partners. Together we can make more'n we'll ever want."

Gamatti listened. In time Schock would try to kill him. Maybe Gamatti could kill Schock first. He knew the man on the other end of the line was thinking the same thing. But it was a lot of credits they were talking about. Next-level credits.

"I'm in."

"Great. You wanna see her? She's a real freak. Pretty hot, or at least she used to be. But now... metal maid. Sad, really. But... the guy wants to make it happen, and I've always been about the customer service. Right, Alfa?"

"Right," Gamatti mumbled.

All that led to here.

At three minutes to noon, Alfa Gamatti is coldly aware of everything that has brought him to this moment. He isn't optimistic... but there is a play here, and that means there's a chance he can make it through this and come out sitting pretty. Maybe.

That chance involves putting Tyrus Rechs down.

Well, Gamatti bought some pretty impressive security bots long before all this. The floors are secure. There's a ship to get away in. At three minutes to noon, Alfa Gamatti feels the odds are in his favor.

Maybe.

Two Minutes to Noon

Pollus and Umari Kazor work until the last moment. Even at two minutes to noon they're both working. Preparing. Bounty hunters need every advantage. If they were given an extra minute, they'd take it. Both are pros. Both are ex-Legion Dark Ops. Both have seen war and all its horror. Both opted to become bounty hunters and are considered the very model of professional.

Now, at two minutes to noon, neither is going down the long trail of bad decisions that led them to this point. That's all in the past. And the past means nothing to a bounty hunter.

"Fraggers?" asks one.

"Full up. You?" replies the other.

"I'm good to go. More to spare at the locs I tagged on your HUD."

"Good thinking. Charge packs?"

"Solid. I'm carryin' at least twenty. You?"

"Less. But they're big. Using the pig on this one, so…"

"Good call. Lay down suppressive. Keep him pinned and I'll get close."

"Copy that."

Gear is adjusted. Weapons loaded. And at the last each stands and looks at the other in full armor. Special aftermarket designs crafted to complement their engagement style. Full capabilities in vision and equipment. Skinned in their own personal styles. One likes matte olive green and the show of battle damage mixed with the names of all the dead branded onto his shoulder plates and down his armored gauntlets. Just like the tattoo he wears underneath. The other prefers a stealth mode that keeps his armor in neutral matte black and then switches over to light refraction for a limited invisibility cloaking effect.

They fist-bump.

"Good working with you, Pollux."

"You too, Umar. Take care."

They part. They're taking separate ends of the main intersection on the strip. It's called Time Square because of the massive digital clock.

Umari turns back. "You think he'd let us…?"

Pollux shakes his head.

"Give us a pass?" Umari tries one more time.

Grim-voiced Pollux speaks. His armor's audible system makes him sound like a nightmare. "Nah. Not his way. We got ourselves into this. The only way through is to shoot it out with him and see who's left standing. It's the only way. We shoulda known better."

Silence. The shining holoscreens gyrate with announcements of events that have been canceled and deals that will never be taken advantage of. All the motion and dead silence seem to be at odds with another as the light shows shift shadows across the square. As though this were a field where some epic sports contest will soon take place.

"Thought so," says Umari. And then he is gone, off to his position to await the coming of Tyrus Rechs.

At two minutes to noon, Umari and Pollux have accepted their fate. Whatever it is to be.

One Minute to Noon

At one minute until the end of the world, Fint sits at his desk drinking the last cup of coffee to be had in the security station. It's hot.

He's cleaned his blaster and has it laid out on the desk before him. The monitors out in the pit, the main area of the watch that keep an eye on the station, show a thousand different images. All seemingly frozen because nothing and no one is moving out there. The few private security personnel that have chosen to remain have been told, along with the unlucky and foolish who have been forced to remain behind, to shelter in place.

Fint pulls the desk bottle from his drawer and tops off the coffee. At one minute to midnight his pension tells him to sit tight and clean up the dead. But somehow, he knows he'll be wading out into blaster fire at some point.

From the numbers, it doesn't look like a fair fight by anyone's stretch of the imagination. And Fint has never liked unfair fights.

At one minute to noon Fint stares at his blaster and takes another sip of the coffee. If just to take the edge off of making a foolish decision.

38

Noon

THE *OBSIDIAN CROW* COURSED TOWARD THE BERTH O1 shuttle pad. Berth O1 was in the spotlight of the docks that could be viewed through the main invisi-steel wall off the grand gambling palaces of the main strip of Cassio Royale. Where twelve hours ago there had been at least three to four of the major liners docked and looking in on the microcosmic snow globe of fun that was Cassio Royale, now there was nothing but the black velvet of space and the underwhelming approach of a tiny pancake-shaped freighter with a central pilot's cupola.

Reversers flared and three landing gears extended as the freighter set down on the shuttle pad next to the main docking berth. Witnessed from inside the hab of the main strip, no arrival could have been less underwhelming and more anticipated.

The four different elements waiting to kill Tyrus Rechs held their collective breath.

Gamatti and his thugs.

Schock and his.

Pollux and Umari.

And Kill Team Predator.

"First Squad to customs," whispered Hess over the Nether Ops comm. "Let's try and pin him down."

***

Rechs, in the Mark I armor, landed atop a hidden docking bay access hatch that housed Gamatti's private ship. He'd jumped from the *Crow* as it came in over the strip to set up for her landing on the shuttle pad. Rechs's access to the city's net had told him early on that Gamatti kept this little get-out-of Cassio card waiting in a secret hangar at the top of his casino, which extended beyond the hab dome.

It was a tricky jump, but the Legion had specialized in this type of EVA boarding operations back during the Savage Wars. And the Mark I armor's jump capabilities made this far easier than it would have been with the average legionnaire armor of today. Unless it was an orbital assault specific variant of the standard-issue. And even then the OAS still required a good amount of pilot training.

He stuck the landing, hitting the top of the tower that stood regally out of the dome's main hab, shooting up into the black void of space. A near miss would have landed him against the invisi-steel glass dome, making him a perfect target for any of the sniper teams the Nether Ops commander had placed on towers along the strip.

Gauntlets magnetized, Rechs was able to grab on to the topside of the docking doors. That was the trick.

Hands first. Then boots. That way you didn't break your legs.

He checked his time clock. The *Crow* would be down on the pad now, and they'd be waiting for him to come out blasting. One of the first rules of bounty hunting was never be where the enemy expected you to be. Which was also one of the first rules of warfare as far as Rechs was concerned.

He crawled across the surface of the dock and reached the manual interface panel. Flipping off the cover, he was rewarded with the soft blue glow of a keypad and control scheme. He tried the coded override he'd had placed in the system… and got nothing.

"Hard way then," he muttered, and moved back out onto the main surface. Standing now, boots magnetically gripping the docking doors below, he removed the plate cutter he'd brought along, a small diamond-edged saw. Working quickly, he cut a four-foot-by-four-foot square, stepped back, and waited for the air to escape, while wondering if any blaster fire or bits of decompressed men would come through the hole.

None did.

With the plate cutter once more stowed on his back, Rechs jumped through the hole and floated down into the bay, hand cannon out and scanning for targets.

***

The only thing Gamatti got from Tolio, the man he'd sent to get his ship ready, was a brief, "He's coming through the hangar, boss!"

And then nothing. No matter how many times he asked for Tolio to come back on the comm, voice rising from concern to anger to outright fear, he got nothing in response. Nothing.

"Shutting down all doors between here and the hangar," announced Kerfa, Gamatti's chief security expert. "I'll deploy the gargantuas that way. Give us enough time to get out of the building."

Gamatti nodded, his throat dry. His mouth beginning to quiver in fear as he wiped the back of his hand across it. He grabbed an impervisteel briefcase from off his desk and allowed his crew to move him out of the building via the safest exit route.

There was an escape pod with one-jump capability located in the lower levels. If they could reach that, they could at least get the boss off the station.

***

Gargantua 1 swarmed down the hall leading to the main elevator. Gargantua 2 was on its six, and 3 and 4 were coming up through the elevator shaft after taking the lift offline.

The Gargantua model was a tactical security bot, a low-level AI private security combat mech with four powerful arms that gripped sections of the walls and floor to move itself forward like a scuttling spider. Twice the size of a human and weighing in at nearly two tons, each machine carried four high-cycle blasters, an imaging suite, and a comprehensive ceramic armor system that made it very hard to take down.

These mechanical monsters were the ultimate pursuit and termination systems. Often they were used on corporate worlds to root out rebels, or to pull hit-and-run raids on expensive corporate assets. They moved in total dark at close to thirty miles an hour, sounding like some infernal machine from a forgotten lighthugger. When they found their target, they would open up with the quad-blasters. Nothing survived that kind of vicious short-range fire in an enclosed space.

Now, pulling themselves along Gamatti's stately hall of dark teak and some of the finest illegally collected art the galaxy had ever seen, the machines were ruining everything. Tearing the teak to splinters, shredding the carpet, smashing statuary, and destroying priceless paintings as they moved to intercept the intruder bent on killing their master.

Rechs heard them as he came down in the lift. He was unsure exactly what they were, but he knew that they were some kind of mech, and it was obvious that they were coming for him.

The lift jerked to a sudden halt.

If the intention had been to trap Rechs and then annihilate him with massed volumes of high-cycle fire, the bounty hunter operated under a different plan.

Rechs used his armor's power to pull the lift doors open with one arm while holding the high-powered medium blaster on the narrowly opening aperture. Nothing visible yet, but he could hear them in the distance. Down the hall and... right below his boots. Two of whatever kind of mechs they were were coming up the shaft and were likely intent on tearing through the floor to get at Rechs.

He dropped to his belly and slid through the narrow opening between the floor of the lift and the hallway beyond. Then he reached back in with a satchel charge and tossed it in the lift just as one of the googly-eyed bot's claw-arms ripped the lift floor in two.

Rechs ran, muttering into the armor's comm, "Detonate now!"

A terrific explosion sent debris and flames all around him and down the well-appointed hall. Rechs's armor was more than enough to handle it, but the rail system that held the lift was not. One metal-groaning second later, the heavy lift, with both bots clawing their way into it, dropped all the way down to the basement garage far below.

As Rechs rounded a corner in the opulent hall, he found two more bots waiting for him. Quad blasters deployed, arms anchoring them along the walls and floors to stabilize the fire, they were preparing to pour down on him as targeting lasers lanced out to range his position.

Rechs dove back around the corner just before a hurricane of blaster fire tore the other passage to shreds. The whine of high-cycle blaster fire ripped through the air as the actual bolts stripped every surface and went on to ruin the underlying structure. A massive glass window shattered out into the skyline, sending shards down on the street below.

***

Captain Hess swore as the tinkling glass rained down on his men's improvised fighting position between the towers. They had brought in sleds and loaded them down with pre-fab liquid-stone barriers. Looking skyward, and seeing the fusillade of blaster fire arching out into the building across the street more than two hundred stories up, Hess knew that Rechs had chosen a completely different way to get at his targets.

"Stand by with the Dragon to engage. We might get a shot here."

Legionnaires scrambled to deploy the system.

***

Only one. Rechs had brought only one electronic warfare banger. He popped and tossed it. The crinkle of an explosion over comm told him that the device had gone off. Hopefully it was enough to fritz out the mechs' targeting systems for a few seconds.

Rechs ran into the crossing hallway and turned away from the machines, racing instead for the shattered glass of the open window at the other end. A second later he was flying out across the brilliantly lit sky of the dome. The wild, gyrating lighting of the non-stop funhouse of the strip strobed and erupted across Rechs's armor as he rocketed across the gap, directly toward Schock's penthouse.

Schock himself, staring with wild-eyed disbelief at Rechs coming straight across the strip—an approach unlike any of the thirty other ways Schock had imagined the bounty hunter might come for him—swore in disbelief.

He tried to pull his gold-plated, comically large blaster, but Rechs pumped the jets on his armor and crashed through the glass, knocking Schock to the ground. Schock, aside from being stabbed in several places by massive glass shards, had also lost three fingers.

Twenty men surrounded Rechs and pulled their blasters, or picked them up from where they'd left them on the gaudy and crass mirrored surfaces Schock favored for interior design. As they began to fire, Rechs rocketed around the room, his armor absorbing whatever hit him.

Among the thugs were the three who'd chased Rechs across the island after trying to throw him of the back of transport. Somehow they'd escaped the game alive; they were never real contestants. The big bruiser smiled like he'd just won the lottery.

Rechs returned fire, engaging as many as he could with the hand cannon while he moved for cover behind a silver-flecked mirror painted to show a comely young girl pouring herself a drink. The hand cannon went off in staccato bursts, sending heavy fifty-caliber slugs into the bodies of the hired blasters. The bruiser's two sidekicks went down in a storm of exploding mirrors and torn couches. Floating feathers mixed with their bloody spray as Rechs thoroughly ventilated them both. Cordite and burnt ozone filled the gaudy room.

Some return fire continued to come Rechs's way, but most of those who'd been smart enough to pull and start firing, knowing it was their only way out of this, had already died within the first thirty seconds. Those who weren't yet killed were now seeking cover. Normally a good decision, except most of the cover that could be found consisted of over-stuffed pleasure couches and giant purple amoeba chairs. Hardly the type of thing to stop a bullet.

Another storm of fifty-caliber fire tore through those defenses as if they weren't even there. Inside Rechs's

HUD, imaging software showed him everyone on IR as the room choked with smoke. The hired guns could only shoot, coughing and choking, at where they thought Rechs was.

The big bruiser came at Rechs from off the floor. He'd taken cover, secured a blaster, and was now making his play.

Rechs, already engaging two others behind cover, flung his boot in a savage kick at the bruiser's blaster and knocked it away. He stepped back and shot the stunned bruiser five times at close range. It emptied the magazine, but it *felt* good.

Not a minute later everyone was dead except Schock. He lay moaning pathetically among the shattered glass on the mirrored floor. A two-fingered hand held his gold-plated blaster, now running bright red with blood. He rolled over and went fetal as he heard Rechs's boots coming for him, crushing the shattered glass to grit.

Schock whimpered softly, planning on telling Rechs, explaining really, how it hadn't been on purpose. It had just… happened that way. He'd had every intention of releasing the skirt. Letting her go. Schock's drug-addled, pain-screaming mind decided he'd trade a name the bounty hunter wanted to hear. Needed to hear. The source of the whole mess really. The entity that had started the whole chain of events in motion. And then, maybe…

Rechs looked down at the pathetic little man on the floor, crying into his boots. Schock's cut face and slashed lips were a mess. Shredded by flying glass. The sounds he made were little more than gurgling and pathetic mewling.

Grabbing with one gauntlet the black-suited dandy who, just minutes ago, thought he was the epitome of evil, Rechs dragged him to the shattered window above the main strip and threw him out.

When Schock realized he was falling, falling thirty stories, he began to scream. A second later he slammed into one of Hess's improvised barriers. Dying, every bone in his body broken, he stared sightlessly skyward like some fallen demon who still couldn't believe he'd been cast out of heaven.

***

Two levels down, Rechs found an observation lounge and reconned the streets below. He tagged the Nether Ops team down there, his HUD updating him on the weapon systems they'd brought to play with, noting in extremely urgent tags the man-portable ground-to-ship torpedo systems. The Dragon X. Two of them.

And then a high-end luxury-type armored sled exited the underground garage of the Gamatti casino. Hired guards wearing armored vests were hanging off the sled from every place they could they find a hold.

They've got another exit route, thought Rechs.

Gamatti would be taken to another location to get off the station now that Rechs had denied them their escape ship. The problem for Rechs was that there was no engagement scenario where he could hit the armored sled from where he stood. He had only a minute, maybe, before it reached a tunnel that led off the strip and down into the main transportation corridors below the hab.

Rechs slapped his last satchel charge against the glass, tuned it for a narrow-cone explosion, and stepped back.

What about the torpedo launchers? that other voice asked him.

Torpedoes chase, Rechs told himself.

The satchel charge exploded, and Rechs followed the explosion out into the air above the strip, not hitting the armor's jets this time. He was falling fast.

Below, he saw one of the Dragon X operators trying to get an engagement solution on him. But the angle was bad, and Rechs was practically falling straight at the guy. Something a Dragon X wasn't designed to engage.

Rechs bumped the jets and fired full at less than fifty meters above the ground. He came down right next to the torp operator, who was stationed on top of an open sled ringed with blaster-proof defensive barriers. Rechs smashed the Nether Ops leej in the throat.

A perfectly tossed fragger came over the edge of the barrier and landed at Rechs's feet. Without thinking twice, Rechs hopped over the barrier, knowing he'd face fire. He rolled away from the truck as the explosive went off.

Rechs scrambled to his feet and rammed himself into the nearest leej, a man strapped with an N-249. He knocked the man down, pulled the weapon system off of him, and tracked Gamatti's speeding, high-end sled as it raced by on the main concourse.

Then he unloaded the whole drum charge.

The men clinging to the side of the sled were hit; most fell away, though a few held on and were dragged. Rechs didn't care them. He targeted the vehicle's repulsors with hot fire. The wild 249 attempted to bump and jerk, but Rechs's armor made him stronger than that. He knocked out one repulsor, and the sled crossed lanes and skidded into a fountain. It was on fire.

The main bulk of Hess's men had been farther down the tiny street that led out into Time Square. But they had quickly organized into teams and were now moving up on Rechs using fire and maneuver.

Rechs covered behind the sled and kicked the leej he'd taken the 249 off of. A swift foot to the bucket and the guy went lights out.

Smoke from the fragger billowed up from the improvised defensive position on top of the sled.

Chucking the spent 249, Rechs pulled his primary, the high-powered medium blaster. Firing from around the corner of the sled, he kept the advancing Nether Ops hit squads' heads down.

Another fragger rolled by his feet and bounced to a stop against marble steps leading up to a jewelry shop just behind Rechs. Taking two steps, he kicked it off in another direction, and it exploded in some verdant topiary.

The hit squad switched tactics from assault to encircle, fanning out across Time Square behind cover to pin Rechs down. There was still one more Dragon in play, and Rechs knew if he used the armor's jets to get altitude and get clear, they'd smoke him with it.

Moving to another position along the sled, Rechs fired at an exposed leej, hitting him in the bucket and punching a hole in it. In return, Rechs got so much blaster fire back that he had to duck behind the sled's barriers or risk taking one in his own bucket. Shots slammed into the street and marble all around.

"Master!" erupted G232 via comm. "I have reached the ship."

Well, that's something, thought Rechs as the volume of blaster fire increased. They'd try to flank him in a rush shortly.

"Good, Three-Two. If I get killed, the ship's yours. It's monitoring my telemetry... so you'll know."

Two fraggers sailed overhead and exploded in the jewelry store, sending marble fragments and glass all over Rechs's armor.

A long pause over comm followed the explosion, and then Rechs heard G232 again.

"Well! I don't really know how to respond to that, Master. A question occurs at what I can only sense is an inopportune time for you: are bots even allowed to own ships?"

Rechs popped out from behind cover, blaster rifle on burst fire. He caught the rush coming for him. Three leejes backed up by some serious suppressive fire from a heavy blaster somewhere off to Rechs's left. He engaged his attackers with a series of rapid bursts, fast-firing more than aiming, knocking down two as they dashed forward in an attempt to get close to the sled Rechs used for cover. One continued firing at Rechs even as he lay on the street, wounded. The bounty hunter had to pull back from the overwhelming suppressive fire rather than finish the guy off.

A second later the leej who hadn't been hit reached the sled and threw himself against the far side of it. Rechs knew the guy was probably cooking a fragger to toss around to Rechs's side. Rechs stuck his blaster around the side of the sled and sprayed the area where he thought the leej was hiding. But in so doing he exposed himself to the rest of the Nether Ops hit squad and took a blaster shot in the shoulder.

And… he was right. The guy *had* been cooking a fragger. It rolled away from the leej's dead gauntlet, and Rechs, who'd been hit and spun around to land on his butt, scrambled to get back around the sled as the explosive went off.

This is going from bad to worse, thought Rechs, thankful for how much of the explosive damage the sled absorbed.

"Master! Master!" G232 was politely, yet urgently, trying to get his attention again despite the ringing in Rechs's comm, or his ears, and the constant whine and sizzle of blaster fire hitting almost everywhere around him now.

Rechs's shoulder was on fire and possibly broken. The Mark I armor was punctured by a nice smoking hole in the outer skin, but the pauldron had stopped the blaster shot. He let go of his rifle and pulled the hand cannon with his off hand.

He switched from auto-fire to single and sent out a few badly aimed shots just to let them know he was still active. Force them to stop and make a new plan.

"Another ship has just set down," announced G232 ominously.

But Rechs had no time for that.

The battle had devolved into almost pure chaos now. Gamatti's men were trying to pull their boss out of the burning sled crashed into the massive fountain, and the kill team was regrouping for what Rechs could only expect would be a coordinated attack to dislodge him from behind his own burning sled. Sniper fire from the towers whined out whenever the shooters saw an opportunity, or just often enough to keep Rechs pinned. Leaning against the sled and covering from the incoming fire, Rechs looked up and saw the two gargantuas he'd previously disabled now coming down the side of Gamatti's tower.

And according to G232, there was a new player involved.

Rechs pulled up the tactical on the Mark I's HUD and looked at an overhead view of the battle space. The armor's processor tracked where incoming fire had originated and the last known movements of hostiles.

That was when Rechs noted the heavy blaster fire, tagged as coming from an N-60 across the plaza and beyond the fountain. Generally the Legion, even the Nether Ops teams, didn't use the Sixty. That was an older weapon system from days gone by. Annotating the N-60's bursts over the course of the last three minutes, it seemed the shooter was moving through the buildings and arcades along that side of the square. Firing to keep Rechs from moving.

It's one of the other two bounty hunters. It was only a hunch, but Rechs had learned to trust his hunches. Besides, it didn't matter. Whoever it was, he would kill them either way.

Rechs checked the load on the hand cannon, which was connected to his armor's redundant magazine feed. He was still in the green on ammunition. He looked up. The gargantuas were still scuttling down the side of the tower, trying to get within range to fire their quad blasters.

Let this go, he could almost hear her saying to him in the lull of the battle. *You got Schock. Let it go, Tyrus. I'm not here anymore. Let it go now.*

"Tyrus Rechs!" called out a voice over external helmet speakers. "This is Captain Hess. I'll give you a minute and then we're coming in after you. Surrender now, and you can take your chances with a House of Reason trial."

But Rechs wasn't really listening to the Nether Ops commander's half-hearted offer. The man knew he had the upper hand. Instead, Rechs was thinking. Thinking hard about how to get his last three targets before he went down. Gamatti, if he hadn't burned alive. And the two bounty hunters.

Then... payback complete.

They could capture him. Or kill him.

They were welcome to try.

"Frankly though," continued Hess from out beyond the burning sled and across the battle-scarred entertainment complex square. "I hope you *don't* surrender. Minute's starting now. Look at the big clock and make up your mind whether you want to live or die, Rechs."

The gargantuas would be within range in less than thirty seconds, let alone a minute.

Rechs got to one knee and readied himself, running through how he was going to play the next thirty seconds...

Then he moved, and everything happened at once.

Running for the side of the sled, he hit the jets and rocketed forward. Sniper fire from the tops of the tower rained down around him, but he was moving too fast, using the jump jets to bump and hop from place to place along the street in an erratic course. He rocketed out into the center of the square, firing at the legionnaires as he moved sideways, hitting a few now that their flank was exposed.

Their plan had gone sideways in a second. Rechs moving from the cover they'd been just about to storm had forced them to abandon their attack and move into a defensive posture.

Rechs spotted the torpedo carrier hoisting the stubby weapon onto his shoulder and flipping open the secondary targeting reticule so that it could connect with his armor's HUD. Rechs drilled the leej through the head with a shot from the hand cannon. It left a smoking hole in the man's bucket, and he collapsed like a sack of unconsidered laundry.

Another leej was running for the torpedo launcher, but Rechs didn't have time to shoot him as he bounced and hopped with what was left of the jump juice to reach Gamatti's wrecked sled. Landing in a spray of shattered plastic and broken glass, black smoke billowing up out of the sled's front, Rechs found two men and Gamatti kneeling down between the vehicle and the fountain, trying to keep their heads down.

Both of Gamatti's men raised their blasters to fire, but Rechs was faster. He ended their lives with two quick trigger pulls. By the time he'd adjusted his aim for Gamatti's head, Rechs was surprised to see it simply explode from a shot coming in from a different direction. Gamatti had been in the act of holding out an open briefcase full of bearer certificates when he died. Paper certificates. Keys to hidden millions of credits located in hundreds of private banks across the galaxy.

That had been his last play. Everything for his life.

Rechs turned to see who had shot Gamatti. And there across the square was Sinnatron, its tattered cloak flying behind it as it engaged the Nether Ops kill team, firing two blasters at once. The specter-like coal-dusted bot briefly raised a smoking blaster to its processor face and feigned blowing on the barrel as it nodded at Rechs.

Then it was back to stand-and-deliver combat with the legionnaires at close range.

The Nether Ops boys, who had been desperately trying to not take Rechs alive, were now fighting for their own lives.

Behind Sinnatron lumbered the massive two-headed industrial-turned-kill-machine bot Tybalt, carrying two anti-armor rocket launchers it had hefted onto its immense metal shoulders.

"Here to save you, Rechsu-san. I am your angel!" cried Sinnatron wildly as it shot down Captain Hess.

Hess, wounded, scrambled for cover as the massive Tybalt raced out and ahead of Sinnatron, firing both rockets at the closing gargantuas, and then lumbered in and among the legionnaires, picking them up and tossing them like rag dolls as they fired at the metal monster's nigh-impenetrable armor.

A stream of heavy blaster fire erupted from the N-60 out of a nearby arcade. It smashed into the late Gamatti's crashed sled and tore up the fountain as it tried to find Rechs. Ducking down, Rechs returned fire from the cover of the burning vehicle, his HUD tagging the bounty hunter in matte olive-green armor as he fired from behind a counter back in the shadows of the building.

Sinnatron deployed another arm unit, this one holding an anti-armor rocket launcher of its own, even as the bot engaged multiple legionnaires in every direction with both its blazing blasters.

"Takaru care of that one, Rechsu-san, I shall!" A rocket whooshed away from the advancing war machine that was Sinnatron, leaving a smoking trail, and the arcade shop containing the bounty hunter went up in a sudden fireball.

Rechs's HUD confirmed the kill.

Signature Match: Pollux.

KIA.

Most of the legionnaires were now dead or dying as the massive Tybalt stomped among their defensive position, wreaking havoc.

And then Sinnatron turned and fired at Rechs, who was limping away from the sled as flames crawled up along its fuel cell. The high-end vehicle was going to explode at any second. But the blaster fire wasn't intended for Rechs. It nailed an invisible target closing on Rechs from behind, smashing the optical deflection system the target had been operating.

Rechs whirled to see Umari made visible. Hit, but not out. Rechs fired with the hand cannon, hitting the man several times in the chest.

Umari slumped backwards and died.

"No needaru to thank me, Rechsu-san. Here to help you is all I am."

And that was when Rechs put it all together, despite the pain in his arm and the glancing shot he'd taken in the thigh and hadn't even known it until he tried to stand up back near the sled.

That was also when Captain Hess fired the man-portable ground-to-ship torpedo system known as the Dragon X at extreme close range at the raging two-headed giant bot, Tybalt.

The bot erupted terrifically in every direction—along with its warhead. The explosion leveled half the square and knocked Rechs back ten meters at least.

He blacked out, knocked senseless by the concussive force of the blast and then the secondary blast. Just like back on Wohan. He lay there, hearing the explosions of other vehicles and bots cook off in the wake of the detonation. Listening as the Cassio Station automated emergency damage control system came online and announced "a situation" in main hab. And a polite request to "please evacuate."

Rechs got to his feet and saw Sinnatron coming through the flames, weapon leveled at him.

It was Sinnatron.

It had been Sinnatron all along.

Sinnatron who had sold Medusa to the highest bidder.

Sinnatron who had wanted—and who was able, due to access to the contract boards—to play both sides of the street. That was why the bot was here. Not to save Rechs. Not to act as Rechs's angel. But to clean up everyone who knew it had been Sinnatron's plan all along.

Or… maybe it actually thought it was both things. The devil, and the savior. Maybe that was possible inside its fractured programming gone completely schizophrenic.

Rechs saw his hand cannon a few feet away. If he moved for it, the bot would shoot him down.

"Last words, Rechsu-san?" asked Sinnatron.

***

Fint moved through the flaming wreckage. Dashing from car to car, passing the wounded and dying legionnaires.

He wasn't sure what he was even doing here. But he knew he was no longer trying to uphold the status quo. That ship had sailed. The tenuous order maintained by the two competing cartels had been shattered beyond repair. Someone would swoop in to fill the vacuum—someone always did—but this détente was over. All he could hope for now was to end the current conflict with as little collateral damage as possible. And there were only two ways to do that.

Kill Tyrus Rechs.

Or help him.

Fint made his choice.

Taking the occasional shot from concealed positions, he struck at some of Rechs's foes. He even managed to knock down a legionnaire or two. But once the big bot was nailed by the rocket, the whole square went up in a terrific fireball.

It was then that Fint moved from safe cover into the square to look for Rechs. To see if the bounty hunter had survived out there. To see if there was a way to get him out. Even though he doubted anyone could have survived that blast at close range.

He spotted Rechs right at the center of the destruction. Rechs and the weird bot. An old THK, carbon-dusted, or cooked coal black by the explosion and the flames. One of its arms had been torn off, and its tattered cloak was on fire. But its intent was clear. Rechs, on the ground, was its target.

Fint fired and hit the thing in the head.

The force of Fint's blaster rocked the processing unit the thing used for a cranium—but nothing more.

The bot turned coldly, fired, and hit the inspector right in the chest. Knocking him to the street.

As Fint lay there, gasping, he could see the bot turn back to its original prey. But now Rechs was holding the hand cannon.

***

"Have you ever seen the sun rise over Lyra?" Rechs asked before he blew Sinnatron's head off.

For a moment Sinnatron's headless chassis almost turned to the left, and then the right. As though it was looking for its missing head. As though it would not accept that all its calculations had somehow ended. Then it fell to its knees, and finally to the street, where it continued to burn.

End of runtime.

Payback.

EPILOGUE

Rechs called the place the Doghouse. He'd once heard a song, an old-timey song, about a man telling another man he was in trouble now. And trouble was called "the doghouse" in that song. As in… you're in the doghouse now. It was a song popular long before Rechs had been a child sifting the ashes of a ruined world once called Earth.

Some person had played it for Rechs decades later. Said it had been recovered from some old lighthugger's memory archives.

Rechs liked the song.

His hiding place wasn't a doghouse, and yet it was, after a sense. It looked like an asteroid, and a large one at that, because it was. It was a rogue body that had broken off from some system long ago and now wandered along out in the dark between systems all by itself. Away from the known and alone. Like Rechs. It was hard to spot unless you knew what you were looking for. The miners who'd discovered and developed it had put in all kind of approach lighting and tracking to help make the difficult landing easier. But after Rechs found them all dead from what they'd dug up deep inside the thing, he'd disabled everything that made it easier for someone to find the big lonely rock. Then he'd purchased it and hidden it as bureaucratically as he could.

This and other places like it, scattered throughout the galaxy, were where Rechs laid low when the kill teams got too close, or he needed recovery time from some hunt that had gotten a little too rough.

In this case, he had returned to the Doghouse for both reasons.

A whole Nether Ops kill team had been wiped out. A major station had been evacuated and critically damaged. Those things would draw attention Rechs didn't need. Even just a little of that would have been enough to drive the bounty hunter into hiding for a while.

And Rechs had been pretty badly injured. Even with his remarkable healing capacities, he needed time to recover.

Time to heal.

Time to forget…

Except that he couldn't.

Fint had made it. Barely. He'd been shot, and he was dying in the aftermath of the battle in Time Square. But Rechs had been through enough practical combat medicine to get a skin patch over the man's sucking chest wound and carry him back to the *Crow*.

There was a station-wide hull breach in progress when Rechs's ship lifted off, and it looked like Cassio Royale was destined to become a new ghost station. Sure, some would stay and try to bring it back to life. But an incident like that had a tendency to scare the tourist trade away permanently. They liked their danger on the rails. Not off and with blaster bolts flying in every direction. That got a little too uncomfortable. Plus, Schock and Gamatti were dead. So who would finance the rebuilding?

Not my circus, thought Rechs.

He'd left Fint with a healer, an old Legion corpsman named Gordon Green who'd patched up enough leejes while fighting with General Rex to be more than capable of taking care of the inspector. He'd heal him, and then Fint could decide where to go next.

And then Rechs got lost because it was time to disappear for a while.

Nether Ops and the House of Reason would double down on finding him, so the trail needed to go cold. Very cold. For a very long time.

Rechs decided six months of laying low was in order. For a start. The truth was, he wondered if he would *ever* be able come back from this one.

He stared at the carbonite block sometimes in the afternoons. After therapy and lots of PT running down in the wonders of the fantastic mines. Avoiding the parts he'd had to block off. Some afternoons he'd go aboard the *Crow*, docked inside the station's main hangar, and just sit with her encased frozen body. He would try to think of something to say. But he couldn't. He wasn't that way. And so he just sat next to the cold block of carbonite they'd frozen her body in.

One evening, late, when he had some old music filling the areas of the station he kept for his own, and he was nursing a Faldaren scotch, he pulled her autopsy report and just studied it, watching what the disease had tried to do to her before she'd been murdered.

He wondered.

Wondered, if the disease had continued on…

If it had not been encased in the time-defying carbonite...

That night he went to sleep and he dreamt of her.

He was swimming on an ocean at night, and she was below the water and couldn't surface. She was trapped and drowning, and Rechs fought in the dream to find her below the dark water. But he could never get enough air to dive deep enough to get her. Someone from the shore kept calling him. Telling him he needed to do some useless and mundane task before he could rescue her.

He was tormented all night long, and in the end he awoke and made breakfast, sitting in the old massive dining facility all by himself and listening to the hum of the industrial machinery all around.

What if she's in there? he thought. *In the carbonite and not really dead.*

He got up and left his food. There was an industrial mineral scanner located in the facility. Within the hour he had it figured out, and he ran a diagnostic scan.

Of course she was dead. Not even the most dormant of life signs were present. All was as it should be...

... except for one thing.

The machine part of her was active. Near her brain was a small EM signature.

One of the dogs, as he thought of them, bayed down in the caverns Rechs had sealed them off in. It was a lonely, inhuman, soul-chilling sound.

Rechs didn't mind it. Frankly, he'd gotten used to it.

But he wondered what that EM signature was.

Probably just the machine virus still working with what it had available. Doing its thing within her biologic matter even though it could never violate the carbonite.

But he had to know.

He loaded her back aboard the *Crow* and took off for a code slicer he knew. The guy specialized in bots and advanced AIs. The nano-plague had been a hobby of his.

"That was years ago," Nathan Davis told Rechs.

Rechs had shown him the scans and pointed out the nano-plague and the EM signature.

"I've learned everything that can be learned about that," declared the pompous savant. Techno Orchestra thundered all about them within the code slicer's "sanctum," as he called it. "I've moved on, Rechs! Quantum consciousness. Infinitely cubing memory. The nature of nothing that had to have once existed, though that's an oxymoron. The nano-plague is child's play. I was a *child* then, Rechs! A mere bumbling idiot feeling my way toward the big important questions."

But Rechs persisted. Because it was important to him. And Davis took a look because Rechs had saved him from some very angry people once.

After an hour Davis declared, "It's a symbiont!"

Nathan Davis declared almost everything as though what he spoke was the only truth the galaxy ever needed.

"What's that?" asked Rechs.

Davis sighed in a dramatic show of disappointment that Rechs would ask such a question. "You can look it up later. But it's actually not that uncommon in plague victims. And here's the interesting part: the virus makes a backup copy of the person it's using as a host. Well, of her personality… as the virus sees it anyway. Stores it within its circuitry—part of the process of turning human into machine. But it's not really a copy, it's a… *design*, really. It's a picture of what the plague intends to become one day, given time."

Rechs must've looked confused, as Davis tried again.

"Look at it this way… it's not her. It's an AI *based* on her and the plague. What the plague was going to make her into."

I want to be a ship, Tyrus.

Rechs sat down and put his forehead on his fist. Staring at the painted mosaic that was the floor of Nathan Davis's mad sanctum.

Davis was the most brilliant man Rechs had ever met. And he was almost unintelligible. To Rechs, who'd met many, many aliens… Nathan was the one true alien in the galaxy.

His intelligence was beyond measure.

Rechs had never thought of himself as smart.

"I can pull it out. We can talk to it, if you want, Rechs. Might be fun."

Davis adjusted his specs and was already rubbing his chubby hands together as though some forgotten hunger had been reawakened within him.

And maybe it was that look on Davis's suddenly feverish face that made Rechs feel like a ghoul, a grave digger. She was gone. At peace now. Beyond all this.

What…

What could it solve?

Except that something left of her was still alive inside that carbonite.

"I can see you're hesitant," Davis said. "Let me just crack her open…" He saw the look on Rechs's face and stopped. "Okay… let me *extract the symbiont*, make a copy, and then I'll keep it in a safe place. Then I'll format the copy for AI imprint. If you ever want to… talk to it… you can. It's an easy install. It won't be her. Aaaaand yet… it will be in a way. It will be a requiem… a remembrance. Like what you're listening to now." Davis turned, closing his eyes to listen, to surrender for a moment, to the music that thundered and swelled about his sanctum, speaking of the struggle of life in every hurtling chord even though everything must come against us in a rage of strings shrieking injustice and violence. And of death, and finally rest. And that we are somehow, in the end, not forgotten.

"This is Verdi's *Requiem*. The *Dies irae*," sighed the mad coder.

Later, when the mad scientist stuff was done, Nathan Davis handed the AI, in a secure impervisteel case, to Rechs.

"Don't expect anything if you ever do install it. It's just... it's like a child, Rechs. I don't mean that it's of that intelligence level. It's actually quite intelligent. Not as intelligent as me... but for you... it'd beat you at 4D chess in six moves."

Davis thought about that for a second.

"No. The game would be decided in three moves. The rest would be you watching your butt get handed to you. By a machine." He laughed. "Sorry, Rechs. You're the toughest man I ever met, but you'll never discover the meaning of life, my friend. Stick with blasters and your big gun. Okay?"

And the Rechs was gone. Back to the Doghouse.

He left the AI in his workshop, next to the table where he maintained his weapons, for two weeks.

And then finally he went out to the *Crow*, pulled the lower maintenance hatch, and uninstalled the old AI. The AI known simply as Ship.

"Did I displease you?" it asked as Rechs went to work.

"No," said Rechs as he auto-wiped all the personality cards one by one. Pulling them and then holding down a button until he got a chime denoting a clean wipe.

"Then… whhhhhhyyy…" It was having trouble as Rechs deleted it. "Urr you doing this?"

"For a friend, Ship. I'm sorry. I'll package your core and sell you to someone nice. No more wars. No more fights. Just jumps from star to star… okay?"

Ship said nothing for a moment. Then: "I www-would like that v-v-v-ery much, Captainnnn. I'm tired now. I think I'll go-go-go to sl-leeeeeep for a bit."

And then it was gone.

Ship was gone.

It took the rest of the day to package up the AI and get it into a new core. The next morning he brought the impervisteel case that contained the AI copy of the symbiont out to the hangar.

All day Rechs worked on his back, looking up at the AI install assembly and data card interface to get the copy in. It was mind-numbing, back-breaking work.

Later, lying in the dark of the main processing core, Rechs booted her up.

Systems came to life.

Blue and pulsing. A warm glow.

Like some night in the water beneath a sinking moon.

Then there was an ominous silence in which he knew the AI was there and awake.

"Hello?" she began. Her voice deep and resonant. A little afraid. Quiet, really.

Rechs felt his voice catch in his throat as he tried to respond. He composed himself and said, "Hello."

"Where am I?"

Rechs wiped away a sudden tear he could not stop.

"You're here," he replied. "With me now."

"That seems... good. I don't know you. But your voice makes me feel safe," replied the AI. "Am I supposed to feel?"

"Yeah," said Rechs.

"I have memories," said the ship, as though she'd just discovered something wonderful. "I know who you are. I know why I feel safe now. You loved her."

I never told her that, thought Rechs. *But I'm glad she knew it.*

If nothing came of this... then knowing that was enough. He thought it would torment him, but somehow knowing that she knew he loved her when he'd never said it comforted him on the other side of all the bad that had happened.

"I am not her."

"I know," whispered Rechs after a moment.

"What function do you need me to perform for you?"

"I was thinking, if you're interested," began Rechs, "I can introduce you to my ship. Once I open the core systems interface, you will have access to become my ship if you want to. Would you like that?"

Silence.

"Yes. I would like that very much, Tyrus."

It was Vexia. It was her voice. It was the way she called him by his first name.

Rechs reached up to throw the interface contact. His hand was trembling.

"Vexia?"

A pause.

"Don't call me that anymore, Tyrus. I'm gone now. But call me something else and we'll sail the galaxy and you can show me all the things she ever wanted to see. Let me stay with you until the heat death of the universe, Tyrus. You'll need someone at the end who loved you because you were... you. You won't have anyone... but maybe I can be the memory of that love when you are alone and surrounded and low on ammunition. I'm free now. Free to be your ship, Tyrus. But you can't call me... by my name. *Her* name. Do you understand?"

"I do," said Tyrus, and flipped the interface switch.

"Oh," she moaned as the ship opened up to her. "This is wonderful. I can fly, Tyrus. I'm a ship. I'm free now."

"Yes," whispered Tyrus. He felt more tears escape from his eyes. "You're free now."

"There are so many, many places to go."

"There are."

"What will you call me, Captain, now that I am your ship? Where shall we go first? I'm ready to run, Tyrus. Ready to try. Ready to see and do everything because I'm not sick anymore. But I need a name first, because... I'm new. I'm safe now. What will you call me?"

"Lyra," whispered Tyrus. And then whispered it again.

"Lyra."

THE END

HONOR ROLL

We would like to give our most sincere thanks and recognition to those who supported the creation of Tyrus Rechs: Requiem for Medusa by subscribing as a Galaxy's Edge Insider at GalacticOutlaws.com

Janet Anderson
Robert Anspach
Sean Averill
Russell Barker
Steven Beaulieu
Antonio Becerra
John Bell
WJ Blood
Aaron Brooks
Brent Brown
Marion Buehring
David Chor
Alex Collins-Gauweiler
Robert Cosler
Andrew Craig
Peter Davies
Nathan Davis
Christopher DiNote
Karol Doliński
Andreas Doncic
Noah Doyle
Lucas Eastridge
Stephane Escrig
Dalton Ferrari
Skyla Forster

Mark Franceschini
Richard Gallo
Christopher Gallo
Kyle Gannon
Michael Gardner
John Giorgis
Gordon Green
Tim Green
Shawn Greene
Michael Greenhill
Jose Enrique Guzman
Ronald Haulman
Joshua Hayes
Jason Henderson
Curtis Horton
Jeff Howard
Mike Hull
Wendy Jacobson
James Jeffers
Kenny Johnson
Noah Kelly
Mathijs Kooij
Evan Kowalski
Mark Krafft
Byl Kravetz

Clay Lambert
Grant Lambert
Paul Lizer
Richard Long
Oliver Longchamps
Kyle Macarthur
Richard Maier
Brian Mansur
Cory Marko
Trevor Martin
Pawel Martin
Tao Mason
Simon Mayeski
Brent McCarty
Matthew McDaniel
Joshua McMaster
Christopher Menkhaus
Jim Mern
Alex Morstadt
Daniel Mullen
Greg Nugent
David Parker
Eric Pastorek
Jeremiah Popp
Chris Pourteau
Eric Ritenour
Walt Robillard
Joyce Roth
David Sanford
Andrew Schmidt
Christopher Shaw
Ryan Shaw
Glenn Shotton

Daniel Smith
Joel Stacey
Maggie Stewart-Grant
John Stockley
Kevin Summers
Ernest Sumner
Tim Taylor
Beverly Tierney
Tom Tousignant
Scott Tucker
Eric Turnbull
John Tuttle
Christopher Valin
Paden VanBuskirk
Andrew Ward
Jason Wright
Nathan Zoss

Jason Anspach and Nick Cole are a pair of west coast authors teaming up to write their science fiction dream series, Galaxy's Edge.

Jason Anspach is a best selling author living in Tacoma, Washington with his wife and their own legionnaire squad of seven (not a typo) children. In addition to science fiction, Jason is the author of the hit comedy-paranormal-historical-detective series, *'til Death*. Jason loves his family as well as hiking and camping throughout the beautiful Pacific Northwest. And Star Wars. He named as many of his kids after Obi Wan as possible, and knows that Han shot first.

Nick Cole is a dragon award winning author best known for *The Old Man and the Wasteland*, *CTRL ALT Revolt!*, and the Wyrd Saga. After serving in the United States Army, Nick moved to Hollywood to pursue a career in acting and writing. (Mostly) retired from the stage and screen, he resides with his wife, a professional opera singer, in Los Angeles, California.